Miss Morton
and the
Missing Heir

Books by Catherine Lloyd

Kurland St. Mary Mysteries

DEATH COMES TO THE VILLAGE

DEATH COMES TO LONDON

DEATH COMES TO KURLAND HALL

DEATH COMES TO THE FAIR

DEATH COMES TO THE SCHOOL

DEATH COMES TO BATH

DEATH COMES TO THE NURSERY

DEATH COMES TO THE RECTORY

Miss Morton Mysteries

MISS MORTON AND THE ENGLISH HOUSE PARTY MURDER

MISS MORTON AND THE SPIRITS OF THE UNDERWORLD

MISS MORTON AND THE DEADLY INHERITANCE

Published by Kensington Publishing Corp.

Miss Morton and the Missing Heir

CATHERINE LLOYD

KENSINGTON
PUBLISHING CORP.
kensingtonbooks.com

This book is a work of fiction. Names, characters, businesses, organizations, places, events, and incidents either are the product of the author's imagination or are used fictitiously. Any resemblance to actual persons, living or dead, events, or locales is entirely coincidental.

To the extent that the image or images on the cover of this book depict a person or persons, such person or persons are merely models, and are not intended to portray any character or characters featured in the book.

KENSINGTON BOOKS are published by

Kensington Publishing Corp.
900 Third Avenue
New York, NY 10022

Copyright © 2025 by Catherine Lloyd

All rights reserved. No part of this book may be reproduced in any form or by any means without the prior written consent of the Publisher, excepting brief quotes used in reviews.

Without limiting the author's and publisher's exclusive rights, any unauthorized use of this publication to train generative artificial intelligence (AI) technologies is expressly prohibited.

All Kensington titles, imprints, and distributed lines are available at special quantity discounts for bulk purchases for sales promotion, premiums, fundraising, educational, or institutional use. Special book excerpts or customized printings can also be created to fit specific needs. For details, write or phone the office of the Kensington Special Sales Manager: Attn. Special Sales Department, Kensington Publishing Corp., 900 Third Avenue, New York, NY 10022. Phone: 1-800-221-2647.

Library of Congress Control Number: 2025936272

KENSINGTON and the K with book logo Reg. US Pat. & TM Off.

ISBN: 978-1-4967-5496-7

First Kensington Hardcover Edition: October 2025

ISBN: 978-1-4967-5498-1 (ebook)

10 9 8 7 6 5 4 3 2 1

Printed in the United States of America

The authorized representative in the EU for product safety and compliance is eucomply OU, Parnu mnt 139b-14, Apt 123
Tallinn, Berlin 11317, hello@eucompliancepartner.com

Miss Morton
and the
Missing Heir

Chapter 1

London 1840

Mrs. Frogerton waved her lace handkerchief at the departing carriage until it turned the corner and disappeared from sight. Her smile faltered as she lowered her hand.

"I've never been so pleased to see someone leave before in my life."

"That's quite understandable, ma'am." Miss Caroline Morton shut the door of the rented house in Half Moon Street and gestured for her employer to proceed her up the stairs. "The last few weeks have been exceptionally busy, what with the wedding and everything surrounding it."

Mrs. Frogerton sighed. "Two years, lass, two years of my life stuck in London waiting for Dotty to make up her mind and marry her viscount."

"I suspect she enjoyed being part of the social whirl, ma'am," Caroline suggested. "And I applaud her for waiting to make certain that her feelings for the viscount were strong enough to translate into a good marriage."

"Her feelings had nothing to do with it," Mrs. Frogerton said. "It took me that long to negotiate the marriage contract. They might be peers of the realm, Caroline, but the dowager countess and her lawyers haggled like fishwives over every penny."

Mrs. Frogerton sat in her favorite chair and reached down to pet her dogs. She wore a morning gown in bronze silk that complemented her dark eyes and chestnut hair. She'd had her children at a relatively young age and still retained her youthful complexion and intense curiosity about life.

To be fair, at this particular moment, she did look rather worn down. Caroline hoped that with Dorothy off on her extended honeymoon, her employer would have plenty of time to recuperate before she decided to return home to run her many businesses. Whether Caroline accompanied her was still not settled.

"I'll ring for some tea, ma'am," Caroline said.

"Thank you." Mrs. Frogerton looked over at her. "And thank you for your support with Dotty. I don't think I would've managed without you."

"You would have managed perfectly," Caroline countered. "You are very well equipped to do so."

Mrs. Frogerton waved the compliment aside. "In business, yes, but dealing with the social niceties of peers and the snobs of society is not my strength, though it is yours."

Caroline smiled. She'd grown up the daughter of an earl, and the subtle nuances of society had been drummed into her from the day she was born. If her father hadn't disgraced his family name and left her and her sister, Susan, destitute and dependent on the charity of others, she would've been married herself by now, presiding over a large household and probably a titled husband.

Instead, she had to earn her living and help others achieve what should have been her birthright while the *ton* pretended she didn't exist. At first, Dorothy, the well-dowered daughter of an industrialist, hadn't been willing to listen to Caroline's advice. She'd learned to consider Caroline an ally only when she realized how invaluable her knowledge was in navigating the intricacies of the *ton*.

And now Dorothy was a viscountess, and Caroline still earned her living while hoping the small inheritance from her aunt would mature enough to offer her security in her old age. . . .

"Did it make you feel regretful?" Mrs. Frogerton asked.

Guiltily, Caroline wondered if Mrs. Frogerton had been reading her thoughts. "I'm not quite sure what you are referring to, ma'am." The butler set the tea tray in front of her.

"The wedding. Seeing all those fancy folk in the pews watching my Dotty get married to a viscount."

"Am I regretful I'm no longer a part of society? Or that I haven't married?" Caroline shook her head. "Not particularly."

Mrs. Frogerton winked at her. "Easy for you to say, lass, when you know Inspector Ross and Dr. Harris would marry you in a second."

"Dr. Harris does not have the means to take on a wife." Caroline poured the tea and took Mrs. Frogerton a cup. "And we are just friends."

"And Inspector Ross?" Mrs. Frogerton sighed. "Although between his work and his brother's bad behavior, he's hardly had a moment to spare to go courting."

Caroline had seen Inspector Ross at Dorothy's elaborate wedding when he'd come to represent his father, but they'd barely had a moment to exchange a word. His older brother's wild excesses were putting an immense strain on his aristocratic family. All the inspector's free time was taken up by the matter. Having watched her own father struggle with his demons, Caroline had nothing but sympathy for the inspector, especially knowing how hard he had fought to stay out of family politics.

"How is his brother doing?" Mrs. Frogerton asked.

"Richard is still alive." Caroline grimaced as she sat down. "But he seems determined to try every means possible to end his earthly existence. Recently, Inspector Ross had to physically restrain him from drinking an entire bottle of brandy at breakfast."

"Many gentlemen drink to excess."

"Not as much as Richard."

"If he does succeed in doing a mischief to himself, Inspector Ross will be his father's heir, yes?"

Caroline shuddered. "I think that's the last thing he wants, but even if he never takes up the title, it will still be his."

"I don't think he'd be able to work at Great Scotland Yard anymore," Mrs. Frogerton observed, "when he'd have a seat in the House of Lords."

"It would be only a hereditary title, ma'am. He wouldn't sit in the Lords until he succeeded his father."

"These titles are so confusing, Caroline. Why have them when they have no particular value at all?" Mrs. Frogerton shook her head. "It makes little sense to me."

"I suspect they matter to the standing of the families involved, but I do take your point," Caroline said. "And in Inspector Ross's case, having that empty title would be such a waste of his abilities."

"I'm sure he could use those in politics, my dear. We could do with a few more sane voices in Parliament."

Mrs. Frogerton was an avid reader of the newspapers and, as a business owner, had strong opinions about how the current government was performing and no hesitation in expressing them to anyone who cared to listen.

The butler came back with the afternoon post on a silver tray and presented it to Mrs. Frogerton. She thanked him and started sorting through the pile. "I'm surprised we're still being invited to things now that Dotty and her fortune are no longer available."

"As I've always told you, ma'am, you are a valued guest in your own right."

Mrs. Frogerton snorted and held out a letter. "There's one for you, my dear."

"Thank you." With a jolt of hope, Caroline took the

letter and examined it carefully. There was no return address, but she already knew it wasn't from the one person she most wanted to write to her.

"Have you heard from your sister yet, lass?" Mrs. Frogerton asked gently.

"No." Caroline stared down at the unopened letter and swallowed hard. "I've had nothing since her first letter telling me she had arrived safely in Maryland. If she doesn't provide me with a forwarding address, I can send letters only via the ship's captain and hope someone picks them up at the port and delivers them to her."

Susan's decision to leave England when she turned eighteen and live with her cousin Mabel in America had devastated Caroline. Despite all her pleading, Susan had never forgiven Caroline for separating her from Mabel in the first place and was determined to depart with her inheritance in hand. In the end, Caroline had given in and allowed her sister to leave, but it had been the hardest decision of her life. The lack of knowing how Susan was fairing was a constant, nagging ache.

She opened her letter and read it carefully, a frown gathering on her brow. "It's from my family's solicitor."

"Good Lord, what's wrong now?" Mrs. Frogerton asked. "I thought you'd taken all your personal business to my Mr. Lewis."

"I have, ma'am, but Mr. Potkins still deals with the Morton family estate. He says someone has written to him claiming to be the next Earl of Morton."

"And what does that have to do with you?" Mrs. Frogerton sniffed. "Your family scarcely deserve your attention."

"He's asking for my help."

"What a nerve! After the bungling of your affairs he and his colleagues made, he hardly deserves your notice, let alone your assistance."

"The gentleman's mother made the claim. Mr. Potkins and the College of Arms are investigating its validity. In the meantime, Mr. Potkins would like me, as the only living representative of the Morton family in England, to meet with these people, preferably at Morton House."

Mrs. Frogerton frowned. "I thought Morton House had been sold off."

"I originally thought that, too, ma'am, but apparently because of the terms of the entail, the property couldn't be sold outright. As far as I understand it, Coutts Bank paid off the debts and currently hold the house in trust for the next earl."

"They probably paid pennies for it," Mrs. Frogerton said. "And intend to sell it back to the earl at a vastly inflated price."

"Considering my father owed them thousands when he died, I can't say I blame them."

"Perhaps we should pay the house a visit. Has it been let to tenants in the last few years?"

"I'm not sure." Caroline stared at her employer. "I thought you said this was none of my business."

Mrs. Frogerton, who had notably brightened, made a dismissive gesture. "The least we can do is take a look, Caroline. It would only be right."

Pleased to see that her employer had cheered up, Caroline decided that a closer inspection of Morton House might do them both good. Mrs. Frogerton would enjoy the outing, and Caroline could lay some old ghosts to rest.

After stopping in Lincoln's Inn Fields to obtain a key from the solicitors, Caroline and Mrs. Frogerton set out for Cavendish Square where Morton House was located. The last time Caroline had been there, the bailiffs had arrived to claim the deceased earl's unentailed possessions. She'd sat on the front steps while the bailiffs carried everything out as she'd tried to explain to her much younger sister why the bad men were taking all her toys.

At one point Susan had cried so much that one of the bailiffs had given her back a doll. Caroline had tried to thank him, but he'd held his fingers to his lips to indicate she should keep quiet, and she'd done as he asked. She'd already sewn her mother's pearl necklace and a silver bracelet into the hem of her travelling cloak, but she didn't have the ability to take anything larger.

As they'd waited for Aunt Eleanor to collect them and their pitiful belongings, even the head bailiff felt sorry enough to invite them back into the house to share their midday meal. It had been strange going past the empty rooms, the furniture now stacked high on the two carts outside. None of the neighbors had come to inquire after the girls' welfare—Caroline's first indication that her social status had irrevocably changed for the worst. She'd expected her fiancé to appear, but despite her recent letter informing him of their current predicament, Lord Francis Chatham had not come.

"Caroline?" Mrs. Frogerton's voice intruded on her memories. "We have arrived."

"Yes, ma'am." She shook off the past and descended the carriage step, offering her employer her hand to help her alight in her turn. "I have the key."

They went up the steps, Caroline carefully avoiding staring at where she and Susan had waited on their last day at the house. The knocker had been removed from the door, there were cobwebs everywhere, and the windows were dirty and shuttered. Caroline set the key in the lock. It squeaked in protest and refused to turn. Eventually, Mrs. Frogerton called on her coachman to use his superior strength, and the door opened with great reluctance. Caroline stepped inside and immediately recoiled at the smell of damp and mildew.

"Good Lord!" Mrs. Frogerton, who was made of stronger stuff, went past her. "It looks like the roof must be leaking." She pointed at the ceiling where a large patch of black mold coated the peeling plaster. "It's probably come right through the house."

Caroline wandered down the central corridor. The

rooms on the ground floor had been used by the earl's secretary and for receiving visitors who didn't merit a trip up the stairs to the drawing room, where the countess and her daughters had received callers. The basement housed the kitchen, scullery, butler's pantry, and housekeeper's sitting room. There was a floor dedicated to the earl and countess's bedroom suites, a nursery floor, and attics above for the live-in staff.

She paused at the bottom of the staircase, her thoughts in turmoil. It was hard to believe that when her mother was alive, this house had been a warm and loving home. Now it was as ruined and desolate as the Morton family itself.

"I don't think this place is fit for ghosts to inhabit, let alone guests." Mrs. Frogerton joined Caroline, her nose wrinkled in distaste. "If this gentleman *is* the new Earl of Morton, seeing his inheritance in this state might encourage him to run away again."

"I agree." Caroline drew an unsteady breath. "It used to be quite elegant, ma'am. My mother had a way of . . . making a place a home despite its grandeur."

Her employer squeezed her arm. "I'm sorry, lass. This can't be pleasant for you. Let's go back to Half Moon Street. I'll compose a letter to Mr. Potkins telling him that his idea to open up Morton House is as ridiculous as most of his suggestions."

"I can write to him, ma'am." Caroline turned back to the front door.

"I wish you'd let me do it." Mrs. Frogerton followed her out. She paused beneath the imposing, white-pillared portico guarding the front door. "I do so enjoy offending his sensibilities."

They returned to the carriage, and Mrs. Frogerton chattered away about inconsequential things, allowing Caroline to regain her composure. If the claimant was indeed the new Earl of Morton, Caroline wished him well. The task of restoring the estate would be enormous. If the new earl didn't have funds of his own, it would be virtually impossible to succeed unless the banks took pity on him. And, if he was anything like his predecessor, or if the banks feared he might be, they would be extremely reluctant to lend him a penny.

To Caroline's surprise, shortly after sending off her note, a rather agitated Mr. Potkins arrived at the house and begged to speak to Mrs. Frogerton and Caroline. He appeared in the drawing room and bowed low before sitting in the chair Mrs. Frogerton offered him.

"I was shocked to receive your note, Lady Caroline. I had no idea that the bank had allowed the property to fall into such a state of disrepair!"

Mrs. Frogerton looked as if there was a lot she might say about that, but after a glance at Caroline, she held her peace.

"It is certainly not suitable to receive guests," Caroline agreed.

"Why can't Caroline meet these people in your office, Mr. Potkins?" Mrs. Frogerton asked.

"We thought that a more . . . social approach with family might reveal more about the claimant than a series of documents," Mr. Potkins said.

"You thought 'the pretender' might give himself away when he was more relaxed," Mrs. Frogerton commented. "And that meeting a real member of the Morton family might shake his resolve."

"There might be some truth in that, ma'am." Mr. Potkins turned to Mrs. Frogerton. "But as the house is obviously uninhabitable, perhaps the meeting will have to take place in my office after all."

"You could invite them to meet us here," Mrs. Frogerton suggested.

Both Caroline and Mr. Potkins turned to stare at her.

"I beg your pardon, ma'am?" Mr. Potkins was the first to find his voice.

"I'm considered a very good judge of character, Mr. Potkins," Mrs. Frogerton said. "It is one of the reasons why I'm a successful business owner." She smiled at Caroline. "Wouldn't you agree, lass?"

"That is very . . . generous of you, Mrs. Frogerton." Mr. Potkins shot to his feet with alacrity. "I'll set up the meeting and send you the details as soon as possible."

"Excellent." Mrs. Frogerton nodded at the solicitor. "Good afternoon, sir."

Caroline waited until Mr. Potkins was heading downstairs before she studied her employer. "That was very kind of you, ma'am, but you do not need to put yourself out for me."

Mrs. Frogerton sighed. "I must confess that I wasn't just thinking about you, my dear. Since Dotty's departure, I fear I am likely to suffer from a lowering of spirits, or at least a lack of things to do. Perhaps this might take our minds off our troubles?" She looked inquiringly at Caroline.

"I, too, feel somewhat at a loss," Caroline acknowledged. "If you are willing to receive the claimant to the earldom, I can only appreciate and applaud your good nature."

Mrs. Frogerton sat back with a contented smile. "Then let's wait to hear from Mr. Potkins, and perhaps you might consider what questions you need to ask to ascertain whether this claim is valid."

"I'll ask Mr. Potkins to provide us with any information he has on the matter," Caroline said. "He is very much in your debt and owes us that."

"I'm actually quite excited, Caroline," Mrs. Frogerton said. "I cannot imagine what kind of a person he will be."

Caroline rang for some tea and resumed her seat. "I wonder if I have ever met this person. If he is a distant connection, he might have attended family events in the past. Perhaps I might recognize him and make Mr. Potkins a very happy man."

"From what you've told me previously, Caroline, the Morton family weren't close. It's possible that this particular branch might have little connection with your own."

"That's probably more likely, ma'am." Caroline was pleased to see the interest in her employer's eyes and relieved to have something to occupy her *own* thoughts rather than worrying about Susan. "But if that is the case, I doubt I will be able to offer Mr. Potkins much assistance at all."

"Let him worry about that, lass. All you can do is your best," Mrs. Frogerton advised as she beamed at Caroline. "I must admit I'm quite looking forward to it already!"

Chapter 2

When the doorbell rang, Caroline glanced over at Mrs. Frogerton before smoothing down the skirts of her second-best gown and rising to her feet. It had taken over a week to find a suitable day for the potential earl's visit. Caroline had studied the meager information Mr. Potkins had given her and drawn up a list of questions with Mrs. Frogerton's assistance.

Jenkins, the butler appeared at the door with Mr. Potkins at his elbow. "Your guests, madam."

"Thank you." Mrs. Frogerton stood and nodded at the solicitor. "Mr. Potkins."

Caroline's gaze had already shifted to the group behind him hovering uncertainly by the door.

Mr. Potkins bowed. "Lady Caroline, Mrs. Frogerton, may I present Mr. Thomas Scutton, his mother Mrs. Scutton, and his sister Mrs. Mary Brigham."

Mrs. Frogerton went forward, her hand outstretched. "You are all most welcome."

Caroline followed her employer, her gaze fixed on Mr. Scutton's face. He was tall and dark with a pale complexion and had a certain impatient air about him that reminded her of every peer she'd ever known.

She went to speak to him, only to have her hand

grasped by his mother. "Lady Caroline! My, you have grown!"

She reluctantly turned to the older woman who was smiling at her. "Have we met, ma'am?"

Mrs. Scutton chuckled. She was a short, round woman with a lively expression, brown hair and vivid blue eyes. Her green day dress wasn't fashionable, but was respectable, as was her daughter's. "You wouldn't remember, dear, you were very young at the time, but there's no mistaking you."

"I must admit, I don't recall having met you before, ma'am. Was it in London?" Caroline asked.

"No," Mrs. Scutton said. "You and your mother were at Morton Hall. There was some kind of celebration—an anniversary, perhaps? And everyone was invited to attend. You were only two or three at the time. You can't possibly remember me."

Caroline eased her hand free and turned to Mrs. Brigham, who showed none of her mother's good humor in her expression. She was tall like her brother, and had dark hair and blue eyes like her mother. She wore unrelieved black and looked quite miserable.

"It's a pleasure to meet you, ma'am," Caroline said.

Mrs. Brigham tentatively offered her hand. "Likewise."

"Oh, don't mind Mary's glum face," Mrs. Scutton said. "She suffered a bereavement and is still in mourning."

"I'm sorry to hear that and offer you my condolences," Caroline addressed Mrs. Brigham.

"Thank you," Mrs. Brigham murmured after a hard look at her mother. "I miss my husband every day, and I cannot wait until we are reunited."

Finally, Caroline turned to Mr. Scutton. He looked steadily down at her, his long nose and brown eyes, reminding Caroline of many of the family portraits in her old home.

"Mr. Scutton."

"Lady Caroline." His voice was pleasantly modulated

without a hint of an accent. He wore a plain dark coat, white cravat, and black waistcoat, which gave him a clerical air. "Thank you for agreeing to see us."

"You must thank Mr. Potkins and Mrs. Frogerton for organizing matters," Caroline said as she gestured for the guests to sit down. "I'm not sure if Mr. Potkins mentioned Morton House isn't fit to receive visitors."

"He did mention it." Mr. Scutton looked at the solicitor. "From what I understand, the affairs of the earldom are in some disarray."

"One might say that." Mrs. Frogerton turned her snort into a cough and rang the bell for tea.

"My father wasn't very good with money," Caroline said. "He left a lot of debt behind."

"So we understand." Mrs. Scutton took up the conversation. "In truth, we thought long and hard before deciding to advance our claim, but it didn't seem right to deny Thomas his birthright." She smiled fondly at her son, but he didn't smile in return.

For the first time, Caroline wondered if the push to revive the earldom came solely from Mrs. Scutton.

"Where do you live currently, Mrs. Scutton?" Mrs. Frogerton asked.

"We're very comfortably situated in Epping in Essex. Mr. Scutton owns a fine house there."

"Ah! By the forest. A lovely area," Mrs. Frogerton said. "Caroline and I drove out there to see the autumn leaves last year. It was quite spectacular."

"It is very pleasant." Mrs. Scutton nodded. "And with the frequency of the mail coaches, we are able to get to London in relatively good time."

From the modesty of their clothing, Caroline had guessed the family weren't wealthy enough to own their own carriage and horses. Claiming the title would offer them a steep rise in social standing even if the earldom was currently in disorder. Caroline could quite understand why Mrs. Scutton had decided to proceed.

"What prompted you to contact Mr. Potkins, Mrs. Scutton?" Caroline asked.

"It was quite by chance, I assure you." Mrs. Scutton smiled as she settled her skirts around her. "I was packing up the Christmas china with old newspaper Thomas had thoughtfully provided for me, and the name Morton jumped out from the obituary section." She glanced at her son, and he nodded. "I must confess that I forgot all about the china and read through the article. I knew, of course, that Mr. Scutton's family had *some* connection with the Morton name, but it was distant enough for me not to have concerned myself greatly about it."

"But, with respect, ma'am, didn't you just say you attended a family function at Morton Hall where you met me?" Caroline asked.

Mrs. Scutton's smile didn't falter. "Yes, that's correct, but at the time I had little reason to suspect *quite* how closely we were related to your family, dear. My husband, William, was very reluctant to speak of it, and I respected his choice,"

"The earl died several years ago, Mrs. Scutton," Mrs. Frogerton said. "One might wonder why you waited so long to make your claim."

"Because it seemed unlikely to succeed, and I suspected my husband would have objected to my getting involved." Mrs. Scutton said frankly. "After William's death, I decided to keep myself informed about the search for the heir, and finally decided, when no one had been announced, that Thomas should make his claim."

"And how did you feel about that, Mr. Scutton?" Mrs. Frogerton looked at him. "Were you behind your mother's efforts on your behalf, or did you think them unlikely to succeed?"

"To be honest, at first I thought she was delusional," Mr. Scutton said. "But once she explained the familial connections, I began to believe she might be correct, and offered no objection to her writing to Mr. Potkins."

Mrs. Frogerton smiled. "How lucky you are to have such a devoted mother."

"Yes." Mr. Scutton didn't smile back. "Very."

Jenkins, the butler, and the parlor maid came in with a tray of beverages and several plates of cakes. Neither Mrs. Scutton nor her son seemed intimidated by their current surroundings and, in Caroline's opinion, they appeared to be exhibiting an appropriate combination of interest in the earldom and slight disbelief that it could actually belong to their branch of the family. The only discordant note was Mrs. Brigham, who had contributed nothing to the conversation and seemed disinclined to try.

"Were you pleased to discover your brother might be in line for an earldom?" Caroline asked Mrs. Brigham as she handed her a cup of tea.

"Not particularly." Mrs. Brigham set the cup down beside her. "It all seems somewhat far-fetched to me."

Mrs. Scutton reached over to pat her daughter's hand before turning to Caroline. "Please don't concern yourself with my daughter's lack of grace. I fear she is somewhat jealous of her brother's good fortune."

"That isn't true, Mama, I simply—"

Mrs. Scutton spoke over her. "Please, my dear, do not embarrass us in such exalted company. Surely you wish the best for your brother?"

"Thomas doesn't want this, either. It's all you."

"I beg to differ." Mrs. Scutton smiled sympathetically at her daughter. "You know quite well that if Thomas didn't want to be here, he wouldn't have come."

"That's only because you've turned his head with your nonsense."

Mr. Scutton gently cleared his throat. "My dear Mary, I am here because I believe in justice. If the earldom is my destiny, then I will have to accept it."

Mrs. Brigham rolled her eyes and turned her attention to her plate.

Mrs. Frogerton held up the teapot. "Would anyone care

for more tea? I'm sure Caroline has a thousand questions she'd like to ask before you leave."

"There is no great hurry, Mrs. Frogerton." Mr. Potkins looked apologetic. "The Scuttons will be staying in London for several days. They originally thought they would reside in Morton House, but that isn't possible. My clerk is currently trying to find them an acceptable lodging house."

"There's no need for that," Mrs. Frogerton said. "They are more than welcome to stay here."

Everyone looked at their hostess with varying degrees of surprise.

Mrs. Frogerton raised her eyebrows. "It is the simplest solution. Caroline can become acquainted with her relatives, and I always enjoy having a houseful of guests." She smiled at Mrs. Scutton. "Do say you accept."

After a quick shared glance with her son, Mrs. Scutton nodded. "That would be immensely kind of you, Mrs. Frogerton. I agree that Lady Caroline needs time to get to know her recently discovered cousins. This arrangement will facilitate that nicely."

"Then it's all settled." Mrs. Frogerton beamed at her new guests. "Caroline, will you ask the housekeeper to prepare the rooms? And please tell Cook there'll be six of us for lunch *and* five at dinner."

"Yes, of course." Caroline rose to her feet. "I'll do that right away." She relayed the information to the household staff and quickly returned to the drawing room.

Mr. Scutton approached her before she could resume her seat. "I do hope you approve of these arrangements, Lady Caroline."

"Mrs. Frogerton has a most generous nature, sir."

"I must admit, when I heard that she employed *you*, I feared the worst, yet she treats you almost like a member of her family."

"As I said, she is immensely kind. I couldn't have found a better employer."

A slight frown appeared between his brows. "With respect, the fact that you had to seek employment as a titled lady is appalling. One has to wonder at the past earl's priorities in life."

"His priority was himself," Caroline said. "He thought only of his needs and his pleasure and had no interest in supporting his family. He even took our doweries and used them to fund his excesses, leaving my sister and me with nothing."

"I . . . am sorry for that."

"It was hardly your fault, sir."

"I know, but the thought that someone I am even remotely connected with did that to his own children doesn't sit well with me."

"Then you are obviously a far better man than my father." Caroline offered him a smile. "Shall we sit down? I am interested in discovering exactly how we are related."

"I believe it's quite complicated." Mr. Scutton joined her on the couch. "My grandfather—or was it my great-grandfather? Mr. Potkins will know—was a younger son of the Earl of Morton. He took a job as the earl's steward for one of his country properties and married his housekeeper, hence the rest of the family giving him the cold shoulder for years."

Caroline sifted through her knowledge of the family tree. "I should imagine it was your great-grandfather. He was one of six boys."

Mrs. Frogerton joined the conversation. "If that is correct, Caroline, then surely the family name should still be Morton?"

"Then I must have missed out a step, ma'am." Mr. Scutton didn't look concerned or sound guilty at being questioned about his birthright. "My mother knows all the details."

Mrs. Scutton nodded. "At one point the family name *was* Morton. But when Thomas's great-grandfather married beneath him, the family threatened to disown him. He ignored their threats and instead took on his wife's family name, probably to annoy his father. He obviously succeeded, because his allowance was cut off, and he used the name Scutton from then on. My husband had Morton as one of his baptismal names, which is why I was aware of some connection to the earldom."

"It's all rather complicated," Mrs. Frogerton agreed. "But that's probably why it is taking so long to untangle."

"The College of Arms are most diligent," Mr. Potkins said. "I have complete faith in their ability to come to the correct decision." He rose to his feet. "I fear I must leave you, Mrs. Frogerton. I have work to do at the office." He turned to Mrs. Scutton. "I will have your bags delivered here, ma'am, and I'll call as soon as I have word from the College of Arms."

"Thank you, Mr. Potkins." Mrs. Scutton smiled at him. "You have been most accommodating."

"I'd like to get this matter resolved as soon as possible. It is never good for an estate to be in flux."

Mr. Scutton stood and went over to shake Mr. Potkins's hand. "Thank you, sir."

After lunch, Caroline took Mrs. Brigham up to her bedroom, which was between her mother and brother's. It had once been Susan's room, and its emptiness and willingness to be occupied by another reinforced the fact that Susan was not coming back.

"I hope you will be comfortable, ma'am." Caroline smiled at Mrs. Brigham. "If there is anything you need, please ring the bell, and one of the maids will attend to you. Dinner will be served at six."

Mrs. Brigham untied the ribbons of her black bonnet and threw it on the bed. "Even though I don't think we're related in the slightest, I'd prefer it if you'd call me Mary."

"You don't believe your brother is the heir to the earldom?" Caroline asked.

"It seems ridiculous to me. But if my mother sets her

mind to something, she's determined it will happen." Mary sighed. "I told Thomas not to go along with her fantasies, but he always listens to her first." There was a note of grievance in her voice that indicated relations between her and her mother were not amicable.

"Did you mention your concerns to Mr. Potkins?" Caroline asked.

"Of course not. My mother would disown me." Mary took off her pelisse to reveal a gown of unrelieved black. "Do you know when my belongings will arrive? I'd like to change for dinner."

"I'll go and check," Caroline promised as she turned to the door. "I assume they'll be here shortly."

She came down the stairs to discover Mrs. Scutton having a heated argument with an older man who had clearly brought the luggage in. He wore an old-fashioned frock coat, well-worn riding boots, and a faded felt hat that had molded itself to the shape of his head. Caroline paused on the turn of the stair, unsure whether or not to interrupt.

"Ah! Lady Caroline." Mrs. Scutton looked up and beckoned to her. "I was just telling Jude we would no longer require his services and that he could return home on the mail coach tomorrow."

Jude took off his hat and bowed. "Pleasure to meet you, miss."

"Lady Caroline is the daughter of the late Earl of Morton, Jude," Mrs. Scutton said.

Jude studied her carefully and nodded. "Aye, I can see it, now."

"Did you know my family, sir?" Caroline asked.

"In a manner of speaking."

Caroline was just about to ask him to elaborate when Mrs. Scutton pointedly cleared her throat. "As I was saying, Jude. There is no reason for you to stay in London."

"But I promised Mr. Scutton I'd always stay with you," Jude said. "Especially in a place like this." He glanced around the pristine hall as if he was in a brothel.

Caroline hastened to intervene. "I'm sure Mrs. Frogerton could find room for—"

Mrs. Scutton spoke over her. "I can't expect her to house my servants, Lady Caroline. It would be too much of an imposition, and Jude is needed at home." She turned to the man. "You can stay at the Blue Boar Cellar in Aldgate where the coach calling at Epping leaves from. I will provide you with the necessary funds for your return."

"It's not safe to leave you and your children here, ma'am." Jude shook his head. "This isn't the right path for you."

Mrs. Scutton took out her purse and counted out some coins. "This should suffice to pay for your accommodation and ticket."

"But Mr. Scutton said—"

"Mr. William Scutton is dead. I am in charge of the family now, Jude, and I am asking you to go home and look after my property until I return."

Caroline glanced at Jenkins, who had silently appeared behind her. "Can you help Mrs. Scutton's man find his way to the Blue Boar Cellar in Aldgate?"

"Yes, of course, Miss Morton." The butler gestured to Jude. "Would you please follow me?"

After one last glare at Mrs. Scutton, Jude reluctantly departed in the butler's care.

Mrs. Scutton let out a breath. "Thank you, I thought he'd refuse to go."

"His care for your welfare is to be commended, ma'am," Caroline said.

"He is a terrible worrier," Mrs. Scutton conceded. "But perhaps not best suited to a life in London." She sighed. "It has all been something of a whirlwind. I'm not surprised he's upset."

"Jenkins will have your bags sent up when he returns," Caroline said. "Would you like me to escort you to your bedchamber?"

"Yes, please." Mrs. Scutton smiled at her as they went up the stairs. "This house is larger than it looks."

"And has far too many flights of stairs," Caroline agreed as they ascended two floors. "Here you are, ma'am. Your room looks out over the back garden and is remarkably quiet."

"Thank you." Mrs. Scutton hesitated. "Is it difficult for you being in such a position in this house?"

"I am very content here." As Mrs. Scutton talked, Caroline walked around making sure everything in the room met Mrs. Frogerton's high standards.

"I meant being employed when you are the daughter of an earl."

"There's no shame in earning a wage when you need it to survive, ma'am," Caroline said. "And Mrs. Frogerton is a generous employer."

"Still . . ." Mrs. Scutton trailed off, her gaze on Caroline's face. "It can't have been easy."

Caroline smiled. She had no intention of sharing confidences with a woman she had just met, especially one who might be connected to the Morton family. "Is everything to your satisfaction, Mrs. Scutton? Dinner will be served at six. If you need anything in the meantime, please ring for one of the maids."

"I will, thank you." Mrs. Scutton paused. "If you do need someone to talk to about your . . . situation, I am more than happy to listen."

"Thank you." Caroline left Mrs. Scutton and went to find Mrs. Frogerton.

Her employer was enjoying a gentle nap in her chair surrounded by her dogs. None of them stirred as Caroline sat opposite her. It was a good opportunity to consider her first impressions of the Scuttons without Mrs. Frogerton's enthusiastic assistance.

Mrs. Scutton seemed pleasant and obviously controlled her family. Mary wasn't happy and was not averse to sharing her discomfort with anyone prepared to listen. And

Mr. Scutton? What went on behind that quiet exterior? Was he as ambitious as his mother, or did he share his sister's reluctance? It was too early to tell.

A bump on the landing as the Scuttons' luggage was taken upstairs woke Mrs. Frogerton with something of a start. She blinked at Caroline as she sat upright and adjusted her lace cap. "Well, what a to-do! I have many thoughts to share about our guests, but I'd rather hear your opinions first."

"I'm not sure what to think, ma'am," Caroline said. "They seem pleasant enough."

"Apart from the widowed Mrs. Brigham. I'll wager she is not a willing participant in this matter, which makes me wonder why they insisted on bringing her along."

"Perhaps they didn't wish to leave her in her bereaved state," Caroline suggested.

"I suppose that might be it." Mrs. Frogerton frowned. "But she can hardly aid their cause."

"She told me she is skeptical of her brother's claims."

"Did she now!" Mrs. Frogerton smiled. "How interesting! It does all seem a little confusing. One might think they'd have their story straight."

"But perhaps that very confusion signals that there is nothing to be investigated?" Caroline suggested. "If they'd all sang from the same hymn book, we might be suspicious of such uniformity."

"Are you inclined to believe them, my dear?"

"I'm not sure," Caroline said slowly.

"Then let's do our best to come to a conclusion over the next few days," Mrs. Frogerton said. "I am in two minds about their sincerity myself."

Chapter 3

The following morning, Caroline and Mrs. Frogerton were joined by Mrs. Scutton and her son for breakfast. Mary hadn't come down, preferring to stay in bed. They were halfway through the meal when the butler came in with a folded note for Mrs. Frogerton.

She read it and frowned. "Please ask Sergeant Dawson to join us, Jenkins."

"Yes, ma'am."

Mr. Scutton looked up from his plate of eggs and ham. "I do hope nothing is wrong, Mrs. Frogerton."

"I fear we're about to find out," Mrs. Frogerton said as a man entered the room. "Good morning, Sergeant, how may I help you?"

"Sorry to disturb you, ma'am, but there has been a fatality."

"In my family?" Mrs. Frogerton pressed her hand to her bosom.

"No, ma'am." The sergeant's gaze moved over the assembled guests. "I believe you have a Mrs. Scutton staying with you?"

"I am Mrs. Scutton."

"I regret to inform you that your servant, Jude Smith, is dead."

All the color drained from Mrs. Scutton's face. "How can this be? He was alive and well barely twelve hours ago."

The sergeant consulted his notes. "From what we can ascertain, Mr. Smith drank rather too much ale, and when he went into the courtyard to . . . relieve himself—begging your pardon, ma'am—he fell beneath the horses of an incoming coach and was trampled to death."

"Good Lord," Mr. Scutton said. "How absolutely horrible."

"It's my fault." Mrs. Scutton produced her handkerchief and dabbed at her eyes. "I was the one who insisted he go home. I sent him to his death at that inn."

"No one can blame you, Mrs. Scutton," Mrs. Frogerton said. "It is simply a tragic accident."

Mrs. Scutton wept in earnest, and Mr. Scutton attempted to console her.

Caroline took the sergeant to the kitchen for a cup of tea. "What needs to be done, Sergeant?" Caroline asked. "Do you want someone to identify the body?"

"Yes, miss. I'll give you the address of the morgue." He shook his head as he wrote the address down and passed it over to Caroline. "It happens all the time. A man takes too much drink, loses control of himself, and ends up face down in the street. Mr. Smith was just unfortunate that a mail coach happened to come along as he was doing it."

"From what I understand, Mr. Smith was a country man and probably not used to the bustle of a London coaching inn," Caroline said.

"That explains it, then." Sergeant Dawson sighed. "God rest his soul." He finished his tea. "I'd suggest Mrs. Scutton not be the one to identify the body. He's not looking his best."

"I'll make sure Mr. Scutton is aware of that," Caroline said. "Thank you for letting us know so promptly."

"No trouble, miss." The sergeant stood up and put on his tall black hat. "Please extend my condolences to the family."

Caroline returned to the breakfast room to find Mrs. Frogerton sitting by herself. "Mr. Scutton took his mother upstairs to bed."

"I'm not surprised she was overset." Caroline resumed her seat and refreshed her tea. "What a horrible thing to happen."

Mr. Scutton returned, his expression grave. He sat opposite Caroline and grimaced. "Mother was very fond of Jude. She's known him for years."

"Yes, she mentioned how much she depended on him when I spoke with her yesterday," Caroline said. "He seemed very protective and reluctant to leave her in London."

"You saw him?"

"Yes, he brought your baggage. Mrs. Scutton was insistent that he return home and gave him the funds to do so."

"Which it appears he promptly drank." Mr. Scutton frowned. "Alcohol is such a blight on our society."

Mrs. Frogerton nodded in agreement. "My family tends toward the Methodist faith, which doesn't allow drinking. I consider it an advantage in both our private and business lives."

"There are elements of the Methodist faith that I cannot approve of, but I do like their prohibition of alcohol," Mr. Scutton said. "Miss Morton, might I trouble you to ask if the sergeant is still in the house? I have some questions for him."

"Unfortunately, he had to leave, but he did give me the necessary details, including the address of the morgue." Caroline hesitated. "He suggested Mrs. Scutton should not identify the body."

"Don't worry. I'll go."

She gave him the sergeant's note, and he read it carefully before rising to his feet. "If you'll excuse me, I'll go and speak to my mother, and then take myself off to the coroner's office and morgue."

"Of course," Mrs. Frogerton said. "And please tell your

mother that if there is anything she needs, including company, then she should ring the bell and ask for me."

"Thank you, ma'am." Mr. Scutton bowed. "You have been most kind."

After he left, Mrs. Frogerton turned to Caroline. "Well, this wasn't quite how I imagined my morning would proceed, but we'll make the best of it. Do you think Mrs. Scutton and her daughter will come down at all today?"

"It's difficult to say, ma'am," Caroline said. "If you wish, I can go and inquire."

"Let's leave them until midday," Mrs. Frogerton said. "There is a milliners shop I'd like to visit, and I'm sure we won't be missed."

Dinner that evening was a subdued affair during which they planned a trip to Morton House on the following day. Even Mary seemed upset about Jude's death and spoke movingly about his presence during her childhood. Mrs. Scutton was most affected and spoke very little, leaving the burden of the conversation to Caroline, Mrs. Frogerton, and Mr. Scutton.

Both of the Scutton ladies retired to bed after dinner, leaving Caroline to entertain the potential earl in the drawing room. Mrs. Frogerton busied herself writing a letter to Dorothy, which meant she could still keep one ear on the conversation behind her.

"I met a Dr. Harris at the morgue who claimed to know you, Lady Caroline," Mr. Scutton remarked as Caroline handed him his cup of coffee. "He recognized Mrs. Frogerton's butler, who accompanied me."

"We are well acquainted with Dr. Harris, sir," Caroline said as she sat down. "He is a frequent visitor to this house."

"That might explain his familiarity with the occupants of this establishment," Mr. Scutton said. "I must admit I thought him quite presumptuous when he demanded to know who I was and what I was doing at the morgue."

"Dr. Harris does have a somewhat forthright manner of speaking," Caroline said. "But he is a good man and an excellent doctor."

Mr. Scutton cast a glance at Mrs. Frogerton's turned back and lowered his voice. "I am surprised your employer allows such a gentleman into the house when you are present."

"I don't understand your concern, sir." Caroline's brow creased.

"You are a delicately bred unmarried lady of a class far above him."

"I'm employed for a wage. There is nothing delicate about that, Mr. Scutton. In fact, Dr. Harris trained in Edinburgh and would consider himself far superior to me."

"This is what happens when a father is remiss in his duties and his daughters have no male to protect them," Mr. Scutton carried on as if she hadn't spoken. "It leaves you open to all kinds of societal abuse."

"I can assure you that I am very capable of taking care of myself."

"I can only applaud you for that, my lady, while still being offended on your behalf."

"Needs must, sir." Caroline held his gaze. "Now, shall we speak of something else? What career did you intend to pursue before deciding to claim the earldom?"

Spots of color appeared on Mr. Scutton's cheeks. "I have offended you."

"Not at all, sir. I am merely attempting to set matters straight between us."

He nodded. "Then perhaps in the present circumstances we should agree to differ, but I warn you that I might have more to say on the matter if things change."

Mrs. Frogerton rejoined them. "Did the police have anything new to disclose about Jude's unfortunate death?"

"They did." Mr. Scutton hesitated. "Apparently someone who witnessed the event is suggesting that Jude was deliberately pushed in front of the coach."

"Who on earth would do that?" Mrs. Frogerton tutted.

"Perhaps another drunkard," Mr. Scutton said. "Or someone who thought it would be amusing to watch a man die horribly."

Mrs. Frogerton shuddered.

"I have arranged for his body to be taken back to his family in Epping and have offered to pay for the burial," Mr. Scutton said.

"That is good of you." Mrs. Frogerton said.

"It's the least I can do when the man has given my family a lifetime of service." Mr. Scutton rose to his feet. "If you will excuse me, I'll go and see if my mother is awake and tell her about the arrangements I've made."

"Of course." Mrs. Frogerton smiled sympathetically at him. "We will see you both in the morning."

Mrs. Frogerton barely waited until the door closed behind her guest before turning to Caroline. "Perhaps Jude had an argument with someone at the coaching inn, and they followed him outside, and contrived to kill him."

"I suppose that could be it," Caroline said. "He did appear to have a temper."

"Alcohol and a fiery temperament are never a good mix." Mrs. Frogerton sighed. "I wonder if Mrs. Scutton will feel well enough to accompany us to Morton House tomorrow?"

Caroline considered what she'd already learned about Mrs. Scutton. "I am fairly confident that she will."

In fact, all the Scuttons, including Mary, were present at breakfast, and very willing to make the short journey to Cavendish Square. They managed to fit all the ladies in Mrs. Frogerton's carriage while Mr. Scutton rode alongside to their destination.

The state of disrepair was even more evident in the sunlight, and none of the Scuttons spoke much as Caroline ushered them into the front hall.

"Oh, dear," Mrs. Scutton said. "I can quite see why Mr. Potkins said the place was uninhabitable at present."

"Who allowed it to get into such a state?" Mr. Scutton looked up at the hole in the ceiling.

"You'd have to ask the gentlemen at Coutts Bank for the answer to that, Mr. Scutton," Caroline said. "I believe Mr. Castle is coming to visit you this afternoon."

Mary had wandered into one of the rooms, and her voice carried back to them. "Where is all the furniture?"

"The bailiffs took everything that wasn't entailed or listed in the will as a family heirloom to pay my father's debts," Caroline answered her. "They filled several carts."

"You witnessed this?" Mr. Scutton looked appalled.

'My sister and I were asked most politely to sit outside and keep out of the way until the job was done." Caroline hesitated. "It wasn't a pleasant experience."

"I should think not," Mrs. Scutton said. "And what did they expect you to do, left in an empty house?"

"We weren't allowed back into the house after they left, ma'am. We waited on the steps until my aunt's carriage arrived to take us to her home."

"How . . . awful." To Caroline's surprise, it was Mary who came over to touch her arm. "I cannot imagine how I would cope with something so terrible happening to me."

Mrs. Scutton cleared her throat. "Shall we investigate the house further? I am quite keen to see what state the basement is in. Do you know if the kitchen contains a proper stove, or were they still cooking over an open fire?"

"Please excuse my mother," Mary said loudly. "She can lack sympathy for those less fortunate than herself."

Mrs. Scutton spun around. "I am well aware of the iniquity of Caroline's treatment by those who should have supported her, Mary. In my opinion, the best way to help, rather than offering platitudes, is to restore the earldom to its former heights, and make sure she is never in want again!"

"Of course, Mother." Mary met her mother's gaze full on. "No one could possibly doubt your loyalty to your family."

Mrs. Scutton didn't reply. She sallied forth with her son at her side.

Mrs. Frogerton inspected the ceiling. "I think I'll find a man to fix this damage and send the bill to Mr. Potkins," she said to Caroline. "It seems only fair."

Caroline let out her breath, and her employer looked quizzically at her. "Something on your mind, lass?"

"I just wish the Scutton family would show less of an interest in me, ma'am. We haven't even established that they are my kin."

"Their concern for your mistreatment does them no disservice in my eyes. You know that I feel the same."

"It's different when it's you, ma'am."

"Family can be quite awkward at times," Mrs. Frogerton agreed. "And perhaps you have become used to your independence and no longer relish being treated like . . ."

"Like a child." Caroline finished the sentence for her. "Mr. Scutton seems to believe I am incapable of making my own decisions."

Mrs. Frogerton looked at her. "If he is confirmed as the new Earl of Morton, he will believe he has the absolute right to dictate such things."

Caroline raised her chin. "Then he should be prepared for a battle."

She didn't have the heart to wander around her previous home and settled on the stairs to await the return of the others. Voices echoed up and down the stairwells as the visitors explored. Mrs. Scutton seemed to be having a wonderful time imagining how the house might be set up if Thomas succeeded to the title and restored it to its former glory. Mary complained all the way around, and Mr. Scutton said very little.

Mrs. Frogerton appeared in the hall very out of breath. She'd climbed to the upper floor to view the damage to the attics where the water was coming in. It took her at least ten minutes of fanning herself before she had the ability to speak again. "I don't believe the damage is as extensive as

I feared. Once the ceiling is fixed, I think the place will at least be habitable."

"There is no furniture and no staff," Caroline reminded her.

"Those things are easily acquired, lass. I rented most of the items in Half Moon Street."

"If you'll excuse my bluntness, ma'am, you had the means to pay for such things."

"Ah." Mrs. Frogerton frowned. "You make a good point." She brightened almost immediately. "I wonder if Coutts would advance the Scuttons some of the funds they hold for the earldom to staff and furnish the house?"

Caroline was about to demur when it occurred to her that Mrs. Frogerton was generously housing and feeding her unwanted relatives, and that her employer had every right to wish to be rid of them. "Perhaps you might advise Mr. Scutton to make the suggestion to Mr. Castle."

"I'll do that." Mrs. Frogerton took out her pocket watch, which had once belonged to her husband Septimus, who had used it every morning to make sure his workers weren't late to the mill. "We'll need to leave in the next quarter of an hour if we are to be back in time for luncheon and Mr. Castle's visit."

"Then I'll go and inform the Scuttons." Caroline stood up, but Mrs. Frogerton shook her head.

"I'll do it, lass. I obviously need the exercise."

As Caroline had the key, she locked the door after the others left the house. She came down the steps just as Mary was about to join Mrs. Scutton and Mrs. Frogerton in the carriage. Before Mary could step inside, a small boy suddenly appeared and ran straight into her. Mary screeched in alarm as she attempted to disentangle herself from his flailing limbs.

"Sorry, miss!" the boy shouted. "No harm done."

He ran off, but not before Caroline saw him hand Mary a folded note that she quickly slipped inside her glove.

Curious as to what had occurred, but unwilling to question Mary in front of her mother, Caroline held her peace until they alighted in Half Moon Street, and the ladies went up the stairs to change for lunch.

"Mrs. Brigham?" She caught up with Mary at her door. "That boy who ran into you . . ."

"What about him?" Mary stiffened.

"Are you certain he didn't steal anything from you? Pickpockets are all too often children in this city."

"He took nothing." Mary opened her bedroom door. "Thank you for your concern, but it is unnecessary." She shut the door in Caroline's face.

Caroline considered what to do. She was quite sure she'd seen the boy pass Mary a note, but it really wasn't her business, and to insist on an answer would show an appalling lack of manners.

She decided not to waste any further thought on the matter and made her way down to the kitchens to ensure that luncheon would be served in a timely fashion. Mr. Castle was due in an hour, and Mr. Scutton had asked if she'd attend the meeting with him. She'd agreed with some reluctance, unwilling to involve herself in the matters of the earldom, but fully aware that she'd already stepped into the middle of it. If things went well, she intended to excuse herself at the earliest opportunity and leave the Scuttons to deal with the bank on their own.

"Good afternoon, Lady Caroline. It is a pleasure to see you again." Mr. Castle bowed as Caroline entered the morning room accompanied by Mr. Scutton and his mother. His shrewd gaze moved past her and settled on Thomas, and he held out his hand. "The presumptive earl, I assume?"

"Yes." Mr. Scutton shook his hand. "And this is my mother, Mrs. Scutton, who originally contacted the Morton family solicitors."

They sat down, and Mr. Castle set out a notebook and pen on the table beside him. "I have all the pertinent details from Mr. Potkins and the College of Arms, and I believe that your claim might well be validated."

"That is gratifying to hear." Mrs. Scutton smiled. "If there is any further proof required, I will do my best to provide it."

"These matters are somewhat complicated and can take time to resolve," Mr. Castle said. "I understand from Mr. Potkins that you have visited Morton House?"

"We visited the house this morning," Caroline said. "Unfortunately, it is currently unoccupied and in sad need of some necessary renovations."

Mr. Castle sighed. "I regret that the property has been allowed to fall into disrepair. We should have put some tenants in to ensure its upkeep."

"I would've been more than happy to stay there with my sister and run the house for you," Caroline said. "Unfortunately, I was not consulted before the bailiffs moved in and took everything away."

"With all due respect, Lady Caroline, the bank would not have considered a young lady such as yourself capable of managing an establishment alone." Mr. Castle looked genuinely apologetic.

"I'm not sure why when I managed it for years during my father's frequent absences."

"If you'd had a husband or an older male relative to advise you, I'm sure the bank would have dealt with the matter differently, but it is of no matter now." He offered her a condescending smile. "We cannot change the past and must think of the future."

Mr. Castle looked at Mr. Scutton. "We might consider offering you the accommodation at a minimal rate until your claim to the earldom is ratified."

Mr. Scutton frowned. "That is very kind of you sir, but I doubt we could afford to staff the house or—"

The banker waved a hand. "I think the bank might consider dealing with those costs for you as . . . repayment for allowing the house to languish in such a way."

Mr. Scutton looked over at his mother. "What do you think?"

"It is a very kind offer," Mrs. Scutton conceded. "Perhaps we should discuss it between ourselves and give Mr. Castle a decision tomorrow?"

"There's no rush, Mrs. Scutton." Mr. Castle rose to his feet and smiled at the assembled company. "It's been a pleasure."

Mr. Scutton stood and offered his hand to the banker. "Thank you for your consideration, sir."

With one last bow to the ladies, Mr. Castle went out, accompanied by Mr. Scutton.

"That went very well," Mrs. Scutton said, smiling.

"Indeed," Caroline agreed.

"You don't sound very impressed, my dear. One might think you would be pleased to see your cousin recognized in such a manner."

Caroline stood up. "I am delighted for him. If you will excuse me, I will attend to Mrs. Frogerton."

"Of course." Mrs. Scutton waited until Caroline was at the door before continuing. "If I might make a suggestion? I don't think your presence will be needed in future meetings with Mr. Castle. Thomas is quite capable of dealing with his inheritance on his own, and you appear to be something of a distraction."

"I only attended because Mr. Scutton asked me to do so," Caroline said. "In truth, I'd be delighted not to be involved in anything to do with the earldom."

"You sound quite bitter, my dear."

Caroline manufactured a smile. "I believe I have a right to be, but rest assured, Mrs. Scutton, I will do nothing to stop your son from achieving his birthright."

She left and went upstairs to the drawing room where Mrs. Frogerton was reading a novel. She shut the door with something of a bang.

"You will be pleased to hear that the unctuous Mr. Castle is so delighted that there might be an heir to the earldom that he and the bank are willing to staff and repair Morton House just for the convenience of the Scuttons."

Mrs. Frogerton set the book aside. "I am rather surprised by such a notion, but I can't say I'll object if they have to leave my house."

"You have been more than generous, ma'am. Never think that I don't know that," Caroline said. "I should not be bothering you with such matters."

"What is setting you all to alt, dear?" Mrs. Frogerton studied her face.

"The fact that Mr. Castle is so willing to help the Scuttons who might not even be Mortons, and yet was fine with turning Susan and me out of our home, a place I could easily have maintained for the future earl, preventing its current state of disrepair from happening."

"Sit down, lass."

Caroline unwillingly complied. "Apparently if I'd been married or had an older male present in my life, I might have been offered the opportunity to stay on as a housekeeper for the future earl, but I was deemed too weak and *female* to manage such a task."

"Ah." Mrs. Frogerton nodded. "Now I understand your annoyance."

"Mrs. Scutton accused me of being bitter."

"And are you?"

Caroline met her employer's inquiring gaze. "I'm far too angry to be bitter."

"I think you have a perfect right to be angry, my dear. I've always said that those who had a duty toward you and Susan let you down appallingly. My concern for you at present is that your resentment will color your relationship with the man who could soon be declared the head of the Morton family."

"I can assure you that if Mr. Scutton succeeds in his desire to secure the title, I will wish him all the best. I just said as much to Mrs. Scutton."

"I'm not sure it will be that easy to disentangle yourself

from the Morton family, lass," Mrs. Frogerton said gently. "Mr. Scutton strikes me as the kind of gentleman who would uphold his family obligations."

"I cannot deny he seems to be an honorable man, but we both know his mother will run his life, and she won't prevent me from absenting myself."

Mrs. Frogerton opened her mouth and then appeared to reconsider her words. She smiled at Caroline. "Would you go and ask Cook for the revised dinner menu? She said she had some difficulty locating a good piece of lamb and might try something else instead."

Mr. Scutton set down his knife and smiled at Mrs. Frogerton through the candlelight. "You have been most kind to us, ma'am. I hope we will be able to move into Morton House within the next week or so and leave you in peace."

"You have been very amiable guests, sir." Mrs. Frogerton, who was wearing her rubies to match the crimson of her evening gown, smiled back. "Caroline and I will miss you."

Caroline didn't miss the swift glance Mr. Scutton gave her as he sipped his wine. Did he expect her to offer to accompany him? The idea was as ludicrous as the notion that his mother would allow it.

"I do hope you will call on us, Mrs. Frogerton," Mrs. Scutton said graciously.

"Of course," Mrs. Frogerton said. "I'm sure Caroline will enjoy visiting her old home, although it's a shame she had to leave it in the first place."

"I agree," Mr. Scutton said. "I mean no disrespect, Lady Caroline, but your father's mismanagement did neither you nor his successors any favors. According to Coutts, if I am the next earl, I'll have to sell everything that isn't entailed simply to maintain the rest." He shrugged. "Not that I have any aversion to such a notion. The maintenance of such great estates and properties is hardly viable in these modern times."

Caroline set down her fork. "I do hope you consider the implications of your choices very seriously, Mr. Scutton. There are many families who have been employed by the earldom for centuries, and—"

"My dear Caroline, that is hardly any of your concern now, is it?" Mrs. Scutton said. "Thomas will know what is best." She smiled fondly at her son.

"I am merely saying that selling off the estate isn't as straightforward a task as Mr. Scutton might think," Caroline continued, her gaze on Mrs. Scutton. "He should consult with those who can advise him best before making any sudden decisions."

"I think Caroline is right, Mama." Mary looked at her mother. "Thomas would do well to consult with her before he makes things worse. Caroline knows far more about the estate than any of us."

Mrs. Scutton's smile thinned. "And I'd respectfully suggest that you know less than anyone at this table, miss, and might consider keeping your thoughts to yourself."

"I know more than you might think, Mother." Mary glared at her mother. "Mayhap you should remember that."

"This is hardly an edifying conversation for Mrs. Frogerton's dinner table, Mary. I suggest you hold your tongue."

"About what? That you made me tell everyone I'm a widow because you're ashamed of me?"

Caroline tried not to look at her employer.

"Mary . . ." Mr. Scutton murmured.

Mary turned on her brother. "And you can hush, because you went along with it!"

Mrs. Frogerton cleared her throat. "Are we to understand that Mr. Brigham is alive and well?"

"He is." Mary raised her chin. "Isn't he, Mother?"

Mrs. Scutton sighed. "I thought it would be easier if no one knew your shame, dear. But if you are determined to share with our hostess, then so be it." She turned to Mrs. Frogerton. "Mary's husband is currently being held in a debtors' prison."

"For debts he incurred due to your bad advice!" Mary said.

"He didn't need my help to make bad investments, dear. That was his own decision."

"That's a lie!" Mary slammed her hand down on the table, making the crystal rattle. "He told me exactly what happened."

"Well, Albert would blame anyone except himself, wouldn't he?" Mrs. Scutton said. "He's never been capable of taking responsibility for anything."

"How *dare* you—"

"Please." Mr. Scutton spoke over both of them. "I can only apologize for the behavior of my sister, Mrs. Frogerton. She is not herself. The stress of her husband's imprisonment has shattered her nerves."

He reached across the table and took Mary's hand. "Please don't worry, love. I was going to tell you later in private, but I've already secured Albert's release."

Mary's gasp was almost overshadowed by Mrs. Scutton's.

"You've done that for me?" She gripped her brother's hand, her eyes filling with tears. "Thank you. I cannot express how grateful I am to you."

"It is of no matter." Mr. Scutton patted her hand and turned to his mother. She didn't look quite as thrilled by the news. "I felt that with my future prospects looking so bright, I could afford to do this to ensure my sister's happiness."

Mrs. Scutton looked at her son. "Mr. Brigham is not to come here. The last time I saw him, he threatened to kill me."

"He did not," Mary said. "You are simply being melodramatic because he has the audacity to stand up to you."

"He wanted me to pay his debts, and when I refused, he told me he would pay me back in another way. How more explicit did he need to be for you to realize he isn't a good man?" Mrs. Scutton asked.

"Mother . . ." Mr. Scutton intervened again. "This is

hardly the place to be discussing intimate family business. We are embarrassing our hostess."

As Caroline knew Mrs. Frogerton's intense interest in gossip, she doubted that but appreciated Mr. Scutton for attempting to put an end to the mortifying conversation. She might not like Mrs. Scutton, but her daughter was putting her in a horrible position. There had been a look of genuine fear on Mrs. Scutton's face when she'd found out her son-in-law was to be released from prison.

Mary rose to her feet and threw her napkin onto the floor. "You should be very careful what you say to me, Mama, because I'm going to tell Albert *everything*." She glared at her mother. "I'm going to my room, and when my husband does come here, I'll welcome him with open arms!"

Mrs. Scutton bit her lip as the door slammed behind her daughter. "My poor girl. She has been so grievously deceived." She dabbed at her eyes with her black-edged handkerchief. "I hope Mr. Brigham takes his freedom, runs away with it, and doesn't bother Mary again. Did you tell him about your good fortune, Thomas?"

"Of course not," Mr. Scutton said. "I'm not stupid."

"One has to wonder whether Mary has performed that duty for you." His mother stood up and nodded to Mrs. Frogerton. "Please excuse me. I must try to reason with Mary."

"Of course," Mrs. Frogerton said. "Having a daughter myself, I can only sympathize."

"Thank you." Mrs. Scutton smiled. "She is a good girl at heart." She looked at her son. "Perhaps you might accompany me? She listens to you."

"Of course, Mother." Mr. Scutton offered her his arm. "Good night, Mrs. Frogerton, Lady Caroline."

Mrs. Frogerton barely waited before the door closed before she turned to Caroline.

"Well! I can't say I anticipated any of that."

"It is somewhat surprising," Caroline agreed.

"But I can also understand why they tried to cover it up at this particular juncture," Mrs. Frogerton continued. "None of it reflects well on the family. Let's hope that Mrs. Scutton is correct and that Mr. Brigham will stay far away from Mary."

Caroline thought about the note Mary had received and met her employer's gaze. "Unfortunately, I don't think he'll be leaving London any time soon, ma'am. In fact, I suspect he knows where Mary is and has already attempted to contact her."

Chapter 4

The next two days passed without incident. Mrs. Scutton and her daughter didn't appear to be speaking to each other, and Mary remained in her bedchamber. Mr. Scutton divided his time between them with scrupulous care while continuing to meet with his solicitors and bankers.

For the first time since the argument, all the Scuttons were present at dinner. Mrs. Frogerton was discussing the progress of the repairs to Morton House with Mrs. Scutton, while Caroline attempted to converse with Mary, who seemed unwilling to speak to anyone. Even as she persevered, Caroline became increasingly aware of a growing volume of noise coming from the front hall.

She turned toward the door just as an unknown man burst in, closely pursued by Jenkins. Mrs. Scutton screeched, and her son shot to his feet.

"Albert!" Mary cried joyfully. "You have come for me!" She rushed over to the man who grinned and planted a kiss on her cheek.

"That's my girl."

Mrs. Scutton pointed at him. "Get the police. This man should not be allowed in this house!"

"Mr. Brigham, I presume?" Mrs. Frogerton asked. "Is

there any particular reason why you felt it necessary to invade my house like a savage rather than leave your calling card like everyone else?"

"I do apologize, ma'am." Mr. Brigham bowed extravagantly in Mrs. Frogerton's direction. He had a strong Irish accent. "Mary says you've been nothing but kind to her, but I knew the old witch wouldn't see me if she thought I'd come calling all proper-like."

Caroline noticed the butler had disappeared, probably to see if he could find a policeman on the street.

Mr. Scutton faced his brother-in-law. "You promised me you wouldn't make a scene."

"I'm not doing anything, Thomas, me lad," Mr. Brigham said. "I'm just putting you all on notice that I'll be back to claim my wife as soon as my affairs are settled."

"She won't leave with you," Mrs. Scutton said. "She has far more sense than that."

Mr. Brigham glanced down at his wife, who was staring at him adoringly, and winked. "She'll do what she wants."

The butler came back with the footman and a police constable.

"Come along now, sir," the constable said, approaching Mr. Brigham. "I don't want to have to arrest you."

"For what? Coming to see my own wife?" Mr. Brigham sauntered toward the door. "I'm leaving. I'm not the one you should be worrying about. Ask Thomas here what happened to Jude at the inn." He smiled. "He should know because he was right there when the 'accident' happened."

He blew Mary a kiss and walked out, leaving a strained silence behind him.

Mr. Scutton cleared his throat. "I'm not sure what Albert is trying to imply about Jude. I did go and see him that evening at the Blue Boar, but only to reassure myself that he had the necessary funds to leave London. He was neither drunk nor dead when I left him."

"Perhaps you should be more thoughtful about how

you spend your money, Thomas," Mrs. Scutton snapped. "Between Jude and Albert, you have made some very poor decisions lately."

It was the first time Caroline had heard Mrs. Scutton publicly criticize her son.

His cheeks flushed as he looked at her. "I did what I thought was best, Mama. That is all. I refuse to feel guilty about trying to help those in need."

Mrs. Scutton rose to her feet, her expression icy. "If you will excuse me, Mrs. Frogerton, I will retire to bed. I have something of a headache."

"Of course, my dear." Mrs. Frogerton looked sympathetic. "I'll send my maid to attend to you."

Mary barely waited until her mother left the room before she smirked at her brother. "That put the wind up her sails, didn't it?"

Mr. Scutton sighed. "Please ensure that Albert doesn't call here again. If you need to speak to him, send a letter."

Mary laughed as she went out the door. "I'll do what I please, brother. You know quite well that neither of you can stop me."

Mr. Scutton sank down onto his chair, put his head in his hands, and groaned. "I can only apologize for the appalling manners of my family, ma'am. The sooner I can get them out of your house, the better."

"All families have their squabbles, Mr. Scutton," Mrs. Frogerton said. "In truth, I much prefer an argument to sulking and silence."

"Your forbearance is much appreciated." He sighed. "I suppose I'd better go and make peace with my mother."

He left, and Mrs. Frogerton picked up her wineglass and drained the contents in one gulp.

"Good lord, Caroline, living with your family is like being in the middle of a torrid novel!" Mrs. Frogerton sounded more delighted than critical.

Knowing her employer, Caroline guessed she might be

enjoying the drama. "I can only add to Mr. Scutton's apologies, ma'am."

Her employer waved off the apology as she refilled her wineglass. "Mr. Brigham strikes me as something of a rogue. His dislike of Mrs. Scutton was very obvious."

"And hers for him," Caroline said. "I did not appreciate his attempts to intimidate Mrs. Scutton and his threats of retribution."

"He's certainly resentful and angry," Mrs. Frogerton agreed. "What did you think of his suggestion that Mr. Scutton was responsible for Jude's death?"

Caroline frowned. "I cannot think of a single reason why Mr. Scutton would want Jude dead."

"Unless Jude knew something that would undermine the Scuttons' claim to the earldom," Mrs. Frogerton said. "You *did* say Mrs. Scutton was very keen to get rid of him, too."

"I am beginning to wish we'd never become involved in this matter at all," Caroline confided. "The Morton family appear to be cursed."

Mrs. Frogerton smiled. "They are certainly an interesting bunch. I must confess that I am quite enjoying all the excitement." She suddenly sat up straight. "We should invite Inspector Ross to dinner. I'd love to hear what he thinks of all this."

"I doubt he'd be willing to express an opinion at the dining table, ma'am. And expecting him to interfere in a matter that is not under his jurisdiction might demand too much of him."

"I won't be asking for his professional opinion," Mrs. Frogerton said. "Just for his ... *impressions*." She rose to her feet and headed to the door. "I'll write him a note directly while you instruct the butler to bring our coffee up to the drawing room."

Caroline couldn't deny that she'd like to see Inspector Ross, but bringing him into close proximity of the aspiring

Morton clan wasn't ideal. She'd have to warn him before Mrs. Frogerton got to him. The last thing she wanted was to make him feel as if he was useful to them only for his profession and not a welcome guest in his own right. Unfortunately, when Mrs. Frogerton got an idea into her head, she was remarkably hard to stop.

To Caroline's surprise, Inspector Ross was able to come to dinner before the end of the week. She made sure to watch out for his arrival and greeted him in the entrance hall before he made his way upstairs to her employer.

"Lady Caroline." He kissed her hand. "How lovely you look tonight."

She smiled up at him. "You always say the nicest things."

"Only when they are true." He kept hold of her hand, his voice low. "I understand there are claimants to the Morton earldom."

"That's correct." Caroline paused. "I suspect Mrs. Frogerton asked you here so that you could observe them and offer her your unofficial report on their suitability."

"So that's it." His slow smile made her heart turn over. "I did wonder."

"She means no harm by it." Caroline rushed to defend her employer.

He set her hand on his arm and escorted her upstairs. "I need no incentive to call on you, Caroline, you know that." He patted her fingers. "As soon as my brother regains his health, I intend to visit you a lot more often."

Ahead of them, someone cleared their throat, and Caroline looked over to see Mr. Scutton standing stiffly in the doorway.

"May I present Mr. Thomas Scutton, Inspector Ross?" Caroline said. "Mr. Scutton believes he is the next Earl of Morton through our mutual great-grandfather."

Mr. Scutton didn't hold out his hand. "You are a police officer?"

"Yes." Inspector Ross looked slightly bemused.

Mr. Scutton addressed his next words to Caroline. "It is a lowly profession usually confined to the goings-on in the servants' quarters. Are you quite certain Mrs. Frogerton wishes this person to be present at her dinner table?"

"Quite, Mr. Scutton." Caroline smiled as she and Inspector Ross went past him into the drawing room. "Inspector Ross is a valued family friend."

As Mrs. Frogerton immediately rose to greet her guest and thanked him for coming, Mr. Scutton was silenced. Caroline was aware that some members of society viewed the Metropolitan Police with great suspicion, but she'd never heard anyone express it so directly.

She touched Inspector Ross's arm. "I do apologize for Mr. Scutton's behavior."

"There's no need," Inspector Ross said easily. "I've heard such opinions many times before. No one likes the police until the day they suddenly need them."

"Still . . ."

He took her hand. "Please don't let it bother you. I rarely have an evening to myself these days, and I'd love to enjoy this one."

"Hopefully he'll keep his opinions to himself from now on," Caroline murmured. "Or I will have a few things to say to him."

"My fierce protector." Inspector Ross smiled down at her. "Do you believe he truly has a claim to the earldom?"

"My opinion scarcely seems to matter, sir. Coutts Bank and the Morton solicitors seem eager to accept his claim as soon as possible."

"They're probably hoping to get shot of administrating an estate that isn't in the best of health. It's hardly a prize," Inspector Ross said. "But I doubt the Royal College of Arms will be in any hurry. They are immune to pressure from anyone. If my father could bribe them to remove Richard as his heir, I'm fairly certain he would have tried it."

"How are your family, Inspector?" Caroline asked.

"In disarray, Lady Caroline." He sighed. "I sometimes fear they're relying on me to fix everything, and I can't. All I can do is try to support Richard until he comes to his senses, but so far there is no sign of that happening."

"It's terribly unfair when you also have a job to do," Caroline said.

"My superiors have been very patient with me, but I fear it won't last forever." He grimaced. "My worst nightmare is that I'm forced to leave my profession and become my brother's keeper again."

Mrs. Frogerton appeared at Caroline's elbow. "I'm sorry to interrupt, dear, but do you think Mrs. Brigham will be coming down to dinner?"

"I'll go upstairs and check, ma'am."

Caroline left the drawing room and went up to Mrs. Brigham's room. She knocked on the door and went in to find Mary fully dressed and sitting at her dressing table, powdering her face and surrounded by the strong smell of the lily perfume she favored. She jumped when she saw Caroline in the mirror and pressed her hand to her bosom.

"You startled me. I thought you were my mother."

"Good evening, Mary. Are you feeling better?" Caroline asked. "Mrs. Frogerton was wondering whether you intend to dine with us."

Mary tossed her head. "I have no intention of sharing a table with my mother ever again."

"Ah, I thought you'd dressed for dinner, but I will make your excuses to your hostess." Caroline turned to the door.

"My mother would much prefer me to stay up here anyway. She's terrified I'll expose her underhand dealings to destroy my marriage and make her and Thomas look bad."

"I'm sure your mother wishes only the best for you," Caroline said.

Mary snorted. "Hardly. All she cares about is Thomas and this bloody earldom. She insisted I had to accompany them here to show a united front when I wanted to stay home and wait for my husband to be released from gaol." Mary set her hairbrush down with a thump. "My Albert is a good man. He might be somewhat . . . high-spirited and take risks *she* doesn't approve of, but he always pays his debts in the end. She just doesn't want me to be with him."

Having experienced Mr. Brigham's "high spirits," Caroline could quite understand Mrs. Scutton's reluctance to believe her son-in-law had the gravity to make a satisfactory husband, but it wasn't her place to mention it to Mary.

Mary smiled. "She'd better watch it, because if she keeps this up, I'm going straight to that solicitor, and I'll tell him everything."

"Everything about what?" Caroline couldn't prevent herself asking.

"Never you mind," Mary said. "But it would certainly put the cat amongst the pigeons and wipe that satisfied smirk from Mother's face." Mary rose to her feet, stretched, and yawned loudly. "I think I'll take myself back to bed. Tell my mother not to disturb me, and ask the maid to bring me up something nice to eat from the dinner party."

"As you wish." Caroline left and went down to the drawing room to rejoin Mrs. Frogerton and give her the news.

"So, Mrs. Brigham is still fighting with her mother." Mrs. Frogerton glanced over at Mrs. Scutton, who was talking to her son on the other side of the room. "At least those two seem to have patched things up." She looked at Inspector Ross. "Caroline's family have proved to be rather exciting guests."

"They will soon be departing, as Coutts Bank has given Mr. Scutton the means to reopen Morton House," Caroline said.

"Have they now?" The inspector raised his eyebrows. "That is somewhat unprecedented."

Mrs. Scutton approached them, her gaze on Inspector Ross. "I don't believe we are acquainted, sir."

Mrs. Frogerton smiled at her. "This is Inspector Ross of the Metropolitan Police, Mrs. Scutton. He has been of great use to us in the past."

"Good evening, ma'am. It's a pleasure to meet you."

"You don't sound like any policeman I've ever met," Mrs. Scutton said.

"That's because his father is a marquess." Mrs. Frogerton winked at the inspector.

"But he's not a bad sort, despite that." A new voice intruded on the conversation, and Caroline turned to see Dr. Harris behind her. "Evening all, and thank you for the dinner invitation, Mrs. Frogerton. It's the only time I get to eat properly."

"Dr. Harris," Caroline said. "I didn't realize you were coming."

Dr. Harris gazed down at her. "I can assure you that Mrs. Frogerton invited me."

"That's not what I meant, and you know it," Caroline said. "It was just a surprise."

"I met your Mr. Scutton in the morgue," Dr. Harris said. "He tried to ignore my impudence in daring to speak to him, but I persevered."

"He did mention he'd seen you, and that you claimed to be acquainted with Mrs. Frogerton." Caroline turned to Mrs. Scutton. "May I introduce you to Dr. Harris, ma'am?"

Mrs. Scutton regarded Dr. Harris with less than enthusiasm. "You and Mrs. Frogerton certainly have a wide variety of 'friends,' Lady Caroline."

Caroline just smiled. Jenkins appeared to tell them that dinner was ready. Mrs. Frogerton took Inspector Ross's arm, and Dr. Harris offered his to a reluctant Mrs. Scutton, leaving Caroline with Mr. Scutton.

He caught her elbow as she turned to follow the others. "May I have a moment of your time?"

Caroline looked up at him inquiringly.

"I am aware that Mrs. Frogerton is a northerner and that perhaps her social circles are eccentric, but I cannot be comfortable with you being exposed to such gentlemen in her house."

"I beg your pardon?"

He set his jaw. "I am concerned for your welfare, Caroline."

"There is no need, sir." Caroline attempted to shake off his hand, but he gripped harder. "Mrs. Frogerton has always had a kind heart and regularly opens her home to a variety of people she considers friends." She paused and made sure to meet his gaze. "In truth, you should be grateful for that, seeing as she invited your entire family to stay."

His mouth thinned. "We will speak of this again when we are established in Morton House."

"We will not, sir." Caroline pulled out of his grasp. "The only person who currently has authority over my actions is my employer—a woman who has been nothing but kind to you. Yet you insult her with your baseless accusations as to the suitability of her friends."

"I meant no such thing. I am merely looking out for your best interests."

Caroline walked toward the door and headed down the stairs to the dining room where everyone was already seated. Inspector Ross looked up as she came in and raised an eyebrow. She slightly shook her head and took her place beside Dr. Harris at the table.

"What do you make of Mr. Scutton, Miss Morton?" Dr. Harris asked quietly.

They'd finished the first course and were waiting for the soup dishes to be removed.

"I have no opinion to share about him, Dr. Harris."

"That's not like you." Dr. Harris drank his wine. "Have you heard any more from Susan?"

"No."

He set his hand over hers and squeezed her fingers. "I'm sorry. That must be hard for you."

She managed to nod but couldn't find the words to make him think everything was fine when it wasn't. She noticed Mrs. Scutton was looking at them and gently moved her hand away. The last thing she needed was another lecture about her morals or lack of them from the Scutton family.

"The worst thing is not knowing her address," Caroline confided. "I suspect Mabel doesn't want me to have it in case I attempt to lure Susan back home."

"I could ask my sister to write to Susan, or she could get one of Susan's old friends from school to contact her," Dr. Harris offered. "She might respond if she doesn't think it's you, and then at least you would have her address."

"I'd appreciate that."

"Good." Dr. Harris nodded and sat back so that the footman could put his plate in front of him. "Oh, it's lamb. My favorite."

Mr. Scutton barely spoke throughout the entire meal, his indignation with Caroline evident in the tightness of his face and his refusal to converse with her. In truth, Caroline was relieved when Mrs. Frogerton invited the ladies to join her in the drawing room so that the gentlemen could enjoy their port at the table.

When they reached the upstairs landing, Mrs. Scutton turned to Mrs. Frogerton. "If you will excuse me for a moment, I'll go and speak to Mary. Perhaps I can persuade her to join us for a cup of tea."

"Of course." Mrs. Frogerton nodded and walked into the drawing room with Caroline. "I do hope Mary stops sulking. Her refusal to come downstairs means a lot of extra work for the staff."

"From what little I've observed, ma'am, she seems quite stubborn," Caroline said. "A trait she shares with her brother."

"What did you say to upset him before dinner, lass?"

"He tried to tell me what kind of people you should be allowed to have in your own house, ma'am."

"Oh, he didn't approve of Dr. Harris?"

"He didn't like Inspector Ross, either. He suggested he should've used the servants' entrance and stayed in the kitchen where he belonged."

"Oh, dear." Mrs. Frogerton tutted sympathetically. "I must confess that I will be glad when they are gone."

Caroline looked over at her. "You could always ask them to leave now, ma'am."

Mrs. Frogerton smiled. "I think I can deal with them for a few more days, my dear. I'm from hardy stock."

Just as the door opened to admit the butler with the tea tray, a horrendous scream echoed down the stairway. Another quickly followed.

"Good Lord!" Mrs. Frogerton pressed her hand to her chest. "What on earth is going on?"

Caroline was already moving past the butler and going up the stairs. As she ran along the corridor, her gaze fastened on the open doorway to Mary's bedchamber. Mrs. Scutton lay half outside the door, one arm outstretched and bloodied.

She fixed a terrified gaze on Caroline. "Help me, please! My daughter!"

Caroline started toward her when Dr. Harris rushed past. "It's all right, Miss Morton. I'll attend to this."

"I'm quite capable—" Caroline began.

Dr. Harris pushed her unceremoniously to one side and went into the bedroom. "Look after Mrs. Scutton," he snapped, his attention on the bed.

Caroline got a glimpse of Mary's frozen face and blood seeping into the cream counterpane beneath her sprawled body.

"Yes, of course." Caroline stumbled to her knees beside Mrs. Scutton.

She moaned pitifully. "They murdered her! Right in front of me! I tried to stop them, but—"

"Dr. Harris is with Mary now." Caroline took Mrs. Scutton's bloodied hand in hers. "He'll do everything he can to help her." She looked up at Inspector Ross, who'd joined them in the corridor. "Could you ask one of the maids to fetch a pillow and a blanket for Mrs. Scutton? She's shivering."

"It's the shock." Inspector Ross went for the items himself and returned quickly. "Let me help you place the pillow under her head." He frowned down at Mrs. Scutton's pale face. She was struggling to remain conscious. "She's still bleeding. I'll ask Dr. Harris what we can do for her."

Dr. Harris spoke from somewhere above Caroline's head. "I'm here. Can you ask one of the maids to fetch up my medical bag? I left it in the kitchen."

Caroline nodded to Lizzie, the parlormaid. She, the butler, and half the staff stood at the end of the corridor with Mrs. Frogerton. The maid hurried down the back stairs.

Inspector Ross moved closer to the doctor and lowered his voice. "Is Mrs. Brigham dead?"

"Yes."

Mr. Scutton came down the corridor at some speed and out of breath. "What is going on? What has happened to my mother?"

Inspector Ross held out his hand. "There has been a terrible tragedy, sir. Perhaps—"

Mr. Scutton ignored the inspector and rushed into his sister's bedchamber. His horrified gasp was audible from the corridor. "My God!"

Inspector Ross followed him into the room and began speaking quietly while Dr. Harris crouched beside Mrs. Scutton.

"Where are you hurt, ma'am?"

She briefly opened her eyes and stared at him without recognition. "I tried to stop him, but he slashed at me, and I fell back."

"It's all right, ma'am." Even as he spoke, Dr. Harris was rapidly examining the slashes on her arms. "We'll soon have this bleeding stopped."

Half an hour later, Inspector Ross had arranged for a constable to stand guard at the front door, alerted the coroner, and started to question the staff about their whereabouts when the screaming had begun. Caroline was sitting with Mrs. Scutton in her bedroom when Inspector Ross appeared, notebook in his hand, and sat down. His expression was sympathetic, but he also conveyed a sense of authority that required answers.

"Mrs. Scutton, I know that this will be very difficult for you, but can you tell me what happened before your daughter was stabbed?"

Mrs. Scutton swallowed audibly. "I went to check that Mary was all right, and I heard raised voices behind the door. When I went in, *he* was there with his brother. Mary was begging him to leave."

"When you say he, whom do you mean, ma'am?" Inspector Ross asked.

"Her husband, Albert Brigham, and his younger brother George."

Inspector Ross wrote in his notebook.

"I shouted for him to get out, but he told me to shut up, and advanced on Mary, and . . ." Her throat worked. "Suddenly, I saw the flash of a blade, and then he was on her, just stabbing and stabbing . . ." Mrs. Scutton started shaking. "When she fell back on the bed, I threw myself at him, and that's when he stabbed me as well. I remember falling to the floor, trying to hold on to one of them to stop them escaping through the door, but I failed."

"That was very brave of you, ma'am," Inspector Ross said as he continued to write.

"It didn't save my daughter though, did it?" Mrs. Scutton's tears fell unheeded down her cheeks. "It's my fault for letting them find us here."

"You aren't responsible for any of this, ma'am," Caroline said gently. "Mr. Brigham chose to come here and murder his wife. You did everything you could."

"Thomas shouldn't have paid his debts," Mrs. Scutton continued. "And where was he when I screamed for help?"

Caroline looked inquiringly at Inspector Ross. He gave his head a slight shake. "I fear it was too late to save your daughter, ma'am. It appears Mr. Brigham came here with the intent to kill her, and nothing would stand in his way."

"He threatened us," Mrs. Scutton said. "I should have taken him more seriously."

Caroline took one of Mrs. Scutton's bandaged hands in her own. "You did nothing wrong, ma'am. Many people make threats when in a rage."

"My poor darling . . ." Mrs. Scutton began to cry again.

Caroline turned to Inspector Ross. "I think Mrs. Scutton should be left to recover, Inspector. Perhaps you might come back tomorrow?"

"Yes, of course." Inspector Ross rose to his feet. "Thank you, ma'am. I am very sorry for your loss. I promise we will do everything possible to find your daughter's husband and bring him to justice."

Caroline joined Inspector Ross outside the bedroom and closed the door so that Mrs. Scutton wouldn't hear anything. "*Was* Mr. Scutton in the dining room with you?" Caroline asked.

"He was not." Inspector Ross said slowly. "He asked to be excused. I thought it was because he considered Dr. Harris and myself beneath his interest."

"He didn't appear for quite some time, did he?" Caroline asked as they slowly walked toward the stairs. "If he'd gone to his room, he would've been right next door to Mary and would've heard everything."

"Perhaps he went into the garden to smoke?" Inspector Ross suggested.

"I've never seen him smoke. One has to wonder if he was the person who let the Brigham brothers in."

"Why would you think that?"

"Because Mr. Scutton always seems eager to please his sister and help her husband."

"It's an interesting point." Inspector Ross considered her. "So far, none of the staff have said they admitted them, but no one claims to have seen them leave either."

"Possibly because everyone was rushing up here to see what all the screaming was about."

Inspector Ross followed Caroline into the drawing room, where Mrs. Frogerton awaited them. She told them that Dr. Harris had gone back to the hospital for his night shift.

"Did you see Mr. Scutton after dinner, ma'am?" Caroline asked her employer.

"I'm not sure that I did. Why? Is it important?" Mrs. Frogerton raised an inquiring eyebrow.

"I believe Lady Caroline is trying to establish where Mr. Scutton was when his mother started screaming." Inspector Ross took the glass of brandy Mrs. Frogerton offered him and sat down beside Caroline on the couch.

"He arrived at the top of the stairs well after I did, and he was breathing hard," Mrs. Frogerton said. "He seemed frozen with shock and almost reluctant to make his way down the corridor toward his mother."

"People behave in many different ways when confronted with violence, ma'am," Inspector Ross said. "It is not uncommon for someone to be paralyzed with fear."

"I suppose that's true." Mrs. Frogerton didn't look convinced. "Perhaps he hates the sight of blood. I am the same, but I doubt I'd stand at the end of the hallway dithering while my family were in great distress."

"Lady Caroline wondered whether he was the one who let the Brighams into the house," Inspector Ross said.

"That might account for his shock," Mrs. Frogerton agreed.

"Or the Brighams could have slipped in while the staff were busy preparing dinner," Caroline suggested. "The back door is not always locked."

"That does seem more likely. Because why would Mr. Scutton wish such horrors on his mother and sister?" Mrs. Frogerton looked at Inspector Ross. "From all accounts, he's devoted to them."

"Perhaps Mary asked her brother to let her see her husband before he left London, and he agreed to help her?" Caroline suggested. "Mr. Scutton could not have known what Albert truly intended."

"Which might also be why he was slow to react, because he couldn't quite come to terms with what he might have done." Mrs. Frogerton nodded.

Inspector Ross finished his drink and rose to his feet. "I'll conclude my interviews with the staff, and I'll come back tomorrow to speak to Mr. Scutton. I hope he'll be able to give me a good description of the Brigham brothers to distribute to my constables."

"I'll let him know you'll need to speak to him when he returns," Mrs. Frogerton said. "Good night, Inspector."

"Good night, ma'am. Lady Caroline." He smiled, bowed, and left the drawing room.

Mrs. Frogerton shook her head. "What a dreadful thing to have happened. Poor Mrs. Brigham."

"Indeed, it is quite horrific," Caroline agreed.

For once, Mrs. Frogerton didn't make light of the matter. "One has to suspect the trouble between Mary and her husband was brewing long before we became involved and was always likely to end in violence and tragedy."

"There was so much blood." Caroline drank her brandy and shuddered. "I don't think I'll ever forget it. I wish I'd heeded Dr. Harris's warning. He was right—I should not have looked."

"Even a stopped clock is right twice a day, my dear, and I suppose it *is* his area of expertise."

"I was just glad he and Inspector Ross were here," Caroline continued. "Imagine if we were dining alone and the Brighams had decided we should *all* die."

It was Mrs. Frogerton's turn to shudder. "Don't think of that, lass, or you'll never close your eyes again."

"I'm not sure I'll be able to anyway." Caroline smiled at her employer. "In fact, I think I'll sit at Mrs. Scutton's bedside, and make sure she has a comfortable night."

"That would be very good of you, my dear." Mrs. Frogerton rose to her feet. "Will you tell the butler to make sure everything is properly locked up tonight? I fear my nerves couldn't stand another invasion."

"Yes, of course, ma'am." Caroline nodded at her employer. "I do hope you are able to sleep."

"Oh, don't worry about me, lass." Mrs. Frogerton waved Caroline's doubts aside as she went toward the door. "I have my dogs to protect me, and I'm as tough as they come."

Caroline wished she could say the same as she tidied the drawing room and took the tray down to the deserted kitchen. Even though she knew the butler would test all the locks before he retired, she checked them all herself. Every sound from the street seemed magnified, every crackle from the coal in the range and drip from the pump made her strain to listen harder, her heart jumping in her chest.

It wasn't until she settled in the armchair beside Mrs. Scutton's bed that she realized she was still shaking. She glanced down at Mrs. Scutton's pale, oblivious face. Her bandaged arms and hands lay on top of the quilt, her fingers curled inward as if still trying to grasp the intruders. Dr. Harris had dosed her liberally with a sleeping draught to keep the horrors at bay. Caroline had always avoided such medication unless it was absolutely necessary, but was tempted to help herself to a spoonful from the bottle beside the bed.

She reminded herself that panicking helped no one and that Mrs. Frogerton was relying on her to keep a calm head and help the Scuttons come to terms with their devastating loss. It had been an awful evening, and for the Scutton family, things would never be the same again. . . .

Chapter 5

"I'm not sure what you're implying, sir." Mr. Scutton looked down his nose at Inspector Ross. "I have no idea how the Brigham brothers got into this house, and I resent you suggesting that I had anything to do with it!"

It was the morning following Mary's murder. Inspector Ross had returned to the house to continue his interviews with the staff and Mr. Scutton. Caroline hadn't intended to be present when the inspector spoke to Mr. Scutton, but after his rudeness the previous evening, she'd reluctantly remained in the drawing room to make sure Mr. Scutton behaved himself.

"It is my job to ask the difficult questions, Mr. Scutton," Inspector Ross said. "One might think you would be willing to cooperate with my inquiries in order to find your sister's murderer." He glanced down at his notebook. "You asked to be excused from the dining room before we had our glass of port. Where did you go?"

"That is none of your business."

"I'm merely trying to establish whether you might have caught a glimpse of the Brighams arriving at the house, or if you saw anything that didn't strike you as unusual at the time but that might turn out to be significant later."

Mr. Scutton set his jaw. "I went into the garden. I preferred my own company to Mrs. Frogerton's choice of dinner guests."

"And you saw no one else there?" Inspector Ross asked. Caroline was impressed by his determination not to take offence. "Was there anything in the garden that seemed out of place?"

Mr. Scutton frowned. "Now that you mention it, the gate at the end of the garden leading to the mews was ajar. The latch was banging against the frame in the wind, and I went to close it."

"I assume that gate is normally locked?" Inspector Ross looked over at Caroline, who was trying to remain inconspicuous in the corner.

"Yes, Inspector. Mrs. Frogerton is very careful about such matters," Caroline said.

"Then one has to assume that might be how the Brighams entered the property," Inspector Ross said. "Thank you, Mr. Scutton. That is most helpful."

"You're welcome." Mr. Scutton looked impatiently toward the door. "Have you finished with me now?"

"Not quite." Inspector Ross consulted his notes. "I understand that you paid off Mr. Brigham's debts."

"Yes, but that doesn't mean I expected him to come here and murder his wife." Mr. Scutton glared at the inspector. "I was attempting to alleviate her distress and hoped Brigham would take the chance offered to him and leave us in peace."

"That is quite understandable, sir." Inspector Ross nodded. "You have obviously known Albert Brigham for some years. Would you consider him a violent man?"

"Hardly, or I would never have allowed him to marry my sister," Mr. Scutton snapped. "He was a little loud and vulgar for my personal taste, but Mary seemed to like him, and I tolerated him for her benefit."

"How did Mr. Brigham end up in such dire financial straits that you were obliged to pay his debts?"

"How the devil should I know?" Mr. Scutton demanded.

"And what in God's name does that have to do with him murdering Mary?"

"Excuse me, Inspector." Caroline cleared her throat. "I was under the impression that Mrs. Brigham believed her husband was given bad financial advice by her family, which led to his incarceration."

Mr. Scutton turned to look at her. "With all due respect, Lady Caroline, I'd appreciate it if you refrained from commenting on my family. It's bad enough that I have to allow you to be here during this pointless interview, but presuming to air your views about a matter you know little to nothing about is beyond the pale."

Ignoring Mr. Scutton, Inspector Ross looked at Caroline. "Did Mrs. Brigham tell you that herself, my lady?"

"Yes, she did," Caroline confirmed. "She was very upset about it."

Inspector Ross wrote something in his notebook while Mr. Scutton scowled at both of them. "Did you know Mr. Brigham's brother well, Mr. Scutton?"

"Hardly at all. He lives in Ireland with the rest of the family and rarely visits."

"Then one has to wonder why he was here now," Inspector Ross murmured. "Did his brother send for him, or was his appearance simply propitious?"

"One might think you are paid to answer such questions, Inspector." Mr. Scutton said. "Not me."

"Oh, I will answer them, sir." Inspector Ross smiled as he put his notebook away in his pocket. "Don't you worry about that." He turned toward the door. "Thank you for seeing me, and for the descriptions of the Brigham brothers. I'll return as soon as I have news."

Caroline followed him out into the hall and waited as he picked up his tall black hat. He didn't have to wear the navy and black uniform of his subordinates, but he tended to wear similar colors to blend in.

"It appears that Mr. Scutton has no liking for me or my profession," he said as he headed for the front door. "Perhaps his attitude will change when I apprehend the Brighams."

"I doubt it," Caroline said. "He seems to take your mere presence as a personal insult."

Inspector Ross shrugged. "It's not uncommon for people to treat the metropolitan police like that. Mr. Scutton has just suffered a terrible bereavement, and no one is at their best in such circumstances."

"You are far more charitable than I am." Caroline opened the front door. Birds were singing in the trees lining the street, and the sun shone brightly. Mrs. Frogerton had ordered the front shutters to be closed out of respect for the dead, and it was something of a pleasure for Caroline to see the light. "Do you think you will apprehend the Brighams?"

"We have both their names and their descriptions, which is a distinct advantage. I'll be back this afternoon to speak to Mrs. Scutton if your physician thinks she will be well enough to receive me."

Caroline nodded. "I believe she is eager to speak to you."

"That's encouraging." His smile was rueful. "Yet again I am visiting you in my professional capacity, Lady Caroline, and not as I truly wish."

She smiled back. "In truth, I am just glad to see you, sir."

He winked and tipped his hat. Then he walked down the steps and onto the street before heading toward the main road, where Caroline presumed he would look for a hackney cab. She went back into the house and discovered Mr. Scutton awaiting her in the hall.

"I assume he'll be back to bother us again tomorrow?"

Caroline looked at him. "Inspector Ross is doing his job, sir."

"His questions are far too intimate to be ignored," Mr. Scutton snapped. "His *impudence* . . ."

"I would have thought you'd want your sister's murderers to be caught," Caroline said. "Inspector Ross is extremely successful at his job and due for another promotion."

Mr. Scutton snorted. "He's an aristocrat. He will receive advancement regardless of his abilities."

"If you dislike him so intensely, sir, I suggest you visit his superiors at Scotland Yard and ask for someone else to deal with the case." She walked toward the stairs and paused to look at him. "Now if you will excuse me? I need to speak to Mrs. Frogerton."

She started up the stairs, leaving him staring after her. She had a sense there was a lot more he wished to say, but she wasn't in the mood to listen to his complaints, and her sympathy for his loss was rapidly dissipating.

Mrs. Frogerton looked up as she came in. "Was Mr. Scutton helpful to Inspector Ross?"

"Not particularly. He seemed determined to take offence at every question Inspector Ross asked him." Caroline sat opposite her employer. "He was most displeased at my presence during the interview as well."

"I suspect he is feeling guilty," Mrs. Frogerton mused. "He's angry at himself for paying Albert's debts, but he's decided to take out his anger on poor Inspector Ross, who is only trying to help."

"I think you are correct, ma'am. I don't know how Inspector Ross remained so calm when he was treated so offensively."

"One assumes that is why he is so successful at his profession," Mrs. Frogerton said. "I hope Mrs. Scutton will provide enough evidence to ensure a conviction." She glanced up as Mr. Scutton came striding into the room. "Good morning, sir."

"Ma'am." Mr. Scutton bowed. "I have decided to have my sister buried as quickly as possible and have spoken to the local vicar and the undertaker. The vicar can hold a funeral service tomorrow at three. I do hope you will both attend."

"Yes, of course." Mrs. Frogerton paused. "Do you think your mother will be able to come?"

"I doubt it, ma'am, and, in truth, it is probably better if she doesn't in her current emotional state."

"Have you spoken to her about the matter?" Mrs. Frogerton asked.

"I'm just on my way upstairs to do so. I saw your doctor in the hall, and he agrees that my mother should stay in bed."

He left, and Mrs. Frogerton looked at Caroline. "Well. Mr. Scutton has been busy."

"He strikes me as the kind of man who prefers action to inactivity."

"I'm surprised he doesn't want to take Mary back to Epping for burial," Mrs. Frogerton said. "She has no roots here in London and will lie among strangers. It's almost as if he wants to forget this tragedy ever happened."

"My father was buried very quickly and without the ceremony normally afforded to a peer," Caroline said. "Aunt Eleanor was worried that if she didn't get him into sacred ground before the inquest into his death, he might be denied his final resting place in the family vault."

"Which makes me wonder again why Mr. Scutton is in such a rush."

"You can't think he had anything to do with her death?" Caroline asked.

"I don't know, lass." Mrs. Frogerton grimaced. "I just feel there is something off with this indecent haste to bury his supposedly much-loved sister."

"Grief can affect people in different ways," Caroline said.

"That's the truth." Mrs. Frogerton sighed. "After he leaves, I'll go and see how Mrs. Scutton has taken the news of her daughter's quick burial."

"Will you ask if she is still willing to see Inspector Ross at two?" Caroline rose to her feet. "I'd hate to waste his time."

Mrs. Frogerton stood, too, and smiled at Caroline. "I don't think he ever minds visiting here, lass, but I'll ask." She sighed. "Mrs. Scutton's the one I have the most sympathy for. Watching her daughter being murdered right in front of her . . ." She shook her head.

"I quite agree, ma'am." Caroline walked with her to the door. "I'll speak to Cook and make sure she sends up something pleasant for Mrs. Scutton's midday meal."

Inspector Ross returned promptly at two, and Caroline took him up to Mrs. Scutton's bedchamber. Mrs. Frogerton was enjoying a quiet nap with her dogs.

"Good afternoon, ma'am." Inspector Ross bowed to Mrs. Scutton, who was sitting up in bed with her pillows stacked behind her. Both her hands were still bandaged, and she was very pale. "I can offer only my sincere condolences for the loss of your daughter and my promise that I will do everything in my power to find the culprit and bring him to justice."

"Thank you, Inspector." Mrs. Scutton's voice was still hoarse from screaming. "Please sit down."

Inspector Ross took the seat next to the bed and Caroline sat on the dressing-table chair near the window. She'd spent a lot of time tending to Mrs. Scutton since Mary's murder and knew she was grieving profoundly for her daughter's loss.

Inspector Ross took out his notebook and pen. "I realize this will be difficult for you, ma'am, but the better the information you give me, the easier it will be to solve this dreadful crime."

Mrs. Scutton nodded. "I will do my best, sir. Although I must admit that some matters are rather hazy in my mind." She hesitated. "At times it felt like a terrible nightmare from which I couldn't wake up."

"Perhaps you could tell me what happened in your own words, and I'll take notes. If I require any clarification, I'll ask you for it."

Mrs. Scutton's gaze went past the inspector and fastened on Caroline before moving back to her hands, which were clasped on the coverlet in front of her.

"Mary and I hadn't been on the best of terms. I was vexed at Thomas for paying off Albert's debts, but Mary rebuffed my concerns. My fears were justified when Albert turned up here and threatened us. Mary thought it all a big joke." Mrs. Scutton looked down at her bandaged hands.

"And what happened on the evening your daughter died, ma'am?" Inspector Ross prompted her.

"Mary refused to come down to dinner, and I decided to go and speak to her after we'd left the gentlemen to their port." Mrs. Scutton glanced at Caroline. "Miss Morton was present at the time."

"Yes, I can confirm Mrs. Scutton was concerned for her daughter and went up to see her after the ladies withdrew from the dining room."

"Thank you, my lady." Inspector Ross wrote something in his notebook. "What happened when you went into your daughter's room, ma'am?"

Mrs. Scutton's hand fluttered to her throat. "I opened the door. Mary wasn't in bed but was standing against the wall facing two men. It sounds ridiculous now, but it took me a moment to comprehend what I was seeing. Mary looked over at me, and I realized she was terrified. She said . . ." Mrs. Scutton swallowed hard. ". . . 'Help me.' Then Albert turned to look at me, and I saw the knife in his hand and moved toward him." Mrs. Scutton moistened her lips. "It all happened so *quickly*. One moment he was jeering at me, the next . . . the light was flashing on the blade as he drove it into Mary's chest and throat. She screamed and fell back onto the bed, blood pouring out of her, while Albert stood over her laughing, and . . . I must have attacked him."

Caroline got up and poured Mrs. Scutton a glass of water, which she took with a shaking hand. "Thank you, my dear."

"And what happened after that?" Inspector Ross asked gently.

"George Brigham started urging his brother to leave, and I tried to stop them." Mrs. Scutton shook her head. "I was so *angry* I wanted to hurt them both, but even though I tried my best, George easily shook me off, and they ran away, leaving me screaming on the floor."

"I arrived shortly after I heard the screaming, Inspector," Caroline said. "And found Mrs. Scutton in the open doorway."

"Did the younger Mr. Brigham participate in the attack?" Inspector Ross looked up from his note-taking.

"Only by being present and not stopping his brother, until it was too late," Mrs. Scutton said. "He must have known Albert had a knife with him."

"He didn't interfere at all?"

"No."

"Do you think he was shocked by what his brother did?"

"I don't know." Mrs. Scutton considered the question. "I must confess that he was the least of my concerns when my daughter was dying in front of me."

Caroline was almost pleased to see Mrs. Scutton regain some of her feistiness as she answered Inspector Ross. She'd been in a daze since the tragedy, barely managing to eat or find the energy to leave her bed.

"Thank you, ma'am." Inspector Ross finished writing and closed his book. "You have been most helpful in very difficult circumstances. Mr. Scutton has provided me with descriptions of the Brigham brothers, which will be circulated widely through London and beyond. I am confident that they will be found."

"Unless they've gone abroad," Mrs. Scutton said as she sipped her water. Caroline was relieved to see some color had come back into her face.

"The major ports have been alerted, ma'am."

"I think they have family in Ireland."

"I'll make sure to add that to my notes." Inspector Ross

got to his feet and bowed. "Thank you again, Mrs. Scutton. I will do my best to apprehend these felons and bring them to justice."

He left, and Caroline went to Mrs. Scutton's side. "You were very brave, ma'am."

"I should have realized what Albert was capable of and made sure he couldn't get near my beautiful daughter." Tears slid down her cheeks. "I failed her."

"No, ma'am." Caroline took Mrs. Scutton's trembling hand in hers. "Mr. Brigham failed to live up to basic standards of human decency and deliberately took a life. The responsibility is entirely his."

"I never liked him," Mrs. Scutton continued. "He was such a bad influence on her."

Caroline gave Mrs. Scutton her clean handkerchief and poured her another glass of water.

"My mother's family heartily disliked my father and only agreed to the marriage because my mother was besotted with him," Caroline said. "That didn't work out happily for her, either."

"At least he didn't murder her." Mrs. Scutton dabbed her cheeks.

"No." Caroline had no answer for that. Draining the life, hope, and love from someone until they no longer wished to live was painful to watch, but not murder. She rose to her feet. "I'll ask Lizzie to bring you up some tea, ma'am."

"Thank you." Mrs. Scutton eased back against her pillows. "I think I need to rest."

Chapter 6

The sun was shining brightly as the small funeral party made its way to Grosvenor Chapel on South Audley Street. It would have taken only ten minutes to walk, but Mr. Scutton was determined to do things properly and had provided a funeral carriage drawn by four black, plumed horses to follow the coffin. When they arrived at the church, they discovered Mr. Castle from Coutts Bank, Mr. Potkins, and Inspector Ross had come to pay their respects.

The recently built chapel was a quiet, austere space unencumbered by the ghosts of the past and provided the perfect place for the short funeral service. As the vicar hadn't known Mary, his remarks were perfunctory, and far easier to bear than personal recollections. Because Mr. Scutton had insisted there was to be no music, the service took less than half an hour. The funeral bearers took the coffin, and the mourners followed them and the vicar to the burial ground at Mount Street.

It was a pleasant site, which Mrs. Frogerton approved of because she hoped it would remind Mary of the forests around Epping where she had lived. Women were not generally welcomed at the side of a grave, but Mrs. Frogerton had insisted they would attend because she had promised Mrs. Scutton a full account of the proceedings.

Inspector Ross, who was immaculately turned out in black, came to stand beside Caroline and Mrs. Frogerton.

"Good morning, Inspector," Caroline murmured. "Have you apprehended the murderers yet?"

"Not quite, my lady, but I have some leads on where I might locate them. They are well known in certain quarters of the city." He paused. "I find it helpful to attend funerals such as this because you never know who will turn up."

"You think the Brighams might be here?"

"You'd be surprised how often the murderer comes to their victim's funeral. Sometimes out of guilt and sometimes because they wish to make certain the person is dead."

Caroline glanced over at the vicar, who was opening his prayer book, and then at Mr. Scutton, whose face was completely blank. Beside her, Mrs. Frogerton took a black lace handkerchief from her reticule and applied it to her eyes.

Caroline patted her arm. "Please don't distress yourself, ma'am."

"I'm just imagining how I would feel if it was my daughter being buried while I still lived," Mrs. Frogerton whispered. "I don't think I could bear it."

The vicar started his final prayers, and the small group fell silent. Around them, the birds continued singing and traffic rolled past. Caroline couldn't help looking around the edges of the graveyard just in case the Brighams had turned up. She caught a glimpse of someone approaching and poked Inspector Ross's arm.

He looked down at her, and she pointed to the entranceway where a tall gentleman was striding purposefully toward them. The inspector nodded and moved quietly to intercept the man while Caroline watched in some trepidation. There was something familiar about the man. . . .

Caroline let out a breath as she realized it was Dr. Harris. He shook Inspector Ross's hand, and they both came over to her.

"Sorry I'm late," he whispered.

"As I didn't know you were coming, I can hardly be concerned about your tardiness, Dr. Harris," Caroline murmured. "You should direct your apologies to Mr. Scutton."

"And interrupt the funeral service?" Dr. Harris made a tutting noise. "I'd have thought you'd been brought up to know better, Miss Morton."

She turned her attention back to the vicar and left Dr. Harris to explain himself to Mrs. Frogerton.

Mr. Scutton spent a moment with his head bowed over the grave before turning sharply on his heel and heading for the gate.

He paused to speak to Mrs. Frogerton when the rest of the party caught up with him. "I think I'll walk back to Half Moon Street."

Mrs. Frogerton nodded. "As you wish, Mr. Scutton. I'll take care of your guests until you arrive."

"Thank you, ma'am."

Mrs. Frogerton looked at Inspector Ross and Dr. Harris. "Do you wish to join us in the carriage, gentlemen?"

Dr. Harris nodded, as did the inspector.

"Come along, then." Mrs. Frogerton led the way after pausing to thank the coffin bearers and pat the horses.

Caroline found herself seated opposite Dr. Harris and Inspector Ross and spent the short journey mentally characterizing their similarities and differences. They were both tall and dark-haired. Dr. Harris tended to dress as if he'd pulled all his garments from a jumbled pile on his floor, whereas Inspector Ross always looked elegant. Dr. Harris's face was as expressive as a stormy day, while the inspector favored a calmer more inscrutable look.

She knew them both to be honest and courageous men who did their best to right wrongs be they physical, material, or emotional. She would trust them both with her life.

"Are you feeling quite well, Miss Morton?" Dr. Harris said as the carriage stopped in Half Moon Street and Inspector Ross escorted Mrs. Frogerton inside. "You look rather bilious."

"I've just attended the funeral of a woman who was murdered in this house," Caroline said. "How would you expect me to look?"

"Ah, good point." He got out of the carriage and came around to offer her his hand to descend. "Did you like Mrs. Brigham?"

"I can't say that I knew her well, but she was always very pleasant to me."

"Do you believe the Scuttons are related to you?" He remained by her side as the butler opened the door and they went into the entrance hall. "I can't say I've noticed any resemblance between you."

"I leave such matters to the College of Arms and the Morton solicitors," Caroline said as she untied the black ribbons of her bonnet and took off her cloak. "In truth, I have no interest in who takes on the title and lands."

Dr. Harris stared down at her. "Well, perhaps you should."

"Why? The Morton family has hardly treated me well."

"But it's your heritage."

"I'm surprised to hear you championing the upper classes, sir. Normally you need no invitation to heap scorn on the institutions that keep them in place."

"Do you want Mr. Scutton to succeed to something that isn't his by right?" Dr. Harris obviously wasn't willing to stop arguing.

"As I have already said—"

He continued. "You do realize that if he becomes the earl, things might change?"

"I'm sure they will, but that will be Mr. Scutton's problem, and nothing to do with me." Caroline glanced around, glad to see that everyone else had ascended to the drawing room.

"I'm not sure if you are being deliberately obtuse, Miss Morton, or really haven't thought this matter through."

Caroline glared at him. "If you are going to be unpleasant, Dr. Harris, I'll leave you to it."

There was a pause, and he set his jaw. She turned away and put her foot on the bottom step of the stairs.

"Caroline . . . he'll be the head of your family."

She looked back at him and immediately regretted it. The look of genuine concern on his face was unsettling.

"He'll consider he has the right to interfere in your life," he continued.

"Don't be ridiculous, Dr. Harris," Caroline said briskly. "He already dislikes me. The last thing he'll want is to see me again once he's established as the earl."

She headed up the stairs and looked down at him from a safe distance. "Are you coming?"

He sighed, took off his hat, and threw it in the general direction of the hall table. "Fine. Ignore me."

"I will." She smiled to show that she wasn't annoyed with him at all, even though he'd perturbed her. "Mrs. Frogerton's cook has made an excellent lunch."

Inspector Ross looked up as they came into the drawing room and walked over to greet them.

"Dr. Harris, I'm glad you came." He lowered his voice. "I know this isn't the right time to ask about medical matters, but it would save me a trip to St. Thomas's to speak to you."

"Mr. Scutton hasn't arrived yet," Caroline said. "There is no one who might take offence."

"Ask away," Dr. Harris said. "I'm always delighted to help the police."

"I wondered whether you had an opinion as to the type of blade that would've been used to stab Mrs. Brigham."

"I assume from the question that you didn't recover one in the bedroom?"

"No. It's highly likely Albert Brigham took it with him."

Dr. Harris pursed his lips. "The blade was long and sharp enough to sever a major artery in Mrs. Brigham's throat.

Once that happens, death is almost instantaneous because of the speed of blood loss."

Inspector Ross nodded. "So, longer than a standard pocketknife, but shorter than a sword."

"Yes, more like a dagger," Dr. Harris agreed. "Not necessarily the type of thing you'd carry around with you unless you perceived you were under constant threat."

"Or you wished to do harm to another," Caroline added and shivered.

Both men looked at her with varying degrees of concern.

"Yes, that, too." Dr Harris reached out and awkwardly patted her shoulder. "There's no need to dwell on it, Miss Morton."

"I wasn't intending to." She stepped away from him and collided with Inspector Ross, who instinctively put his arm around her waist to steady her. "I do apologize."

Dr. Harris looked at them and bowed. "I'll offer my respects to Mrs. Frogerton and take a glass of brandy."

Caroline eased away from Inspector Ross.

"He's quite fond of you, isn't he?" he said, staring after Dr. Harris.

"In his own way." Caroline smiled. "It's like having an irritating older brother who is intent on sticking their nose in your business, and totally oblivious to any hints to keep out of it."

Inspector Ross chuckled and set her hand on his sleeve. "Come and get something to eat. I'm sure you'll need your strength for dealing with the Scuttons."

"They have turned into something of a trial," Caroline acknowledged. "I regret allowing Mrs. Frogerton to become involved with them."

"I suspect she's quite content with the situation." Unconsciously, Inspector Ross echoed what Mrs. Frogerton often told Caroline. "She likes to be needed and busy, and the Scuttons have certainly offered her plenty to do."

"I suppose so." After making sure her employer was already supplied with both food and drink, Caroline picked up a plate and helped herself, Inspector Ross still beside her. "It still seems a dreadful imposition."

"But they'll be moving into Morton House at some point," Inspector Ross reminded her.

"When Mrs. Scutton feels able to cope," Caroline said. "And if Mr. Scutton truly is the earl."

"She seems to be a strong woman. I'm sure she'll come about." Inspector Ross looked back at the door where Mr. Scutton had just come in. "Will you excuse me? I'll go offer Mr. Scutton my condolences, speak to the vicar and then I need to be on my way. The search for the Brigham brothers is a priority. I'm sure Mr. Scutton will be delighted to hear that one of the stable boys saw the Brighams coming into the garden through the unlocked gate to the mews."

"I suppose that depends on whether he was the one who unlocked it. Thank you for coming," Caroline said.

"It's my pleasure, Lady Caroline." He walked with her to where Mrs. Frogerton was chatting to the vicar and his wife and bowed. "I have to leave, ma'am. Thank you for inviting me."

"It's always lovely to see you, Inspector Ross, even on a such a sad occasion as this." Mrs. Frogerton offered him her hand, and he bent to kiss her fingers. "I'm sure we'll see you soon."

"I hope so, ma'am. The quicker we find the Brigham brothers, the better it will be for everyone." He inclined his head and went over to Mr. Scutton, who looked less than pleased to see him. It took but a moment for the men to exchange words, and then Inspector Ross left.

Duty compelled Caroline to go over to Mr. Scutton, who was standing with Mr. Castle, and attend to his needs. "Would you care for some refreshments, sir?" Caroline asked.

"Just some tea, please." He visibly straightened his back. He looked exhausted. "I need to go tell my mother how the ceremony went."

Caroline nodded and was just about to turn away when he touched her arm. "May I ask a favor of you?"

"Yes, of course."

"My sister's belongings."

Caroline took a moment to consider exactly what he was asking her before venturing a guess.

"Would you like me to pack them up for you?"

"I'd like you to sort them out—give the personal items to me and get rid of her . . . clothing and such. I don't think my mother is in a fit state to accomplish this task, but I dread her going into Mary's room and seeing everything still there."

"That is very thoughtful of you, Mr. Scutton," Caroline said. "I'll speak to Mrs. Frogerton and attend to the matter as soon as she gives me leave."

"Thank you." He bowed stiffly. "I'd appreciate it."

"You're most welcome, sir," Caroline said. "Now, let me get you a cup of tea while you thank the vicar, and then you can take it up with you to visit your mother."

After the last guest departed, Mrs. Frogerton went for her afternoon nap, leaving Caroline with plenty of time to deal with Mary's possessions. She opened the door into Mary's bedroom with some trepidation. The last time she'd been in there, the smell of congealing blood had been overwhelming, and she'd feared she might faint.

To her relief, Mrs. Frogerton had ordered the disposal of the mattress and all the bed linen and instructed the maids to scrub the room until no trace of the tragedy remained. It smelled strongly of lye soap, and the sun was filtering in through the open window along with the gentle roar of traffic from Piccadilly. There was still evidence of Mary's presence scattered around the room. but otherwise it looked perfectly bland.

Caroline had asked the butler to bring up Mary's bags from the basement, and they stood underneath one of the windows. She opened the wardrobe and took out Mary's gowns, skirts, and petticoats, placing them on the bed. As she folded each garment, she methodically checked the pockets and the fabric for any attached pins, jewelry, or loose items. There was a small brooch in the shape of a rose attached to the collar of Mary's favorite church dress, which Caroline unpinned and set on the dressing table, but little else. From what Caroline knew of the family, they hadn't been wealthy, and Mary's belongings bore that out.

Her petticoats and gowns were darned, the hems turned, and various adornments had been added or taken away to keep the garments within the bounds of recent fashion. It appeared Mary had been an excellent and careful needlewoman.

She investigated the bottom of the wardrobe where there was a line of boots and shoes in similar condition—patched, well polished, resoled, and carefully looked after. Caroline placed everything from the cupboard onto the bed.

Mary's possessions reminded Caroline vividly of her own. Learning to be frugal had taught her some valuable lessons of economy, but they had been hard learned. She'd never realized how fortunate she was until the family funds were abruptly cut off, and she was left to fend for herself, or serve others simply to survive.

Caroline shook off her thoughts and turned her attention to the chest of drawers. At the back of the underwear drawer, she found two long jewelry cases and set them aside. There was a well-thumbed bible and a prayer book with several pages marked with spills of paper.

Caroline hadn't thought of Mary as particularly religious, but it appeared she had a strong faith. There was also a catechism for the Roman Catholic Church, which gave Caroline pause. Was Mr. Brigham a Roman Catholic? Mrs. Scutton had mentioned he had family in Ireland. Had Mary agreed to accept his religion when she married him? Caroline had a sense that it was non-negotiable.

She couldn't imagine Mrs. Scutton being pleased about

that. To many people, popish heretics could not be trusted and were justly barred from holding office or marrying into the Royal Family. Had Mary pretended to go along with Mr. Brigham's demand that she renounce her faith and take on his? Would such a deception have led her husband to decide she should no longer be allowed to live? There was no divorce for the common man. . . .

From all she'd heard and seen of Mr. Brigham, he hadn't struck her as a particularly religious man, but faith could run deep. Caroline set Mary's prayer books beside the jewelry cases on the dressing table. Clearing out the drawers, she found a small bottle of rose water, a tin of red lip tint, and a glass vial filled with a clear liquid. She had little knowledge of the practices of the Roman Catholic Church but assumed the bottle held something significant.

Mary's cloak and coat hung on the back of the door, with her leather gloves in the pocket along with a curiously regular string of black oval beads on a circular chain. There was no sign of her purse or any money. Had the Brighams taken that from her before Mrs. Scutton came upon them? Or had Mary offered them everything simply to buy her freedom? When Inspector Ross apprehended the Brighams, she'd have to ask him to check if Mary's purse was in their possession.

She checked the back of the drawers and under the bed, but didn't find any correspondence, personal or otherwise. Had Mary burned every letter or note she'd received while in London? Caroline's gaze went to the fireplace, but Mrs. Frogerton's staff were too efficient to leave any evidence behind in the grate. She could ask Ellie the housemaid if she remembered any paper being burned, but was it important? Caroline didn't know, and Ellie had gone away to help her mother.

It wasn't until she packed the first bag with Mary's boots and gowns that she realized the dress Mary had worn when she'd been murdered had been her best dress. Caroline frowned. When she'd spoken to Mary just before dinner, she'd been wearing a brown silk and lace evening gown. She'd told Caroline she was too tired to come down and was off to bed.

Why had Mary remained in all her finery? Caroline closed the first bag and buckled the straps. Had she been expecting someone? Had she been murdered by a man she'd deliberately invited into the house?

Chapter 7

There was a knock on the door, and Caroline jumped as Mrs. Frogerton peered in at her.

"What's wrong, lass? You look as if you've seen a ghost."

"I suspect sorting the possessions of someone who has been murdered is likely to encourage the worst kind of thoughts, ma'am." Caroline folded Mary's cloak and coat and laid them in the bottom of the second bag. "There are some puzzling anomalies."

"Such as?" Mrs. Frogerton had moved over to the dressing table and was examining the bottles with an interested eye. "Good Lord! Why does she have this popish thing?" She held up the small glass vial. "That's the Virgin Mary."

"I wondered that myself, ma'am, as she also has a Roman Catholic catechism and a string of what I assume must be prayer beads."

"A rosary? Perhaps Mr. Brigham was forcing her to convert!" Mrs. Frogerton shuddered.

"Have you seen such things before, ma'am?" Caroline asked as her employer set the vessel down. "I was wondering what the liquid is inside it."

"What those heathens insist on calling Holy Water. It supposedly has healing powers." Mrs. Frogerton didn't sound convinced. "They scoop it up in their churches where it's blessed by the priest and bring it home to dab on themselves at the first sign of illness or trouble." She noticed Caroline was staring at her. "I know all about these customs because we employ many people from Ireland in our mills and potteries."

Caroline nodded. "Ah, that makes perfect sense. I wonder if Mr. Scutton was aware that his sister had such popish leanings."

"He'll certainly know when you hand over her possessions to him."

"Do you think I should?" Caroline asked somewhat hesitantly. "Mr. Scutton once mentioned he'd been considering entering the Church of England before the matter of the earldom came up."

Mrs. Frogerton turned to look at her. "He can't do anything about it now, can he, lass? His sister is dead, and none of us can know her mind."

"Yes, of course," Caroline said. "I don't know what I was thinking."

"You were thinking about protecting Mary, and there's no shame in that." Mrs. Frogerton's eye was caught by the jewelry boxes. "These are very fancy."

"I haven't looked inside them yet, ma'am," Caroline admitted. "I thought, perhaps . . ."

She needn't have bothered, as Mrs. Frogerton was already undoing the clasp and reading the inside of the padded lid. "Ooh! Rundell, Bridge and Company are some of the finest jewelers in London. Dotty was always going on about them having made the Lingard family tiara." She paused. "Oh, there's nothing in here."

"That seems odd, ma'am," Caroline said. "Why would she keep an empty box?"

"Perhaps she was wearing the items on the evening she died." Mrs. Frogerton frowned. "I'm sure I would have noticed the quality of this jewelry if I'd seen her wear it."

"We'll have to ask Inspector Ross." Caroline hesitated.

"Although the lack of jewelry does call attention to something that was already puzzling me."

"What is that?" Mrs. Frogerton carefully examined the inside of the satin case, but there didn't appear to be anything hidden within.

"Her purse isn't here either."

"Do you think those braggards robbed her as well?" Mrs. Frogerton shook her head. "The depravity!"

"Or Mary gave them everything of value she possessed to try to persuade them to leave her alone."

"Blackmail."

"Possibly." Caroline set the second empty box down on top of the first. "I'm beginning to wonder whether she invited Mr. Brigham here thinking she could persuade him to give her up in exchange for all her worldly possessions."

"If Mary was expecting them, it might explain how those villains gained access to my house so easily," Mrs. Frogerton said. "None of my staff are careless about their own safety, let alone mine."

"Yes, while the staff were busy preparing dinner, Mary could've sneaked down the back stairs to the lower levels and left both the garden gate and the back door unlocked. She told me she intended to go to bed, but she was dressed in her best dinner gown and was very eager for me to leave. She didn't seem to want her mother to visit her, either."

Mrs. Frogerton smoothed her fingers over the velvet-covered jewelry box. "The poor lady."

"Yes, if she willingly invited her murderer into this house, she made a terrible mistake."

Before Mrs. Frogerton could respond, the door opened, and Mrs. Scutton came in. She still wore her nightgown and had one of Mrs. Frogerton's shawls wrapped around her shoulders. Her hair hung loose around her shoulders, and she looked exhausted.

"I heard voices, and for a moment I thought it had all

been a terrible nightmare and my Mary had returned to me." Mrs. Scutton swayed on her feet.

Mrs. Frogerton hastened to Mrs. Scutton's side. "I'm so sorry we disturbed you."

Mrs. Scutton stared at Caroline. "Why are you touching my daughter's things?"

"Mr. Scutton asked me to pack Mary's possessions away so that you would not have to worry about it," Caroline said. "I didn't mean to offend you."

"What is this?" Mrs. Scutton pointed at the stack of prayer books and the glass vial.

Behind her back, Caroline and Mrs. Frogerton exchanged concerned glances.

"Perhaps you should speak to Mr. Scutton about these personal matters, ma'am?" Caroline suggested. "He asked me to bring everything to him."

Mrs. Scutton raised her chin. "I don't know what is wrong with the boy, burying her in haste, and now attempting to erase her very existence." She staggered slightly, and Caroline rushed to take her arm and guide her to a chair. "It's as if he's trying to pretend she never lived."

Mrs. Frogerton caught Caroline's eye. "Why don't you go see if Mr. Scutton has returned from his errands, Caroline, while I help Mrs. Scutton back to her room."

"Yes, of course, ma'am."

Caroline left the bedchamber in some haste and went in search of Mr. Scutton. Somewhat to her relief, he had just entered the hall and was removing his hat and gloves when he looked up and saw her.

His expression was inscrutable as she approached him. "Good afternoon, Lady Caroline."

"Mr. Scutton." She paused at the bottom of the stairs. "Your mother came upon me while I was packing Mary's belongings and didn't take it well."

He sighed. "I would've hoped you'd be more careful." He started up the stairs. "Is she angry with me?"

"I cannot say, sir. She just seems distressed and wishes to speak to you." Caroline followed him. "Mrs. Frogerton is with her now."

"Then I'll go and see her." He paused long enough to look back at her. "Can you at least ensure that Mary's belongings are put in my room?"

Caroline resisted the impulse to curtsy like a parlor maid and instead nodded before he continued down the corridor to his mother's bedchamber. He knocked sharply on his mother's door and went in. Caroline expected Mrs. Frogerton to appear, but there was no sign of her, so Caroline continued into Mary's room to gather Mary's belongings and transfer them to Mr. Scutton's room.

She hadn't been in Mr. Scutton's bedroom since he'd taken possession of it, but she wasn't surprised to see he kept it in good order. There was a small standing cross on the dressing table beside a common prayer book and a candle, but no other ornamentation. His clothing was all put away, and even his hairbrush was immaculate.

Caroline set Mary's bags beside the bed and left her more personal possessions on the coverlet. There was little else she could do to help the murdered woman, but she had great faith in Inspector Ross's ability to bring her killers to justice.

She left Mr. Scutton's room and paused in the corridor, listening. There were no raised voices from Mrs. Scutton's bedroom, which was a relief, but there was also no sign of Mrs. Frogerton. It was possible the Scuttons were holding their fire until their hostess removed herself from their vicinity. Caroline considered whether to knock on the door and inquire after Mrs. Frogerton but decided against it. If anyone could extricate themselves from a difficult situation, it was her employer.

Her faith was rewarded as Mrs. Frogerton emerged from the room, closing the door firmly behind her. Then she immediately craned her neck so that her ear was as close to the door as possible.

"Mrs. Frogerton," Caroline whispered in consternation. "What are you doing?"

Her employer held her finger to her lips, and Caroline went to stand beside her. It wasn't long before Mrs. Scutton raised her voice and was immediately countered by her son. Unfortunately, it was still impossible to hear what they were arguing about.

"Ma'am," Caroline said urgently. "Forgive me, but this is highly inappropriate."

Mrs. Frogerton sighed and moved back. "I can't hear them anyway. I should've gone up the back stairs."

"For what purpose, ma'am?" Caroline asked

"Because they were dying to shout at each other and they couldn't wait to get rid of me. I almost felt obliged to leave them to it."

They headed down the stairs to the drawing room, and Mrs. Frogerton took her usual seat by the fire. Caroline rang for some tea and sat opposite her employer. "Was Mrs. Scutton angrier than her son?"

"Oh, no, she was upset. He was the one who was angry, and, like most men, he made little effort to conceal his true feelings." Mrs. Frogerton allowed her favorite pug dog to sit on her knee while she talked. "In truth, he blamed you for the whole debacle."

"Me?" Caroline sat up straight. "He *asked* me to pack Mary's things."

"He blamed you for drawing his mother's attention to his actions. He claimed that he'd merely been attempting to mitigate her grief and that you had somehow bungled it by being too loud or something equally laughable."

"What a . . ." Caroline couldn't think of a suitable word to utter in front of her employer.

"Sanctimonious buffoon comes to mind," Mrs. Frogerton mused. "I must say that Mr. Scutton has failed to endear himself to me in any way."

"Did you get any sense about what they were arguing about?" Caroline couldn't resist asking.

Fortunately, Mrs. Frogerton was more than willing to indulge Caroline's curiosity. "Mr. Scutton seemed inclined to believe his mother had known about Mary's flirtation with 'heretical beliefs' and wanted to know why she hadn't mentioned it to him. *Mrs.* Scutton was far more interested in discussing her son's indecent haste in burying his only sister."

"I wonder who will win the argument?" Caroline asked.

"Mrs. Scutton."

"Even in her current state?"

"Yes, because I might not like Mr. Scutton, but he does treat his mother with respect." The door opened, and the butler appeared with the tea. Mrs. Frogerton put the dog on the floor and thanked Jenkins as he set down the tray.

The butler turned to Caroline. "Mr. Lewis has called and wondered if he might come up and speak to you for a moment."

"*My* Mr. Lewis?" Mrs. Frogerton asked.

"Yes, ma'am. Your man of business." The butler bowed.

"Then please show him up and fetch some more cups." Mrs. Frogerton sent the butler on his way and glanced over at Caroline. "I wonder what he wants to speak to you about?"

"I have no idea," Caroline said. "I can only hope it isn't bad news."

"You are such a pessimist, my dear."

"I wonder why?" Caroline rose to her feet as Mr. Lewis came into the drawing room. "Good afternoon, sir."

He strode over to shake her hand and then turned to Mrs. Frogerton. He was a small, dapper man with a pleasant expression and a spring in his step. "Thank you for receiving me. I was on my way to my office and thought I'd see if you were entertaining guests."

"You're hardly a guest," Mrs. Frogerton said as she gestured for him to sit down. "Would you care for some tea?"

"That would be most welcome. It is surprisingly warm out there today."

"Well, if you will insist on walking everywhere, sir . . ."

"I enjoy a good walk, ma'am." Mr. Lewis patted his stomach. "I sit at a desk for most of the day, which is not good for my health."

Mrs. Frogerton didn't look convinced. Persuading her to take a short walk in the park with the dogs was as much as Caroline could manage.

Caroline poured tea for him and Mrs. Frogerton, and then for herself when the extra cups arrived.

She listened quietly while Mr. Lewis and Mrs. Frogerton exchanged pleasantries and updated each other on family news. She had no particular desire to hear what he wished to talk to her about. In her experience, legal matters rarely worked in her favor.

Eventually, Mr. Lewis returned his attention to her, and she mustered a smile and gave him her full attention.

"Lady Caroline, I have some news to share with you about the African mines."

Mrs. Frogerton set down her cup. "I just realized I am being rather rude in assuming that either of you require my presence while you discuss this private matter."

"I am more than happy to proceed with you here, ma'am," Caroline said quickly. "I value your counsel."

"That is very wise of you, my lady," Mr. Lewis said. "Mrs. Frogerton is one of my most astute clients."

"Then I will stay." Mrs. Frogerton beamed at both of them. "But I will resist the urge to comment unless specifically asked for an opinion."

Mr. Lewis turned back to Caroline. "I've recently been in correspondence with the DeBloom family lawyers. As you are no doubt aware, since the demise of her mother and the incarceration of her brother, Miss DeBloom is the only member of the family who still owns shares in the company."

"Did Mr. DeBloom relinquish his shares to his sister?" Caroline asked.

"Yes, but he had little choice in the matter. After his

prosecution for fraud, he was deemed no longer fit to run a business, and barred for the remainder of his life from doing so."

"And quite rightly so," Mrs. Frogerton murmured.

"Miss DeBloom has no interest in running the mines, and her lawyers have been looking around for a potential buyer. I can't say I approve of such tactics when you and your sister Susan are the majority shareholders, but that is what they've been doing."

As he appeared to be waiting for her to say something, Caroline nodded for him to go on.

"They wrote to me to say they'd been approached by a potential buyer and that Miss DeBloom was more than willing to accept their offer."

"If she sells her shares, what happens to ours?" Caroline asked.

Mr. Lewis smiled. "Well, that's the question, isn't it? I'm happy to tell you that the new mining company wants to discuss buying you out, too."

"Well, I cannot claim to be attached to these mythical mines, so I would be willing to consider their offer," Caroline said. "I assume the DeBloom lawyers can vouch for the credibility of this new company?"

"Yes, they've been extremely diligent in their investigations and have passed everything over to me," Mr. Lewis said. "If you like, I'll send over what I received so that you can look through it."

"Please send it over," Mrs. Frogerton said. "I'd be more than happy to go through it with you, Caroline."

"I'd appreciate that, although I'm not quite sure what the fuss is about," Caroline said. "The likelihood of that land being profitable is very small."

"I wouldn't be so sure about that, my lady. As the sole landowner and part business owner, the offer you receive from the mining company should be significantly higher than the one Miss DeBloom is ready to accept," Mr. Lewis continued. "I will make sure to consult with every expert I can find to ensure that the financial compensation they offer you reflects the potential value of the land."

"Thank you." Caroline smiled at Mr. Lewis. "I know that you will do your best for me."

"Of course." He finished his tea and turned to Mrs. Frogerton. "I won't keep you any longer, ma'am."

"It's been a pleasure." Mrs. Frogerton nodded as Mr. Lewis rose to his feet. "Caroline deserves some good fortune in her life."

Mr. Lewis winked at Caroline. "Then I'll do my best to provide it for her."

After he left, Mrs. Frogerton turned to Caroline. "Well, lass, this is exciting, isn't it?"

"Is it?" Caroline set Mr. Lewis's empty cup on the tray. "I've learned not to get too stirred up about such matters, ma'am. They tend to lead to disappointment."

Mr. Scutton came into the drawing room and paused. "I do apologize. Am I interrupting?"

"No, please come and sit down and take some tea with us," Mrs. Frogerton said. "We just had a visit from my Mr. Lewis who manages my business affairs. He also manages Caroline's affairs, and we were merely discussing possibilities."

"I wasn't aware that you had affairs that were separate to the Morton estate." Mr. Scutton looked inquiringly at Caroline.

"Your family solicitors allowed the earl to break every legal rule to take money that didn't belong to him, leaving Caroline and Susan without funds or doweries," Mrs. Frogerton spoke before Caroline could think what to say. "Caroline had a perfect right to move her personal affairs to someone who wouldn't be so easily duped."

"I had a small bequest from my Aunt Eleanor," Caroline said. "Mr. Lewis deals with that and some of my father's other investments."

"Your father?" Mr. Scutton paused. "Surely such matters are part of the Morton estate?"

"Not these particular things, sir. They are not covered by the entail." Caroline silently scolded herself for even mentioning the matter.

"Are you quite sure? Perhaps I should speak to this Mr. Lewis and ask him to apprise Mr. Potkins as to the state of your affairs."

"When you become the earl, you are more than welcome to speak to Mr. Lewis," Caroline said. "There is nothing worth discussing at this point."

"Then one might wonder why Mr. Lewis came to call today and why he wished to speak to you." Mr. Scutton sipped his tea.

"He was passing and came in mainly to see me," Mrs. Frogerton said. "My son has been helping him invest Caroline's inheritance, and he wanted us to know how successful that strategy has been."

"Perhaps you might ask your son to help with the Morton estate, ma'am," Mr. Scutton said rather sarcastically. "From what I can see, there will need to be harsh economies if the earldom is to survive and become profitable."

"I'll mention it to Samuel next time I write, Mr. Scutton, but he is a very busy man," Mrs. Frogerton refused to be ruffled by his tone. "He certainly inherited my head for figures."

"I'll bear that in mind, ma'am." Mr. Scutton cleared his throat. "Has there been any news about the Brigham brothers from the police?"

Caroline was slightly surprised at his abrupt change of subject, but she was more than willing to go along with it.

"We've heard nothing from Inspector Ross today."

"Typical," Mr. Scutton tutted.

"I'm sure the police are doing their best," Mrs. Frogerton chimed in. "I have complete faith in Inspector Ross."

"With all due respect, ma'am, that's because you like him. You have no knowledge of his ability to catch criminals."

Mrs. Frogerton chuckled. "Oh, you'd be mistaken about that. I've been on the wrong side of Inspector Ross on more than one occasion, especially when he arrested Dr. Harris on suspicion of murder."

"I can quite believe Dr. Harris would arouse suspicion in anyone," Mr. Scutton murmured as he stood up. "There is something distinctly disreputable about the man and his appearance."

"He's an excellent doctor," Caroline said.

Mr. Scutton looked down at her. "You have a soft heart, Lady Caroline, and, I fear, a tendency to be taken in by those who might not have your best interests at heart."

"I beg to differ, Mr. Scutton," Mrs. Frogerton said. "Caroline is no fool. Now, does your mother intend to come down to dinner tonight?"

"I doubt it, ma'am. I fear our disagreement exhausted her, and she has retired to bed." He bowed and looked at Caroline. "Thank you for dealing with Mary's possessions, my lady."

He left the room and shut the door behind him.

Mrs. Frogerton turned to Caroline, her expression full of dismay. "I do beg your pardon. I should never have mentioned that Mr. Lewis called to see you."

"It is of no matter, ma'am," Caroline said. "In fact, it might be worth asking Mr. Lewis if the assets I currently hold *are* mine and not part of the earldom."

"From what I understand, if the matter isn't mentioned in the entail, then it belongs to the person who was bequeathed it in the will. But I agree that Mr. Lewis would be the best person to confirm that opinion."

"I'll send him a note," Caroline said. "The last thing I want is to be embroiled in any further legal trouble with the Morton estate."

Chapter 8

Two days later, Caroline joined Mrs. Frogerton in the breakfast room.

"There you are, lass." Mrs. Frogerton refilled her coffee cup. "Mrs. Scutton feels well enough to visit Morton House to see how the renovations are coming along. I said that you would accompany her."

"Yes, of course. What time does she wish to leave? I'll go order the carriage."

"There's no particular rush." Mrs. Frogerton pointed at the chair opposite hers. "And you have a letter from Mr. Lewis to read."

Caroline sat down and took the letter. It was relatively short, which was a blessing. "Mr. Lewis says that my father was very careful to list the shares and land in our names and not his, which means they are not considered part of the Morton estate."

"Excellent news." Mrs. Frogerton smiled. "I did think of one benefit of you selling that land, dear. You'll have to inform Susan of her good fortune, and if that doesn't raise Mabel's interest, nothing will."

"Yes, I'd have to insist on her giving me a proper home address and the name of a reputable financial institution in Maryland where the money could be deposited in Susan's name." Caroline folded the note and placed it back on the silver salver.

"And if she is unwilling to provide such information, you should ask Mr. Lewis to hold on to any money until she does."

There was a steely note in Mrs. Frogerton's voice, reminding Caroline that beneath her pleasant exterior, her employer was a shrewd negotiator and successful business owner.

"Don't you think it's strange that the Scuttons haven't put a notice in the newspaper about Mary's death?" Mrs. Frogerton asked. "One has to wonder if they've told anyone at all, because they certainly haven't received any letters of condolence and none of their acquaintances were invited to the funeral."

"That is odd, isn't it?" Caroline said slowly. "Perhaps Mr. Scutton is waiting for his mother to recover sufficiently to deal with such matters."

"What matters would those be, Lady Caroline?" Mr. Scutton said from the doorway. He entered the room and loomed over the table. He wore black, as befitted his current state of mourning, and had the somber expression to match.

"We were wondering whether Mrs. Scutton needed our assistance to share the news of her daughter's death," Caroline said. "It appears there has been no formal announcement in the newspapers yet."

He visibly stiffened. "My mother is quite capable of dealing with our family affairs."

Caroline smiled. "Then we shall leave everything in her capable hands. Are you accompanying her to Morton House this morning, sir?"

"I wasn't aware that she felt well enough to go out."

For a moment, Caroline regretted engaging him in conversation. Everything she said made him poker up even more, and she was tired of being conciliatory. She poured herself a cup of tea from the pot the butler placed in front of her and mentally rearranged the tasks she had to deal with for the rest of the day to accommodate her outing with Mrs. Scutton.

"Any news from Scotland Yard?" Mr. Scutton asked after helping himself to a substantial breakfast. He took a seat beside Mrs. Frogerton.

"Not so far," Mrs. Frogerton answered him. "But I'm sure they'll apprehend the culprits soon."

"That would be nice," Mr. Scutton said drily. "As we are all forced to pay for this ridiculous policing service, the least they could do is attempt to catch the odd murderer."

Caroline set her cup down rather hard in the saucer and abruptly stood up. "If you'll excuse me, I need to speak to Mrs. Scutton and send a message to the mews about our departure time."

"Thank you, my dear." Mrs. Frogerton smiled sunnily up at her. "I have a few letters to write this morning, so I will see you when you return."

Caroline took her time ascending the stairs. The last thing she wanted was to bring her annoyance with Mr. Scutton into her dealings with his mother. She knocked on the bedroom door and went in to find Mrs. Scutton sitting in the chair beside the bed. She wore one of Mrs. Frogerton's black gowns, and her hair was arranged in a neat, low bun at the back of her neck.

"Good morning, ma'am." Caroline smiled at her. "I understand that you wish to visit Morton House?"

"Yes, I need to leave this room." Mrs. Scutton looked toward the windows. "Or else I fear I will go mad."

"Have you had your breakfast, ma'am?" Caroline asked gently.

"I have, and I wish to leave as soon as possible."

"Then I will send a message to the coachman and ask him to bring the carriage around."

"Thank you."

"You are most welcome." Caroline inclined her head. "I will return to escort you down the stairs when the coach has drawn up outside the front door."

* * *

It seemed Mr. Scutton had decided not to accompany them to Morton House, for which Caroline was grateful. Mrs. Scutton was silent on the way to Cavendish Square, her gaze on the busy streets beyond the carriage, her gloved hands clasped tightly in her lap.

After they alighted, Caroline produced the key, but as they approached the front door, it opened to reveal a workman.

"Morning, miss, ma'am." The man beckoned them inside. "Be careful now, won't you? We've been fixing that hole in the roof, and we've stirred up a lot of dust."

"We will endeavor to keep out of the way of your workers, Mr. Murphy," Caroline said. She regularly communicated with the Irishman whom Mrs. Frogerton had hired to repair Morton House. "This is Mrs. Scutton. She will be living in the house when it is completed."

"Good morning, ma'am." Mr. Murphy touched his cap to Mrs. Scutton, who was looking around the entrance hall. "It will be lovely when it's finished."

"I'm sure it will." Mrs. Scutton offered him a brief smile.

"Would you care to come down to the kitchen, ma'am?" Caroline asked. "Mrs. Frogerton wanted your opinion on which stove to put in."

Mrs. Frogerton had said no such thing, being a woman who made quick decisions and stood by them. Caroline had a sense that Mrs. Scutton desperately needed something to engage her interest, and a discussion about the merits of various stoves might animate her.

Mrs. Scutton set off down the corridor and paused at the top of the stairs, her hand going to the inconspicuous door that led to the narrower servants' staircase.

"I think we can use the main stairs now, ma'am." Caroline said. "Mr. Murphy assures me that the banister has been strengthened."

"It was rather wobbly last time we came," Mrs. Scutton agreed. "I felt safer on the back stairs."

They went down into the basement. The light immediately diminished, and Caroline opened all the doors and followed Mrs. Scutton into the kitchen.

Mrs. Scutton looked around the large room with its stone-flagged floor. Light entered through two barred half-windows at either end of the room. A pine table occupied a third of the space, and one wall contained the immense hearth, the old bread oven, and the mechanism used to turn a joint of meat over the fire.

"Mrs. Frogerton was insistent that the kitchen was the first place that needed restoring," Caroline said. "She had the maids from Half Moon Street in here scrubbing all yesterday."

"She is very kind." Mrs. Scutton trailed her fingertips over the surface of the table; her expression was hard to read. "I remember visiting this house, once." She smiled. "Not the kitchens, obviously, but I was rather overawed."

"I came down here quite a lot when I was a child," Caroline said. "Cook was always willing to feed me little treats."

"It must seem strange that you have no claim to the house you grew up in."

"Not really, ma'am," Caroline said. "I grew up knowing that, as a female, I wouldn't inherit the earldom or this house. I confidently expected to be managing my own home."

"And yet you ended up with nothing."

Caroline smiled, determined not to take offense. "My sister said I should've hurried up and married during my first Season and then none of my misfortunes would have happened."

"She was right." Mrs. Scutton paused to look at her. "Is your sister at school? You rarely speak about her."

"After finishing her education, Susan decided that she wished to live in America with our cousin, Mabel," Caroline said.

"I suppose she thought there was no place for her while you were employed in another woman's house."

"Mrs. Frogerton was more than happy to have her and pay her school fees until I could reimburse them," Caroline said. "But Susan made her own choices."

"That must have been . . . difficult for you."

"Yes, I would've preferred it if she had chosen to stay with me, but she had her own inheritance and decided otherwise. She grew up with Mabel at Greenwood Hall and considered her a sister."

"Thomas would've done anything for his sister, but his efforts to appease her simply made things worse." Mrs. Scutton moved her attention to the chimney breast.

Caroline's instinctive urge to defend her decisions about Susan made her want to reply. She reminded herself that Mrs. Scutton was speaking about her own family and that there was no need to take offense. "It is rare that we understand the ramifications of our decisions until it is too late." Caroline said eventually. "All we can do is make them in good faith and hope for the best."

Mrs. Scutton didn't reply and walked through the interior door into the butler's pantry where the silverware had been kept. The glass cabinets were empty now, as everything not entailed had been sold at auction to pay the last earl's debts. Caroline wondered how the new earl would fill those cupboards again. Mr. Scutton wasn't a fool, but he didn't strike her as a man equipped to deal with the intricate problems of maintaining an earldom.

"Is there a key to the cellar?" Mrs. Scutton asked as she moved through the housekeeper's room and on to the scullery where the newly installed pump gleamed brightly against the old stone sink.

"I believe the door is open!" Caroline called out as she hurried to catch up.

Mrs. Scutton gazed down into the blackness of the cellar. "I suppose the earl's wine was sold off as well?"

"Yes. Apparently, it made a surprisingly large sum of money."

Mrs. Scutton snorted. "Men like to drink."

"If you wish to go down, I can fetch an oil lamp," Caroline offered.

"No, I'm not quite that brave today." Mrs. Scutton stepped back. "Shall we go upstairs?" She retrieved a notebook and a pencil from her reticule. "I need to consider what furnishings we will need to make it habitable."

"Mrs. Frogerton rents all her furniture in Half Moon Street," Caroline mentioned as they skirted Mr. Murphy's workmen and edged up the stairs. "I'm sure she would recommend the company that supplied her."

"That might be a short-term solution." Mrs. Scutton walked over to the double windows at the front of the drawing room overlooking the square. "I don't think the fixtures and fittings from our house in Epping will work with these proportions."

"The ceilings are quite high." Caroline looked up at the intricate plasterwork above her head.

Mrs. Scutton stared out of the window. "I assume that if Thomas does succeed to the earldom, he'll have to sell our house in Epping simply to raise some capital before he embarks on his reforms."

Aware that she'd been rebuked before for involving herself in the Scuttons' affairs, Caroline remained silent as Mrs. Scutton walked back toward the door. She paused, her hand on the wall, and smiled.

"Isn't there a secret door here?"

"Yes, there is." Caroline looked at Mrs. Scutton in surprise. "How did you . . . ?"

"When Mr. Scutton and I came to call, we were brought up here by the butler, and there was no one in the room." Mrs. Scutton smiled. "We were somewhat disconcerted at being left in an empty room, and then suddenly your father came through this door and gave us both a terrible fright."

"That does sound quite like him," Caroline said. "He did love a good joke."

"He did seem to find it amusing, although he was nothing but kind to us during the rest of our visit." Mrs. Scutton sighed. "I fear I am too tired to do anymore. May we leave?"

Caroline nodded and led the way down the stairs. The workmen had disappeared, leaving the lingering smell of sawdust and paint behind. They stepped over various bits of wood, and tools, and went out of the front door to find Mr. Murphy and his men sitting on the steps enjoying the fresh air.

Mr. Murphy rose to his feet. "Just enjoying a brew before we get back to work, miss."

"It all looks to be coming along nicely," Caroline said. "I'll make sure to tell Mrs. Frogerton." Her employer had given up waiting for Mr. Castle to organize the repairs and had dealt with the matter herself. She forwarded all the bills to Coutts where they were paid without comment. "Thank you, Mr. Murphy."

"We'll be done in a couple of weeks, I reckon." He had a strong Irish accent and the black hair and blue eyes to match. "Once we get the stove in and the new privy, there's not much else to do."

"I'm sure Mr. Scutton will be delighted to hear that." Caroline smiled and turned to assist Mrs. Scutton into the waiting carriage.

They set off, and Caroline sat back against the seat. "At least you'll be able to give Mr. Scutton a positive report on the progress of the house repairs."

"Yes, he'll be delighted." Mrs. Scutton twisted her hands together. "I can't believe I won't have to furnish a room for Mary."

"It is indeed sad, ma'am," Caroline said gently.

"Thomas won't mind. He was all too keen on sending Mary off with that vicious husband of hers." Mrs. Scutton sounded bitter, and Caroline couldn't blame her. "If only he hadn't paid off those debts...."

There was nothing Caroline could say to that, and she was relieved when Mrs. Scutton relapsed into silence until their journey was completed at Half Moon Street.

After making sure Mrs. Scutton was safely ensconced in her room, Caroline made her way down to the drawing room where Mrs. Frogerton was sitting reading the newspaper.

"Caroline! How did it go?" Mrs. Frogerton set the paper aside.

"The work is progressing well, and Mr. Murphy sends his regards." Caroline sat down. "Mrs. Scutton is still not quite herself but definitely improving."

"Good. In all honesty, I can't wait for the house to be ready to receive them."

"Mr. Murphy said it would be within the next two weeks once you've decided on the stove."

"Did Mrs. Scutton have an opinion on that?"

"No, she was far more interested in what had happened to the contents of the wine cellar."

"Good, then I will pick the range that I like and bill Coutts Bank for it." Mrs. Frogerton paused. "Have you seen Mr. Scutton?"

"Not since breakfast, ma'am."

Mrs. Frogerton lowered her voice and glanced over at the door. "I suspect he might be up to no good."

Caroline stared at her. "How so?"

"I saw him take the letter Mr. Lewis sent you."

"The one I read and discarded?"

"Yes, it was on the tray the butler brings the post on and then it wasn't."

"Did one of the staff take it down to the kitchen to be disposed of?" Caroline asked. "It seems unlikely that he'd be reading my private correspondence."

"I did doubt it myself, lass, but when Mr. Scutton went

out quite soon after breakfast, I asked the butler where he'd taken his hackney cab to, and it was the same street as Mr. Lewis's offices."

"That *is* quite close to his own solicitors, ma'am."

"Yes, but still . . ." Mrs. Frogerton studied her face. "It is rather peculiar, isn't it?"

"I suppose I'll have to ask him when he returns." Caroline sighed.

"I wouldn't worry. Knowing Mr. Scutton, he'll be eager to seek you out if he has something he wishes to tell you."

Caroline nodded. Mr. Scutton certainly felt he had the right to interfere in her affairs even while he warned her to keep out of his. "I think that's good advice, ma'am. I can assure you that I have no wish to discuss my business dealings with him."

"Why should you? He is not proven to be related to you at this point." Mrs. Frogerton returned her attention to her newspaper. "I wonder if Mrs. Scutton will come down to lunch? Perhaps you might inquire, Caroline."

After lunch, when Caroline was writing another letter to Susan she feared her sister would never receive, Mr. Scutton came into the drawing room and shut the door behind him.

"Lady Caroline, I wish to speak to you."

She set down her pen with some reluctance, wondering how long it would be before Mrs. Frogerton returned. "How may I help you?"

He went to stand in front of the fireplace, his hands linked behind his back as he regarded her. "I took it upon myself to visit Mr. Lewis this morning."

Caroline considered what to say. Part of her wished to accuse him of reading her personal correspondence, while the rest of her was curious about what he might reveal.

"I know you will consider my intervention in your affairs as improper, but for all intents and purposes, I currently stand as the head of the Morton family, and thus your interests are mine."

"I beg to differ."

"Lady Caroline, we both know that women require the protection and guidance of men—the stronger sex—and that Mrs. Frogerton might be formidable in her own way, but she is hardly of your class."

"I'd much rather listen to her advice than any man's."

"Which is precisely my point. You have been living in her house for quite some time now. It is not surprising that you have come to depend on her counsel when there is no one else to turn to."

"That's why I have Mr. Lewis, sir."

"But Mr. Lewis's interests are primarily those of Mrs. Frogerton, are they not? Didn't she recommend him to you?"

"I'm quite capable of making my own decisions, Mr. Scutton."

"I'm not saying you aren't, Caroline, I'm simply suggesting that you don't have to do so any longer because I am more than willing to stand as your advisor in all matters." He sighed. "I'm aware that we haven't always seen eye to eye, but I sincerely care for your interests, my dear, and I wish to see you succeed in this world."

Caroline turned to look more fully at him and gripped the back of the chair so tightly that her fingers hurt. "And which particular interests are those?"

"All of them." A slight frown overlaid his concerned expression. "Mr. Lewis confirmed that he represents you and your sister for matters that have nothing to do with the earldom or the Morton estate. I can assure you that he refused to tell me anything more than that."

"I'm glad to hear it."

"I'm simply offering myself as your representative if you need me." Mr. Scutton held her gaze. "Mr. Lewis is a highly regarded professional, but he is Mrs. Frogerton's man."

He bowed and left the room, nodding to Mrs. Frogerton as she came in. "Ma'am."

Mrs. Frogerton looked inquiringly at Caroline as she sat down. "From the expression on your face, I can only conclude that Mr. Scutton did visit Mr. Lewis. I sincerely hope he was sent away with a flea in his ear."

"Mr. Scutton wanted me to know that he stands ready to provide protection and guidance when I need it because women are too feeble to manage their own affairs."

"Did he now." Mrs. Frogerton raised her eyebrows. "And yet I didn't hear raised voices when I came in. Did you let him get away with such ridiculous blather?"

"I think he was trying to be conciliatory," Caroline said. "I wonder why?"

"Probably because he wants whatever assets you have for his own use." Mrs. Frogerton said bluntly. "And he's finally worked out that fighting with you won't help his cause."

"Yes," Caroline said. "I believe you are completely right."

Chapter 9

The next morning, Mrs. Frogerton passed the newspaper over to Caroline at the breakfast table with the page folded back to the society announcements and obituaries.

"I thought it was time to hurry things along."

Caroline read the black-edged announcement of Mary's death and stared at Mrs. Frogerton. "With all due respect, ma'am, do you think that was wise?"

"I did ask Mrs. Scutton for permission."

"And Mr. Scutton?"

Her employer shrugged. "He wasn't my concern. I'm sure his mother will tell him."

"He won't appreciate your interference," Caroline said.

"I know, but Mrs. Scutton was very grateful for the suggestion and more than willing to allow me to proceed. I also put notices in the *Epping* and *Essex Gazette*." Mrs. Frogerton reclaimed the paper. "I'm thinking it might stir things up a little."

"How so?"

"The Brighams might think they've gotten away with it. There's been no public outcry, no newspaper articles, and no death announcement for Mary. Now this matter is in the public eye, they might be more vulnerable."

"And those around them might wonder at their silence,"

Caroline said. "And hopefully take their disquiet and their concerns to the authorities."

"Exactly." Mrs. Frogerton looked up as Mr. Scutton entered the room. "Good morning."

He stood over her and jabbed at the folded newspaper with his fingertip. "I understand from my mother that you are responsible for this."

"Yes indeed." Mrs. Frogerton smiled at him.

He took in a deep breath, and Caroline tensed. "I suppose I should thank you, ma'am. In my grief I admit I have forgotten to address some of the necessary formalities."

"You are most welcome, Mr. Scutton."

He nodded and set the newspaper on the table. "The sad news might generate some interest from those who are acquainted with the Brigham brothers."

"That was my thought, too, sir." Mrs. Frogerton nodded.

"Let's hope your strategy is more successful than that of the Metropolitan Police."

Mr. Scutton went to get his breakfast. Behind his back, Mrs. Frogerton raised her eyebrows at Caroline. Both of them had expected him to take the news badly.

"My mother intends to get up for the day," Mr. Scutton said as he sat down. "I believe she wishes to make an appointment with a dressmaker to provide her with her own mourning clothes."

"If it is acceptable, sir, I'll ask my own dressmaker to call on us today. She is an excellent seamstress," Mrs. Frogerton offered.

"I'll relay that offer to my mother, ma'am. Thank you." He paused. "I suppose, as the mother of the Earl of Morton, such people would come to her."

He turned his attention to the newspaper and didn't speak again as Caroline and Mrs. Frogerton planned out the days' events.

"When does Ellie come back from visiting her family?" Mrs. Frogerton asked.

"I believe she is due back at the end of this week, ma'am.

But you did tell her to stay with her mother until she was well enough to cope."

"I could hardly do anything else. Poor Ellie already sends most of her wages to her mother, and losing that money would be catastrophic for the family."

"I'm sure Ellie will be back as soon as she can, ma'am." Caroline said.

"Good, because Lizzie will be glad to see her. Looking after the house all by herself has been something of a trial. I did consider hiring another parlor maid, but as I don't intend to be here for another year, it seemed unnecessary."

Caroline stood up. "Shall I take the letters from your desk to be posted, ma'am?" She glanced down at the dogs, who were eating more of Mrs. Frogerton's toast than their owner. "I could take the dogs with me for a walk."

Three of the dogs looked up at the word, while the other one hid under the chair.

"Don't take Pug. He doesn't have the strength," Mrs. Frogerton said.

Privately, Caroline thought he would have the strength if Mrs. Frogerton didn't feed him so many treats, but she would never say it out loud.

"I'll just fetch my bonnet."

"Thank you, dear. I'll send the dogs out to the hall with the butler."

Caroline retrieved all the correspondence and then set off with the dogs toward the receiving office in Charles Street.

The weather remained mild, and it was something of a pleasure to escape the sad atmosphere hanging over Half Moon Street. Caroline wished with all her heart she'd never heard of the Scuttons and that her father's solicitors hadn't involved her and Mrs. Frogerton in their schemes. She was even beginning to wish she'd encouraged her employer to leave immediately for the north after Dorothy's wedding.

The clerk at the receiving office was very helpful and accepted the letters into his care. Before she left, he informed her that he had something for her. "I was just about to send it out for delivery, miss, but perhaps you'd like to take it with you?" He went to the back of the office and retrieved what looked to be a letter.

She took it, noting that it seemed as if it had been dropped in the mud at least once, glanced at the address, and went still. "It's from America."

"Yes, it's the first one I've seen in a long while." He regarded her with a friendly eye. "Do you have family over there, miss?"

"Yes, my sister and my cousin live in Maryland." Caroline was surprised her voice wasn't shaking as she put the letter in her reticule. "Thank you, Mr. Chisolm."

"You're most welcome." He hurried around the desk to open the door for her, clucked indulgently at the dogs, and bowed with a flourish as she went by him. "Have a pleasant day."

Caroline nodded somewhat absently and walked to the corner of the street before she took in her surroundings and remembered to head for Green Park. She found the nearest bench and let the dogs explore while she composed herself. After a few moments, she opened her reticule and took the letter out. Despite the grime, she could make out Susan's handwriting rather than Mabel's, which was something of a relief.

She undid the string that bound the pages, cracked the wax seals, and spread the single sheet of paper out on her lap. She was surprised at the smallness of the script, as her sister normally communicated as little as possible. It appeared that Susan was inspired by her new surroundings and had decided to tell Caroline all about them. Caroline read through the letter and then read it again more slowly, trying to catch the nuances she might have missed. Despite all Caroline's fears, it appeared that her sister was happy and well. She knew she should be relieved by such news but admitted to herself that she'd almost hoped Susan had written begging to return. . . .

Caroline set the letter on her knee and smoothed it with her gloved fingers. Was that what she was becoming? Someone who begrudged others success and good fortune? It wasn't a pleasant thought, and Caroline was unwilling to indulge her own grievances.

She called the dogs, reattached their leads, and set off to Half Moon Street deep in thought.

"Miss Morton!"

She paused as a familiar figure came striding toward her.

"Dr. Harris."

He swept off his hat and bowed before smiling down at her. "I'm glad to see you getting some exercise in the fresh air."

"It is always pleasant to be out of the house, Dr. Harris. I enjoy it." She noticed he was wearing what passed as his best coat and that he'd made some attempt to tame his hair. "Where are you off to today?"

"I just had an interview for a new position." He grinned.

"At a different hospital?" Caroline asked.

"Yes. The Royal Free. I consider them the most radical and innovatory teaching hospital in England."

"That sounds like it would be a perfect for you." Caroline hesitated. "Are they in London?"

"Of course they are." He looked vaguely insulted that she didn't know. "Camden."

"Not quite so central. I suppose you might have to move lodgings if you get the position you applied for."

"I'm fairly certain I've got it," Dr. Harris said.

"It will be harder for you to visit us in Half Moon Street." One of the nearby churches chimed the hour, and Caroline turned toward the park gates. "Do you wish to accompany me back to Half Moon Street so that you can tell Mrs. Frogerton your good news?"

"I'm sure you can tell her for me."

Caroline frowned. "I can, but she is very fond of you, and said just yesterday that she hadn't seen you for quite a while."

"You've got a houseful of guests," Dr. Harris pointed out.

"Yes, but—"

"And Mr. Scutton insinuated that I was not welcome in the house."

"Mr. Scutton has nothing to say about Mrs. Frogerton's guests, Dr. Harris. You know that."

"He implied that he spoke for all of you."

"And you should know better than to believe I'd allow a man—especially one who might not even be related to me—to speak for me." She stared at him. "If you have better things to do than spend a moment with your benefactor, then I'll wish you good day."

Dr. Harris let out a long-suffering sigh. "I don't visit as much because you seem far too cozy with Inspector Ross."

"What does that have to do with anything we've been discussing?" Caroline asked. "I believe I am allowed to have friends, am I not?"

"You know what I mean, and who could blame you? He's the right class, he's a man of good character, and he'd take good care of you."

Caroline resisted the urge to stamp her foot. "Why is everyone obsessed with finding someone to care for me? I am quite capable of looking after myself."

"*I* know that. The rest of them are fools."

"And yet it seems you are behaving in exactly the same manner by telling me who I can be friends with and trying to control me."

Caroline realized she'd raised her voice when Dr. Harris winced, but she wasn't in the mood to be conciliatory. "To be perfectly honest, I am sick and tired of the lot of you!" She started walking. "Come along, dogs."

Dr. Harris kept pace with her. "I didn't mean to make you cross."

"Then please go away."

"I'm making a right mess of this, aren't I?" he muttered. "Typical!"

Caroline kept walking. "I thought we were supposed to be friends. I *thought* you, at least, wouldn't attempt to control my actions."

"Caroline . . ." He caught hold of her elbow, and she had to stop. "Is that how you think of me? As just a friend?"

She refused to look up at him, and after a moment he sighed and released her. "I suppose I have my answer." He stepped back and bowed. "Please give Mrs. Frogerton my best wishes and tell her I will come and visit when I know my new employment is secured."

She watched him walk away. The desire to call him back and ask him to explain himself warred with her fear that he wanted what she was unwilling or unable to offer him. Why couldn't they just stay friends? He was the only person she could truly be herself with, and now it appeared that his friendship came with conditions and would not be available to her if she strayed from the path he had decided on.

"Men," Caroline muttered to the dogs as she picked up her pace. "Let's get back to Half Moon Street so you can tell Pug all about your walk in the park."

She released the dogs when she came into the entrance hall, and they immediately started up the stairs. Caroline took off her bonnet and gloves as the butler came toward her.

"Inspector Ross has called, Miss Morton. He is with Mrs. Frogerton in the drawing room."

"Thank you, Mr. Jenkins."

Caroline found the dogs scratching at the closed door and opened it to let them in, where Mrs. Frogerton welcomed them with great enthusiasm. While her employer was busy cooing at her dogs, Inspector Ross came over to greet Caroline.

"Lady Caroline." He paused to scan her face. "Is everything all right?"

"Yes, thank you." She smiled brightly. "Has Mrs. Frogerton offered you some tea, or have you just arrived?"

"Tea is on its way," Mrs. Frogerton said. "But Inspector Ross has yet to tell me why he is here." She gestured for both of them to sit down. "Have you news of the Brigham brothers?"

"Actually, I came to tell you about an interesting development in an earlier case involving the Scutton family," Inspector Ross said. "The driver of the coach who ran over Jude Smith and was injured in the melee himself came to see me. He was thrown off the box, broke his arm, and has been recovering at home."

"Has he been charged for his part in this matter?" Mrs. Frogerton asked.

"No, because all the witnesses say he had no ability to prevent what happened. He was maneuvering a large vehicle and four horses through a narrow arch into a small, cobbled yard and couldn't bring the coach to a halt at such short notice."

"Then why did he come to see you?"

"He wanted me to know that after having time to reflect on what happened, he was certain that someone deliberately pushed Jude in front of the horses."

"I suppose that even if he couldn't prevent the accident, he was in an excellent position to see what happened from his elevated position on the box," Mrs. Frogerton said. "And was he able to describe who pushed Jude?"

Inspector Ross grimaced. "All he could tell me was that the person wore a cloak with the hood pulled up over their head, obscuring their face."

"I suppose if I intended to deliberately murder someone, I wouldn't want my face to be seen either." Mrs. Frogerton sighed. "Could he tell if it was a man or a woman?"

"He thought it was a man." Inspector Ross hesitated. "I did wonder if there was any connection with the Brighams. They are known to frequent the Blue Boar."

"That would tie things up rather neatly, wouldn't it?" Mrs. Frogerton glanced at Caroline. "What do you think, my dear?"

"I think this information is better shared with the Scuttons, ma'am." Caroline looked at Inspector Ross. "I'm not sure how it became our concern."

There was a slight pause before Inspector Ross turned toward her, his expression very professional. "I decided to share the news with Mrs. Frogerton to see if she thought Mrs. Scutton was in a fit state to hear it herself. I am aware that she is still mourning her daughter."

Caroline felt heat rise in her cheeks as they both looked at her. The door opened to admit the parlor maid with the tea tray, giving Caroline the opportunity to jump to her feet and fuss over its placement in front of Mrs. Frogerton.

"Thank you for your consideration, Inspector. I'll tell Mr. Scutton about this matter," Mrs. Frogerton said. "He knows the state of his mother's mind better than anyone."

"Thank you, ma'am." Inspector Ross sipped the tea Mrs. Frogerton handed him. "I'm hoping the notices in the newspapers will garner some response from those associated with the Brighams."

"If the death announcement doesn't generate any interest, I might be willing to offer a reward," Mrs. Frogerton said.

"I'll bear that in mind, Mrs. Frogerton." Inspector Ross finished his tea, set his cup back on the saucer, and stood up. "I apologize for the brevity of this visit, but I have to be in court at two and must be getting back."

Mrs. Frogerton smiled at him. "Thank you for taking the time to come see me. I appreciate your consideration."

Inspector Ross bowed and left the room without further acknowledging Caroline. She continued to drink her tea and studiously avoid her employer's gaze.

"I think that's the first time Inspector Ross has left this house out of sorts with you, my dear," Mrs. Frogerton commented.

"Hardly the first time, ma'am. He was very cross with me for traveling around London without a chaperone. Like most men, he seems to think I'm incapable of looking after myself."

Mrs. Frogerton carefully broke a biscuit in four pieces and fed one to each of her dogs before she looked back at Caroline. "Did something happen to upset you this morning?"

"I will admit that I am having a rather trying day, but I don't expect you to listen to my problems, ma'am. They are hardly worthy of your concern."

"But your state of mind is my concern when you behave in such an uncharacteristic way," Mrs. Frogerton said.

"I apologize if I was rude. I will try to do better." Caroline summoned a smile. "May I pour you another cup of tea?"

"There's no need to poker up, lass. I'd rather hear what's on your mind than deal with you sulking all day."

"I am not sulking."

Mrs. Frogerton regarded her for a long moment. "No, you're angry, aren't you?" She set her cup down on the side table. "You might as well tell me what's wrong, Caroline, or else I'll be bothering you about it all day."

Knowing her employer's relentless tenacity, Caroline gave into the inevitable. "I met Dr. Harris in the park."

"Oh, dear," Mrs. Frogerton said. "He does have a tendency to bring out your stubborn side. What did he want?"

"It was a chance encounter. He was on his way back from an interview at the Royal Free Hospital in Camden where he is seeking a new position."

"It's an excellent hospital." Mrs. Frogerton nodded. "I can imagine him doing well there."

"He was fairly certain he'd be offered the job. I suggested he should walk back to Half Moon Street with me to share his good news in person. He implied that Mr. Scutton had told him not to call on us, and I told him that Mr. Scutton had no jurisdiction in your house."

"What did Dr. Harris say to that?"

"He said I was too cozy with Inspector Ross, which had nothing to do with what Dr. Harris and I were discussing."

"Perhaps he felt that, between Mr. Scutton and Inspector Ross, he was no longer welcome in this house," Mrs. Frogerton suggested.

"His *welcome* is due to you, ma'am. It's your house, and you decide who gains access to it," Caroline said. "Dr. Harris was insinuating that I was somehow at fault for considering Inspector Ross a friend."

"Ah." Mrs. Frogerton nodded. "Now I understand what went on."

"He has no right to comment on my friendships or lack of them," Caroline said fiercely. "And to attempt to tell me who I can associate with is beyond the pale."

"And what did he say when you told him that?"

"He . . . wasn't best pleased with me," Caroline admitted. "He attempted to justify his reasoning but just made things worse."

"Of course he did." Mrs. Frogerton sighed "I've never met a man more likely to shoot himself in the foot than Dr. Harris." She paused. "I think he cares for you a great deal and has some difficulty knowing how to express himself."

"I don't want him to . . . care about me," Caroline said.

"Now, that's a different matter entirely, lass. You can decide only your own feelings, not his," Mrs. Frogerton said gently.

"I thought he was my friend." Caroline studied her hands, which were twisted together on her lap. "The first real friend I made after I lost my entire world."

Mrs. Frogerton didn't say anything, and after a while Caroline had to look up at her.

"May I be frank, my dear?"

"You usually are, ma'am."

"Dr. Harris is in no position to take a wife."

"I am aware of that."

"I suspect he is struggling between his desire to make his feelings known to you with the knowledge that he can't do what is necessary to provide for you at this time." Mrs. Frogerton paused. "Or in simpler terms—despite knowing he can't court you himself, he considers Inspector Ross a threat."

Caroline considered her employer's words. "In truth, he's acting like a dog in a manger."

"Exactly."

"And with no cause. I have never encouraged him to think of me in a romantic way, nor has he ever behaved in such a manner toward me. In fact, he's the opposite of romantic."

"Yes." Mrs. Frogerton paused. "As I mentioned earlier, he obviously has no idea how to deal with you."

"Which is hardly my fault." Caroline sighed. "And now he probably won't talk to me for weeks, and even if he does, things will be awkward between us."

Mrs. Frogerton poured herself another cup of tea as Caroline contemplated Dr. Harris's anticipated absence.

"If he's got any sense, he'll turn up and try to make amends in his own way," Mrs. Frogerton said. "Which, knowing the pair of you, will probably result in further misunderstandings."

"He did say he would call on you if he secured the new job," Caroline said.

"Then I'll expect to see him fairly soon. I'd suggest you treat him exactly as you always have, Caroline, and that will show him how to go on."

Mrs. Scutton came into the drawing room, and Caroline jumped to her feet. "Would you care for some tea, ma'am? I can ask the butler to bring a fresh pot."

"That would be most welcome." Mrs. Scutton sat down. "Thomas came to tell me Inspector Ross's news about poor Jude's death." She shook her head. "I can't believe anyone would be cruel enough to deliberately push him in front of a coach and four."

"Inspector Ross wondered if it had anything to do with the Brighams," Mrs. Frogerton said. "Did Jude know them?"

"Yes, he did. Mr. Brigham and Mary were still living in my house after their marriage, and they saw him every day."

"Mary seemed very fond of Jude, ma'am." Caroline added the hot water the butler brought to the teapot and stirred it vigorously. "She spoke very movingly about him after his death."

"They were close when she was young. After Mr. Scutton's death, Mary regarded Jude as a father."

"Was Jude related to Mr. Scutton?" Mrs. Frogerton asked.

"I believe they grew up together, although I'm not certain if there was a familial connection." Mrs. Scutton paused. "William never mentioned one. But Jude stayed with us after my husband passed away, and I will always be grateful for that."

Mr. Scutton came into the room and, after greeting Mrs. Frogerton and Caroline, he took a seat beside his mother.

"Are you discussing Jude, Mother?" Mr. Scutton asked as Caroline passed him a cup of tea. "It's a sorry business and a terrible indictment of the state of crime in London."

"I was telling Mrs. Frogerton how Jude was with us throughout my marriage and beyond," Mrs. Scutton said.

"He must have known you all very well, ma'am," Caroline said. "Did he have a family of his own?"

"Yes, he had a sister who acted as our housekeeper in Epping." Mrs. Scutton sipped her tea. "Sarah very kindly sent me a clipping from the *Essex Gazette* which gave details of Jude's funeral at our parish church of St. John the Baptist. I haven't told her about the suspicion that Jude was deliberately pushed into the path of that coach, but I fear I might have to do so now in case Inspector Ross decides to tell her himself."

"I'm sure Inspector Ross will handle the matter with great care and compassion, ma'am," Mrs. Frogerton said.

Mr. Scutton made a dismissive noise. "I agree with my mother that she should write and tell Sarah the news before the inspector blunders in."

Mrs. Frogerton looked as if she wished to say more on the subject, but instead smiled at Caroline. "Did you post the letters, my dear?"

"Yes, ma'am." She smiled in return. "I also received one from America."

"From your sister?" Mrs. Frogerton clapped her hands together. "How wonderful! Is Susan well?"

"Apparently so," Caroline said. "I'll give you the letter to read after dinner, ma'am, and you can tell me your thoughts."

Mrs. Scutton glanced between them. "I must say, Mrs. Frogerton, that you do treat Caroline with extraordinary kindness, considering she is employed to be of service to you. I doubt other employers would be interested in the intimate details of their inferiors' families."

"Perhaps that's because I don't consider myself superior to anyone, ma'am," Mrs. Frogerton said. "I come from humble beginnings, and I have never appreciated being seen as a lesser being."

"With your wealth and status, I doubt that happens to you very often these days," Mrs. Scutton said.

"Then you'd be surprised." Mrs. Frogerton set her cup down and rose to her feet. "Mr. Lewis is coming to talk to me about some business matters, Caroline. Tell the butler I'll see him in the study so as not to disturb anyone."

She left the room, her dogs trailing after her while Caroline set the tea tray to rights.

"That's all very well." Mrs. Scutton lowered her voice. "In truth, I suspect Mrs. Frogerton's been kind to you only because you offered her daughter access to a level of society she would have otherwise been barred from due to her lowly origins."

"Mrs. Frogerton would have accomplished her goals

without me, ma'am," Caroline said. "She is well liked and respected in society."

Mrs. Scutton raised an eyebrow. "Your loyalty does you credit, dear, but I suspect you will be relieved to leave your employment once Morton House is available to us."

"I'm sure you will be delighted to move into Morton House, ma'am, but it has nothing to do with me." Caroline took Mr. Scutton's discarded cup and set it back on the tray.

"Nothing to do with you?" Mrs. Scutton looked over at her son. "Thomas? Have you not made your position on this matter clear to Caroline?"

"I have been rather busy dealing with other matters, Mother," Mr. Scutton said somewhat acerbically. "And to be honest, it didn't occur to me that I'd have to say anything when it's obvious that Caroline should return to the protection of her family."

"I beg to differ, Mr. Scutton," Caroline said. "I have an employment contract with Mrs. Frogerton, and I intend to honor it."

"She won't object if you leave." Mrs. Scutton smiled. "In truth, you've served your purpose in getting her daughter married to a peer, and she probably has no more use for you."

"Thank you for your concern, but I intend to stay until Mrs. Frogerton tells me otherwise." Caroline walked toward the door.

"Are you worried that the College of Arms won't find in our favor and you'll be tossed out on the street again?" Mrs. Scutton asked in a sympathetic voice that set Caroline's teeth on edge. "Because I have it on very good authority that our claim will be verified before the end of the month."

Caroline grabbed the door handle and half-turned to curtsy to Mrs. Scutton. "If that is the case, I am very glad for you, but it doesn't change my decision."

"This is what happens when a young woman isn't under the protection of her family." Mr. Scutton looked at his mother. "She develops alarmingly independent thoughts and habits."

There was much Caroline wanted to say to Mr. Scutton, but all of it would only confirm his suspicions of her desire for independence. She reminded herself that both he and his mother would be gone soon. She was an adult, and they had no legal reasons to compel her to return to Morton House. The notion of returning to the north with Mrs. Frogerton was becoming more compelling every day.

Chapter 10

The next morning, they were all at the breakfast table when Inspector Ross was announced by Jenkins.

Inspector Ross entered the room and bowed to Mrs. Frogerton. "Good morning, ma'am, Mrs. Scutton, Mr. Scutton, Lady Caroline. I have good news. Mr. George Brigham has been apprehended."

"Just George?" Mrs. Scutton, who always found the negative in any positive, asked. "Where is Albert?"

"I'm sure we'll find out when we interview George," Inspector Ross said. "He was discovered in a brothel in a state of drunkenness and claims to have no knowledge of anything relating to Mrs. Brigham's death."

"I suppose he would claim he's innocent." Mrs. Scutton sniffed. "He *is* a Brigham after all."

"As soon as I have more information, I'll pass it on, ma'am," Inspector Ross said.

"Thank you, Inspector," Mrs. Frogerton said. "Caroline? Why don't you walk Inspector Ross down the stairs and see him on his way?"

"Yes, of course, ma'am." Caroline rose to her feet but gave her employer a challenging stare.

Inspector Ross held the door open for her, and they

went down, side by side, to the entrance hall in silence. Caroline paused as he picked up his hat and gloves.

Aware that things weren't quite right between them, Caroline ventured a remark. "I do hope Mr. Brigham can provide some clarity on this matter."

"Once he sobers up, so do I, my lady." Inspector Ross headed for the front door.

"I'm sure you'll quickly find the other Mr. Brigham now."

He looked down at her without his usual smile. "I thought you weren't interested in hearing about these matters."

"I was merely attempting to congratulate you on your excellent police work, sir." Caroline didn't look away from his gaze.

"Thank you for your confidence in me." He set his hat on his head and opened the front door.

"Inspector Ross . . ."

"Yes, my lady?"

Her desire to set things right between them rapidly receded. It was the third time this week she had offended a man's dignity, and she was becoming remarkably tired of it. Why was it always the woman's job to soothe ruffled male feathers?

"Nothing." She offered him a bright smile. "Have a good day."

He tipped his hat and left the house.

Caroline shut the door and went down to the kitchen. Mrs. Frogerton's dogs should have returned from their walk and finished their breakfasts. At least they would be happy to see her.

Later that afternoon, Inspector Ross returned and asked if he might speak to the Scuttons again. As Mr. Scutton had gone out, his mother requested Mrs. Frogerton and Caroline join her.

Mrs. Scutton barely waited until he took his seat to start

speaking. "Well? What news do you have? Has Albert been arrested yet?"

"Not yet," Inspector Ross said. "George claims his brother is in Ireland."

"I know exactly where his family is from in that benighted country if you need that information," Mrs. Scutton said. "He's probably gone back to them."

"But would he leave his brother behind to take the blame for his actions?" Mrs. Frogerton wondered.

"I wouldn't put it past him," Mrs. Scutton said. "He isn't a good man."

"Mr. George Brigham is still denying he was involved in the murder," Inspector Ross said. "He claimed he didn't even know your daughter was dead."

"That seems absurd," Mrs. Frogerton said. "Perhaps after the tragic event, Albert knocked his brother unconscious and left him at the brothel, hoping that if George did wake up, he wouldn't remember a thing."

"With respect, ma'am, that seems unlikely," Inspector Ross said. "Albert would have no guarantee that George would forget everything."

"Then he must be lying." Mrs. Frogerton pressed her lips together in a thin line.

"I suspect that is the case, and that he's simply trying to buy time for his brother," Inspector Ross said. "If he has the funds, Albert might be considering fleeing the country."

"Mary's purse was missing from her bedroom," Mrs. Scutton said.

"And there were those empty jewelry boxes," Mrs. Frogerton added. "I should expect those items would fetch a pretty penny if they were pawned."

"Jewelry boxes?" Both Mrs. Scutton and Inspector Ross spoke at the same time.

Despite her reluctance, Caroline spoke up. "I found two velvet boxes that I handed over to Mr. Scutton with the rest of Mary's possessions."

"He didn't mention them to me." Mrs. Scutton frowned. "I have no idea where Mary would've gotten such jewelry."

"Maybe Mr. Brigham gave it to her?" Mrs. Frogerton suggested.

"If he did, it was probably stolen or won over a gaming table." Mrs. Scutton sniffed. "He wasn't a wealthy man."

"I will ask Mr. Scutton about the matter when I return, ma'am," Inspector Ross assured her. "But to your point, if Mr. Brigham had given Mrs. Brigham the jewelry, he would've known how to retrieve it."

"By murdering my daughter in front of my eyes." Mrs. Scutton dabbed at her cheeks with her handkerchief. "Perhaps that's why he came back in the first place."

"How so?" Inspector Ross asked.

"Maybe he needed the jewels to get out of the debtors' prison, but Mary refused to give them to him. So he thought when he got out, he'd come and get them anyway and take his revenge."

Inspector Ross wrote a few more words in his notebook and nodded.

"What else did George Brigham say?" Mrs. Frogerton asked. "Did he deny visiting her here?"

"He's refusing to answer that until he can find a lawyer."

"I don't understand why you are allowing him to prevaricate, Inspector!" Mrs. Scutton snapped. "Officers are not known for being temperate with criminals. Perhaps you are too gentlemanly to deal with this case."

Inspector Ross said, "I've never found that threatening or torturing a subject leads to a truthful confession, ma'am. And I would never allow it under my watch. George Brigham isn't as clever as he thinks he is. We'll get the truth out of him eventually."

"You'd better. Because while he runs rings around you, his brother is preparing to leave the country without a care in the world." Mrs. Scutton rose to her feet. "I am gravely disappointed in you, sir. Please return only when you have a full confession and Albert is in your custody."

Inspector Ross stood as well. "Perhaps in future I would do better to update Mr. Scutton, ma'am, and spare you the necessity of dealing with me."

Mrs. Scutton ignored him and sailed out of the room, her nose in the air. Inspector Ross grimaced.

"Sit down, Inspector." Mrs. Frogerton waved him into a chair. "Mrs. Scutton might be offended, but I am not, and I have questions for you." She turned to Caroline. "While Mr. Scutton is absent, why don't you go up to his bedroom and see if Mary's belongings are still there."

"Mrs. Frogerton . . ." Caroline bit her lip. "It would not feel right to invade Mr. Scutton's privacy in such a way. Perhaps we should wait—"

"Don't bother." Mrs. Frogerton stood up and headed for the door. "It's my house. I'll do it myself." She left the room, shutting the door behind her.

Caroline stared at the door and sighed. "Oh, dear."

Inspector Ross cleared his throat. "In truth, I think your objections were valid, my lady. If Mr. Scutton had returned while you were investigating the luggage and discovered you, he could have you charged with theft."

"And what if he discovers Mrs. Frogerton doing the same thing?" Caroline turned to look at him.

"As the owner of this property, she retains certain rights."

"She rents it."

"But she is the legal tenant."

Caroline walked across the room to the windows that overlooked the street. "Perhaps I should keep watch for Mr. Scutton so that I can warn her if he returns."

Inspector Ross followed her over to the window and, after a moment, spoke. "I don't like being at odds with you."

Caroline kept her gaze on the street below and didn't reply.

"As you might imagine, I have been under considerable strain recently, what with Richard and the trials of my profession. Being reprimanded by you was . . . difficult to hear." He sighed. "On reflection, I've come to realize that the fault was mine. I should not have been offended when you voiced your concerns."

She turned slightly to look up at him, searching his face for the truth of the matter.

His smile was wry. "I apologize unreservedly."

"I was not in a particularly good mood that day, myself, Inspector," Caroline said. "But, as you were not one of the people who caused my state, I should not have become vexed with you." She swallowed hard. "I am heartily sick of all the trouble the Scuttons have brought upon this household, and I wish I'd never set eyes on them."

He reached out and cupped her chin, bringing her gaze up to his. "Then can we forgive each other and move past this?"

"I'd like that."

"Good." He leaned closer, and she held her breath.

The drawing room door opened, and Mrs. Frogerton came back in. "I couldn't find those boxes anywhere, Caroline! What on earth do you think Mr. Scutton has done with them?"

While Mr. Scutton took his mother out for a drive in the park. Caroline wrote a letter to Susan and Mrs. Frogerton perused the financial section of the morning newspaper.

Jenkins came in and addressed Mrs. Frogerton. "There is a person wishing to speak to Mrs. Scutton."

"Did you tell them that the Scuttons aren't home?"

"Yes, of course, ma'am, but she insisted she needed to speak to someone before she left."

"Then we'll come down and speak to her." Mrs. Frogerton set her newspaper to one side and stood up. "Come along, Caroline."

They descended into the hall to find an older woman dressed in black awaiting them. She looked up as they approached, her expression determined.

Mrs. Frogerton went toward her. "I'm sorry the Scuttons aren't here, but if you wish to leave a message with me, I'll make sure they receive it."

"Thank you, ma'am." The woman bobbed a curtsy. "I traveled to London on one of the brewery carts, and I can't stay much longer as he'll be leaving again at five."

"I'm Mrs. Frogerton, and this is Miss Morton."

"I'm Sarah Smith. Jude's sister. Mrs. Scutton might have mentioned me."

"Yes, of course," Mrs. Frogerton said. "Will you please join us for tea?"

Caroline opened the door into the small morning parlor and nodded for Jenkins to bring some refreshments.

"Are you from Epping?" Mrs. Frogerton inquired.

"That's right. I keep house for the Scuttons."

"We are so sorry for your loss," Mrs. Frogerton said. "Everyone who has spoken about your brother says he was an admirable man."

"He did his best, ma'am, in difficult circumstances." Miss Smith pressed her lips together. "He was loyal to a fault."

"What message do you have for Mrs. Scutton?" Mrs. Frogerton asked. "Would you prefer to write it down, or will you trust us to repeat your words to her?"

"I trust you, all right." Miss Smith looked at them both. "First off, tell her we were sorry to hear of Mary's death, which we read about in the *Epping Gazette*." She paused. "It would've been nice if she'd written to tell us, but I suppose we're not good enough anymore now she thinks her son will be an earl."

"Mrs. Scutton was bedridden after Mary's death," Mrs. Frogerton tried to explain. "The shock of her daughter's murder—"

"Murder?" Miss Smith blinked. "What on earth are you talking about?"

"Mrs. Brigham was murdered by her husband."

"No." Miss Smith shook her head. "Albert *adores* her."

"There were witnesses to the fatal attack, Miss Smith," Caroline said.

"Good Lord." Miss Smith sat down very suddenly, one hand pressed to her bosom. "I don't believe it! We saw Albert not three days ago!"

"In Epping?"

"Yes. He came by to collect the rest of his clothing." Miss Smith looked shaken. "He seemed perfectly normal and didn't mention a thing about Mary, except to say she was keeping well." She paused. "Now that I think about it, he was remarkably tight-lipped."

"Did he mention where he was going?" Caroline asked.

"I believe he was headed for his family home in Ireland," Miss Smith said. "He said he and Mary were intending to live there. How could he have been so *brazen*? My poor, dear Mary. Dead at his hands. She was always Jude's favorite."

"She spoke very highly of him," Mrs. Frogerton said.

"Oh, dear Lord." Miss Smith fanned her face. "I'm coming over all peculiar."

"I'll fetch some brandy, ma'am." Caroline was already moving toward the door where she almost collided with Jenkins and the tea tray. "There's a decanter in the dining room."

Miss Smith was coaxed into taking a small glass of brandy followed by some heavily sweetened tea. She slowly recovered her equilibrium.

Mrs. Frogerton leaned forward to replenish her teacup. "Do you still wish to leave Mrs. Scutton a message? Whatever you have to say must be important if you came all the way to London to deliver it."

"It doesn't feel right anymore." Miss Smith made a face. "I was angry with her for not telling us about Mary herself. Now I understand why she might not have felt ready to share such a terrible thing, even with her own family."

Mrs. Frogerton nodded sympathetically. "Still . . . is there anything you wish us to pass on?"

Caroline had to admire her employer's persistence.

Miss Smith took a restorative breath. "When we were unpacking Jude's belongings, we found several items and letters he'd been keeping for Mary. We think she must have given them to him to take back to Epping."

"As he tragically didn't leave London, I assume they weren't found on his person," Mrs. Frogerton said.

"No, he'd packed them in his trunk, which was delivered to our house in Epping by carrier the day after he was supposed to have arrived. We were concerned because he hadn't returned himself. We only found out he was dead when Mr. Scutton sent us an urgent message that very evening."

Mrs. Frogerton made sympathetic noises and reached over to pat Miss Smith's gloved hand.

"I intended to ask Mrs. Scutton if she wished the items to stay with us in Epping or if she wanted them returned." Miss Smith paused. "I suppose you could still ask her that without causing offense?"

"Certainly." Mrs. Frogerton paused. "Are there any details about those things you wish me to share with Mrs. Scutton?"

"I think she needs to see them for herself." Miss Smith rose to her feet as the clock chimed the quarter hour. "I have to go."

"Thank you for coming, Miss Smith." Mrs. Frogerton shook her guest's hand. "I'll tell Mr. and Mrs. Scutton you called."

"Don't tell him. I'll write to her when I get back to Epping." Miss Smith had almost reached the door when she turned back and took in a deep breath. "In fact, I've changed my mind. I'd be obliged if you didn't mention I'd been here at all."

Mrs. Frogerton frowned. "You don't want me to give Mrs. Scutton any message?"

"You've been very kind, but on reflection, my presence here won't make anything better, will it? Mr. Scutton won't appreciate my interference, and I don't want to deal with his temper. Both Jude and Mary are dead now, and there's no need to upset Mrs. Scutton any further. I'll write and tell her what we found and leave it up to her if she wants to reply to me."

She left the room, and shortly after, Caroline heard Jenkins showing her out the front door.

Caroline and Mrs. Frogerton regarded each other in some disbelief.

"How odd," Mrs. Frogerton said.

"Yes, indeed, ma'am." Caroline said. "It does make one wonder exactly what Mary entrusted Jude with."

"That is a puzzle, isn't it?" Mrs. Frogerton said. "I wonder if Mary had more jewelry?"

"Or if she placed all her personal papers in his care. I found nothing of that ilk in her belongings." Caroline frowned. "But why would she do such a thing?"

"To keep everything safe from Mr. Brigham? Although it sounds as if he was nosing around Epping anyway."

"I must write a note to Inspector Ross to inform him of what Miss Smith told us about Albert's whereabouts and plans," Caroline said.

"And why didn't Miss Smith want Mr. Scutton to know what was going on?"

"Yes, she was quite adamant about that," Caroline agreed. "Perhaps she and Mr. Scutton don't get on."

Mrs. Frogerton pursed her lips. "I think we should take a trip to Epping, lass. I've always been a great admirer of nature, and a drive through the forest will set me to rights."

"Do you think it is wise to interfere, ma'am?"

"If it helps clear up this muddle without inflicting further distress on Mrs. Scutton, then yes." Mrs. Frogerton held Caroline's gaze. "And I've thought of a way to manage it without telling a single falsehood."

Caroline raised a skeptical eyebrow.

Mrs. Frogerton smiled. "We'll offer to take Mary's belongings back to Epping and save the Scuttons a journey."

Mrs. Frogerton sat back, looking very pleased with herself. "Now which of them do you think we should approach with this good news? Mr. Scutton or his mother?"

After dinner that same evening, they gathered in the drawing room, and Mrs. Frogerton smiled at Mr. Scutton. "I do hope you and Mrs. Scutton will be able to amuse yourselves tomorrow. Caroline and I have to visit an old friend of mine in Theydon Bois who is rather poorly."

"Theydon Bois?" Mr. Scutton looked up. "That's quite near Epping."

"Is it?" Mrs. Frogerton asked. "If it is close to your home, perhaps we could offer our services to deliver letters to your kin?"

Mr. Scutton looked over at his mother. "What do you think, ma'am? Is there anything you need from home?"

"Not particularly, Thomas, but I have started writing a letter to Sarah that I could finish tonight."

"Is Sarah your housekeeper, Mrs. Scutton?" Caroline asked.

"Yes, but more importantly, she is Jude's sister. I have been sadly remiss in keeping her informed about recent developments in the family."

"You have been unwell, ma'am, and under a great deal of stress," Caroline said. "I'm sure she'll understand once you write to her."

Mrs. Scutton stood up. "If you would be so kind as to deliver the letter for me, I'd be most grateful. I'll finish it now, and I'll write the direction on the back."

"Is there anything we can do for you, Mr. Scutton?" Mrs. Frogerton asked after Mrs. Scutton's departure. "If you are still concerned about Mrs. Scutton seeing Mary's possessions in your room, we could deliver them to Epping."

Mr. Scutton considered her, a muscle flicking in his cheek. "Out of sight, out of mind, eh?"

"And to be frank, it would make it easier for my maids

to clean your room, Mr. Scutton. They are already complaining about the luggage collecting dust," Mrs. Frogerton continued brightly. "Or perhaps you mean to move them to Morton House? That would be another solution."

"No, take them to Epping," Mr. Scutton said rather abruptly before he remembered his manners and attempted a smile. "If you would be so kind."

"Of course." Mrs. Frogerton nodded. "We'll be on our way before breakfast. I'll ask Jenkins to bring everything down from your room so that we don't disturb you in the morning."

"Thank you." Mr. Scutton bowed. "There's no need to mention this to my mother. I don't want to cause her further distress."

"I wouldn't dream of it." Mrs. Frogerton pressed a hand to her bosom. "The poor lady has dealt with quite enough in the past weeks."

Mr. Scutton excused himself, leaving the drawing room to Caroline and Mrs. Frogerton, who looked rather pleased with herself.

"You see, lass? I can be quite the diplomat when I put my mind to it."

"I think Mr. Scutton has already been through Mary's possessions, taken what he wants, and is happy to have the rest in Epping," Caroline said.

"Out of sight, out of mind, indeed." Mrs. Frogerton nodded her agreement. "But it does give us a legitimate reason to visit the Scutton family home and perhaps form a clearer picture of what is going on."

"If there *is* anything going on," Caroline reminded her. "Inspector Ross seems to have the matter in hand. He already has one of the perpetrators in custody."

"He's being his usual competent self, but he can't be everywhere, can he?" Mrs. Frogerton asked. "We're simply investigating matters outside his sphere of influence. I'm sure he'd approve of that."

Caroline was certain Inspector Ross would not approve,

but she'd never found a way to dampen her employer's enthusiasm once roused and had resigned herself simply to making sure Mrs. Frogerton remained safe.

"I wonder why Miss Smith didn't give Albert Mary's things," Caroline mused. "At that point she had no idea he was suspected of murdering his wife."

"To be fair, we don't know whether she did or not," Mrs. Frogerton said. "All we know is that Mary left specific instructions about who might or might not see the things she entrusted to Jude. Miss Smith was quite insistent that Mrs. Scutton should be the recipient of that information."

"Yes, and very reluctant to allow Mr. Scutton any knowledge of it." Caroline sighed. "For a family that claimed to be so united, they seem remarkably at odds."

"Every family has its secrets, lass." Mrs. Frogerton rose to her feet. "Now, I'm off to bed. We have an early start in the morning, and I want to be well on our way before either of the Scuttons begin to doubt our sincerity in this matter."

Chapter 11

It was a very pleasant day for a drive out into the countryside. Caroline tried to set her misgivings aside as the crowded tenements of Stepney and Bethnal Green lining the London Road disappeared behind them and the wider vista of Hackney Marshes and beyond appeared.

"It should take us between three and four hours to get there," Mrs. Frogerton said. She wore her new bonnet. The cherries on the brim rattled every time the carriage went over a bump. "We'll stop and change the horses in Woodford and go on from there."

"I seem to remember that it is a fairly straight road, ma'am," Caroline said. "Perhaps one day we'll be able to travel all over the country in a steam locomotive."

Mrs. Frogerton shuddered. "I've been on one of those awful contraptions. The noise, the soot, and the stomach-churning speed were not to my taste. I'd told Samuel he'd never get me on one again."

"I haven't been on a train yet, ma'am. Dr. Harris said that he would take me, but—" Caroline paused. "I doubt that will happen now." They hadn't heard from him since Caroline had argued with him in the park.

"He'll come around, lass. He always does." Mrs. Frogerton patted her knee. "Now, do you think we should stop in Theydon Bois just in case Mr. Scutton asks any awkward questions when we return?"

"I assume you don't have a friend in Theydon Bois." Caroline fought to restrain a smile. "I thought you said you told no falsehoods."

"I said I wouldn't tell the *Scuttons* any lies about my intentions for Mary's belongings, and I'm quite sure I didn't."

Caroline smiled. "I'm sure you're right, ma'am."

"I'm from the north, lass. None of my friends live in these parts." Mrs. Frogerton winked before looking out of the window. "Luckily, Mr. Scutton doesn't know that."

The high street in Epping was wide, allowing the weekly market to take place. There was little activity as they passed the black-and-white thatched inns and small shops, their only obstacle a man herding a flock of geese across the street.

"The Scuttons' house is down a lane at the end of the high street," Mrs. Frogerton said. "Mrs. Scutton gave the coachman excellent directions."

The carriage turned slightly to the left and went along a narrower lane until it dipped down into a hollow on the side of the hill. There was a long, red-bricked house set back from the road with space for the carriage to pull up on the drive. It was a very pleasant dwelling with a well-established wisteria climbing gracefully over the front door.

"I believe this might be it." Mrs. Frogerton opened the window and looked around. "It's an elegant house."

"And just the sort of thing the fourth son of an earl might end up in if he's alienated his father," Caroline said. "It's grand enough not to make the family look bad, but relatively easy to maintain on his restricted income."

Mrs. Frogerton looked at Caroline. "The things you know astound me sometimes, lass. That would never have occurred to me."

They got down, and Caroline instantly stretched out her spine. Mrs. Frogerton's hired carriage might be very comfortable, but some of the roads they'd traveled had been less than kind.

Closer inspection revealed a well-tended thatched roof and rows of small diamond-paned windows glinting in the sun. There was a blue front door set slightly off-center at the front of the property that had an air of disuse. It wasn't a large house, but it was very charming.

"Did you send a note to Miss Smith about our impending visit, ma'am?" Caroline asked as she straightened her skirts.

"I didn't have time," Mrs. Frogerton said innocently. "I wonder if there is a stable yard through that archway on the left. Shall we investigate?"

She walked through the arch, looked back at Caroline, and gestured to the coachman. "Collins can bring the carriage around once we've made ourselves known to our hosts." She glanced at Caroline, who had followed her. "Shall we try the kitchen door?"

The door was slightly ajar, and the faint sound of singing came through the gap. Mrs. Frogerton knocked twice and then pushed the door open. "Hello? Is there anyone here?"

Footsteps sounded on the flagstones of the dimly lit hall, and Miss Smith came toward them, wiping her floury hands on her apron.

"Mrs. Frogerton?" Her bewildered gaze swept over Caroline. "Miss Morton. Has something happened?"

"I do apologize for this unexpected intrusion, Miss Smith," Mrs. Frogerton said. "We were visiting a friend of mine in Theydon Bois today, and Mrs. Scutton asked if we could deliver a letter to you from her."

"Good Lord, please forgive my manners and come through to the kitchen!" Miss Smith said. "Did you come by carriage?"

"Yes, indeed."

"Then tell your man to seek out young Basil in the stables. He'll make sure the horses are taken care of."

"I'll go and speak to Collins, ma'am," Caroline murmured to her employer and went back out into the sunlight.

When she returned, she followed her nose through to the kitchen, where Mrs. Frogerton had already established herself at the table while Miss Smith continued kneading her bread.

Miss Smith looked up briefly as Caroline came in. "I'd take you through to the parlor if I wasn't covered in flour."

"We're fine as we are," Mrs. Frogerton reassured her. "Shall I make some tea?"

"I can do that, ma'am," Caroline offered. She preferred to be on her feet after hours in the carriage. "If Miss Smith doesn't object."

"Please be my guest. There's tea in the caddy next to the kettle on the stove. It should already be hot, as I've been promising myself a cuppa for the last hour."

"Are you all on your own today, Miss Smith?" Mrs. Frogerton asked.

"The kitchen maid's gone to buy more flour from the mill, and her brother is out in the back garden picking vegetables for our dinner." Miss Smith pummeled the dough with the strength of a prize fighter. "I keep meaning to ask Mrs. Scutton whether she wants to take someone on to replace Jude, but I haven't had the heart."

"Perhaps Mrs. Scutton will have some directions for you in her letter," Mrs. Frogerton said. "She was most insistent that we drop it off to you today."

"You didn't tell her that I came to London, did you?" Miss Smith patted the dough into a ball and set it on a tray to proof. She immediately started on another.

"No, she had already begun to write to you of her own accord," Mrs. Frogerton assured her. "Mr. Scutton asked us to bring you the belongings Mary left in London."

"Did he." Miss Smith thwacked the dough hard against the tabletop, and flour flew everywhere. "I'd still like to know why he buried poor Mary in London and didn't bring her home to lie with her kin."

"Do you not... care for Mr. Scutton, Miss Smith?" Mrs. Frogerton asked.

"I find Thomas a very humorless man with a nasty temper," Miss Smith said. "When he announced he'd had a calling to enter the church, I couldn't think of a better place to put him. Now his mother has him all stirred up with ideas of an earldom, he's suddenly not so keen on the church anymore."

"I suspect most gentlemen would prefer to become a peer than a priest, Miss Smith," Mrs. Frogerton remarked. "One can hardly blame him for wanting to advance in the world."

"Jude didn't like it at all." Miss Smith washed her hands and set the filled teapot on the table, along with a jug of milk and some earthenware cups. "He warned Mrs. Scutton that meddling with the past would lead to no good." She sighed. "It didn't do Jude any good, did it? If he hadn't followed Mrs. Scutton to London, he would still be alive and well."

"Do you think he had good reason to be concerned as to Mrs. Scutton's decisions?" Mrs. Frogerton accepted her tea with thanks. "There must be sufficient evidence for the claim that Mr. Scutton is in line for the earldom, or the College of Arms would not bother investigating it."

"That's not what Mary told Jude." Miss Smith sipped her tea. "She said she'd tried to tell Thomas to take no heed of his mother, but he wouldn't listen to her."

"One has to wonder what Mary thought she knew that her brother did not." Mrs. Frogerton made a face. "Unless she was prescient enough to write her suspicions down, I suppose we'll never know."

"She might have said something to Albert. They were

very close." Miss Smith shook her head. "I still can't believe he murdered her."

"I believe Mr. Scutton was equally shocked," Caroline said. "But Mrs. Scutton appeared to be frightened of Albert, perhaps with good cause."

"Like most mothers, she didn't think anyone was good enough to court her daughter," Miss Smith said. "If you don't mind me saying, Mrs. Scutton thought her family were a cut above the Brighams."

"Perhaps she had cause if she knew her husband was descended from a family with an earldom," Caroline said.

"But that wasn't *her* family, was it?" Miss Smith pointed out. "It's the Scutton side. Hetty refined her accent over the years, but when she first arrived from London, she was quite common herself."

"Mrs. Scutton came from London?" Caroline asked.

"Yes, I believe she was in service there."

"Then how did she come to meet Mr. Scutton?" Mrs. Frogerton asked.

"She came down with the family she worked for when they left London after the Season and met Mr. Scutton here." Miss Smith smiled. "From what Jude told me, it was a very quick courtship, but they seemed happy enough together."

"I suppose she needed to make up her mind quickly before she signed up for another year of employment," Mrs. Frogerton commented. "It's happened with my staff in the past."

"Jude took a while to come round to her, but she always treated him with respect, and he appreciated that," Miss Smith said. "When Mr. Scutton died so suddenly, Hetty leaned on Jude something terrible, but he didn't mind."

"My son was a great comfort to me when my husband, Septimus, died," Mrs. Frogerton said. "My daughter was far too self-absorbed and rather cross that being in mourning curtailed her social activities."

"Mary and her mother had their disagreements, but I

never thought they'd fight over Mr. Brigham," Miss Smith said. "Albert's such a charmer."

"Perhaps Mrs. Scutton saw through his charm and feared, quite rightly, for her daughter's safety," Mrs. Frogerton said. "Did Jude like Mr. Brigham?"

Miss Smith considered the question, her gaze directed out of the window. "I've never thought about that, but now that you mention it, they were never close. Jude wasn't one for clever words or jokes at other people's expense, and Albert liked to tease. Jude put up with Albert only because he cared for Mary."

"It is always difficult when a beloved family member finds a mate." Mrs. Frogerton set her cup down. "I had to rely on my own wits to decide which gentleman was fit to court my Dotty."

"And you did very well, ma'am," Caroline reminded her. "Viscount Lingard is a fine gentleman from a respected family. I think Dorothy will be very happy."

"I hope so, but even if she isn't, she'll have little to complain about," Mrs. Frogerton said. "I tied that marriage contract up so tightly in her favor that he won't dare misbehave on her."

Caroline set down her empty cup. "Perhaps I should ask Collins to bring in Mary's bags. Did she have a bedchamber where we can place them, Miss Smith?"

"Yes, I'll show you where it is." Miss Smith went out of the kitchen into the wide front hall and pointed up the shallow oak stairs. "Mary's room is the one of the far left of the landing."

"Then we'd better get started," Caroline said. "We have a long drive back to London."

She left Mrs. Frogerton and Miss Smith chatting happily in the kitchen and oversaw the bringing up of the bags. While the other women were occupied, she took a quick look around Mary's bedroom. Half the drawers and the wardrobe were empty, indicating where Mr. Brigham had removed his clothes. There was nothing worth noting in Mary's remaining possessions and no sign of any other jewelry boxes.

There was a small desk in the corner of the room. Caroline tried the lid, but it appeared to be locked, which was somewhat annoying. She could hardly go downstairs and ask Miss Smith for the key.

She went back out onto the landing and called down the stairs. "Mrs. Frogerton? Do you have the keys for Mary's trunk? I don't want to accidentally take the keys away with us."

Her employer came up the stairs, her expression hopeful, her voice lowered. "Have you found something, lass?"

"No." Caroline drew Mrs. Frogerton into Mary's bedchamber and closed the door. "I do want to make sure we leave the right keys behind, but I'm also wondering if you might know of a way to get into Mary's desk."

"Is it locked?" Mrs. Frogerton set the keys to the trunk on the lid and walked over to the desk.

"Yes," Caroline said.

Mrs. Frogerton removed one of her hairpins and inserted it into the lock.

"What on earth are you doing, ma'am?"

"If you are ever blessed with a daughter, Caroline, it's very useful to read locked-away journals to prevent any catastrophes."

"Isn't that an invasion of their privacy?"

"When your daughter is set to inherit a fortune, I'd call it a necessity." There was a slight click, and Mrs. Frogerton smiled. "Ah, that did the trick."

She opened the drawer. "There is some correspondence in here. Do you want to help me look through it?"

"Should we?" Caroline glanced back at the door.

"Seeing as we've come all this way, lass, I'm loathe to leave with nothing to show for it." Mrs. Frogerton took out a pile of paper and leafed through it. "Most of this appears to be her personal correspondence." She paused. "Now, why would she be speaking to a priest?"

"Perhaps she really was intending to convert to Catholicism," Caroline said.

"This appears to be an answer to a theological question." Mrs. Frogerton set it aside. "I can't understand a word of it."

Caroline helped her sort. "And this is her marriage certificate from the local parish church."

"I wonder why Mr. Brigham didn't take that with him?"

"Perhaps he didn't have the key to the desk, either," Caroline suggested.

"Or he knew it was no longer important." Mrs. Frogerton sighed. "I wish she'd written a daily journal. That would've been most helpful."

"There's a letter here addressed to her mother," Caroline said. "I wonder if that's the one Jude brought back here for her?"

"I do wish it wasn't sealed." Mrs. Frogerton made a face. "I'm very interested in what Mary had to say to her mother, but I wouldn't feel quite right about opening it."

Caroline was glad her employer had some principles left. . . .

"Shall we put everything back?" Caroline suggested.

"Yes, we should," Mrs. Frogerton agreed. "But I have thought of a way that we might get another look at that letter."

They locked the desk and went downstairs to the kitchen, where Miss Smith was taking loaves of bread out of the oven and putting more in to bake. The kitchen smelled delicious.

"Would you care for a slice of bread and cheese?" Miss Smith offered. "To see you on your way?"

"Yes, please." Mrs. Frogerton sat back down at the table. "I can't think of anything I'd like better."

A thick slab of yellow butter appeared on the table, and

Miss Smith skillfully cut the still warm bread into substantial chunks. After she topped up the teapot, she sat down again and asked, "Have the police caught Albert yet?"

"They believe he's still in Ireland." Caroline managed to speak around a mouthful of the best bread she'd ever tasted. "They did arrest his brother, George."

"George was in on it, too?" Miss Smith shook her head. "I still can't believe it. Mary didn't want to go to London with her brother because she was waiting for Albert to come and collect her. She trusted him absolutely."

"I thought he was still in prison at that point?" Mrs. Frogerton murmured discreetly.

"Mary said it was all a misunderstanding engineered by her mother and that Albert did have the money to pay off his debts," Miss Smith explained. "She went to London only when Thomas begged her to accompany them."

"I did notice that Mr. Scutton and Mrs. Brigham appeared to be close," Mrs. Frogerton said. "I have a son and a daughter myself, and it's always nice to see brothers and sisters getting along."

Caroline couldn't quite recall Dorothy and her brother being together without a lot of arguing, but she couldn't deny their affection for each other.

Miss Smith nodded. "Thomas and Mary were always very close, which was why she was so upset when Thomas went along with his mother about the earldom."

"Mary did mention that she had some doubts about the validity of his claim," Caroline said. "Did she express such doubts to you?"

"Many times. She even asked Jude for his thoughts on the matter."

"And what did Jude think?"

"I know he was worried. I think that's why he decided to go to London with them in the first place." Miss Smith sighed. "He'd be alive today if he hadn't gotten involved."

Mrs. Frogerton sipped her tea. "One has to wonder what Mary was so worried about."

"She wouldn't tell me exactly what was bothering her," Miss Smith said. "She liked her secrets, and having something to hold over her mother probably appealed to her."

"Mayhap she told her husband," Mrs. Frogerton mused. "Perhaps he didn't appreciate what she had to say."

"He was in a good humor when I saw him," Miss Smith said. "But perhaps that was because he'd silenced her secrets for all eternity."

Caroline shivered, and Mrs. Frogerton reached out to pat her hand. "It's all right, lass. Whatever Mary's secrets were, she paid a terrible price for them." She turned to Miss Smith. "You mentioned Mary had left some correspondence for her mother's attention. Would you like us to take it to Mrs. Scutton?"

"Yes, that would be an excellent idea." Miss Smith stood up. "I'll go find the letter."

Caroline glanced at Mrs. Frogerton as their hostess went up the stairs. "I do hope you relocked that desk."

"Of course I did." Mrs. Frogerton wasn't perturbed at all. "I've had plenty of practice."

Miss Smith returned with the letter and set it on the table beside Mrs. Frogerton. "I did think of something when I was looking for this."

"And what was that?"

"It was only after her marriage that Mary changed toward her mother and no longer supported Thomas's aspirations to the peerage."

"Was Mr. Brigham a bad influence on her, do you think?" Mrs. Frogerton asked.

"I'm not sure." Miss Smith pursed her lips. "Perhaps she simply saw things differently when she was with him."

"It's a mother's worst nightmare that her daughter will marry someone who takes her away from her family," Mrs. Frogerton commented. "But I can sympathize with both of them." She put the letter in her reticule. "We should probably be getting back to London, Caroline. Thank you so much for seeing us, Miss Smith."

"It was a pleasure, Mrs. Frogerton, Miss Morton." Miss Smith sighed. "I'm still not used to the quietness in this house. It used to be filled with family, and now—if the Scuttons succeed in their bid for the earldom—I'll be all alone."

"Perhaps Mrs. Scutton will require your company in London?"

Miss Smith shook her head. "Oh, I couldn't live there. But she'll sell this house, and then where will I be?"

"If such a thing comes to pass, please write to me. I would be delighted to assist you," Mrs. Frogerton said.

"That's very kind of you, ma'am, but you are under no obligation to help me."

Mrs. Frogerton rose to her feet, and so did Caroline. "Miss Smith, you have been very good to us. I shall repeat my offer—if you are in need, please write to me, especially if you think of anything that might help regarding Mary."

"Thank you." Miss Smith stood, picked up a loaf of bread, and wrapped it in a cloth. "Please take this with you. I've baked far too much again."

Mrs. Frogerton took the proffered loaf with some alacrity and tucked it under her arm. "How delightful! I'm not sure this bread will make it back to London in one piece, but I will do my best."

Miss Smith saw them out the door, and they climbed into the carriage again. It wasn't until they'd meandered through Epping and into the forest beyond that Mrs. Frogerton glanced over at Caroline and asked, "What did you think of Miss Smith's account of things?"

"I thought she was surprisingly open with two women she barely knew, but you do have a way of getting people to confide in you, ma'am."

"She was also quite lonely," Mrs. Frogerton said. "And, I think, worried about what had befallen her brother and Mary. She probably appreciated having someone to share her concerns with."

"It was interesting that she believed Mary changed after

she married Mr. Brigham," Caroline commented. "Mrs. Scutton said the same thing."

"It certainly doesn't show Albert Brigham in a good light," Mrs. Frogerton said. "Perhaps he married her *because* of her brother's prospects and didn't want her trying to undermine them."

"I suppose that's possible," Caroline said thoughtfully.

"You sound doubtful, lass."

"It just doesn't make much sense to me," Caroline said. "From all accounts, Mary adored Albert, and I'm fairly certain she would've done anything he asked of her without the need of threats."

"Perhaps you're looking at this from the wrong perspective," Mrs. Frogerton said. "What if Mary's desire to hurt her mother overrode everything else?"

"I suppose the drive to claim the earldom did come from Mrs. Scutton," Caroline agreed. "If Mary wanted to destroy her mother's ambitions, she certainly believed she had the ammunition to do so."

Mrs. Frogerton eased back into the corner of the carriage as the road got bumpier. "There is another person to consider in all this."

"Are you speaking of Jude?" Caroline asked. "If Miss Smith was correct, and Mary confided in him, he probably knew far more than we assumed about the Scutton family."

Mrs. Frogerton nodded. "And perhaps he died for that. In truth, I was thinking of someone else."

"Who, ma'am?"

"Mr. Scutton, of course." Mrs. Frogerton folded her hands in her lap.

"What does he have to do with this matter?"

"We know who murdered Mary, but who really stands to win the most, Caroline?" Mrs. Frogerton raised her eyebrows. "Mr. Scutton. Have you noted his connections to Jude and the Brighams?"

"You might need to explain more, ma'am."

"He admitted going to the Blue Boar to see Jude even

after his mother had clearly dealt with the matter, *and* he paid off Albert's debts."

"Are you suggesting he is somehow involved in his own sister's death?"

Mrs. Frogerton shrugged. "I'm just speculating, lass. He's the one who has the most to lose if Mary tells everyone his claim to the earldom is false."

"You're suggesting he might have used the Brigham brothers to do his dirty work for him," Caroline said slowly. "I can't quite believe that, ma'am. He doesn't seem the type, and he clearly cared for his sister."

"Then perhaps he thought releasing Mr. Brigham would encourage him to take Mary away and thus keep his secrets safe."

"That sounds far more like him," Caroline said.

"And maybe everything that happened after that wasn't meant to happen, but it was too late to stop it."

Caroline considered her employer. "Mr. Scutton certainly wasn't pleased when Mr. Brigham turned up at your house."

"He wasn't happy at all, was he?" Mrs. Frogerton agreed.

"I don't think he mentioned the jewelry boxes I found amongst Mary's things to his mother, either," Caroline said. "She seemed quite surprised when I told Inspector Ross about them."

"She did, didn't she?" Mrs. Frogerton concealed a yawn behind her hand. "Let's try to make sure that one of us is in the room when she opens that letter from Mary and hope that she is in a confidential mood."

"I doubt Mrs. Scutton would confide in either of us. She is quite reserved." Caroline took a book out of her reticule and settled down to read.

"I was quite surprised to hear that Mrs. Scutton came from London."

"Yes, that was odd, wasn't it? She made it seem as if she'd spent most of her life in Epping. Perhaps she is a little self-conscious about her roots, ma'am."

"One would assume so, seeing as her son might be about to become an earl." Mrs. Frogerton yawned again. "There is much to think on. I intend to close my eyes for a while and consider this matter. Please wake me up when we reach Woodford."

"Yes, of course, ma'am."

Mrs. Frogerton subsided gracefully into her corner, and within a few moments, a tiny snore escaped her.

Even though Caroline was tired, she found it impossible to close her eyes. Mrs. Frogerton's comments about Mr. Scutton had unsettled her greatly. It was true that Mr. Scutton had much to gain if he won the earldom, but was he ruthless enough to permanently silence his sister's misgivings about the situation? He seemed far more obsessed with doing the right thing and lecturing others on their behavior than plotting cold-blooded murder.

But maybe behind that austere mask lurked a man that she didn't really know at all. Miss Smith disliked him and said he had a temper. Caroline shivered and resolved to be far more careful in her dealings with Mr. Scutton in the future.

Chapter 12

The next morning Caroline was still stiff from the long carriage ride and was more than happy to take the dogs for a walk in the park for her suffering employer. She enjoyed Green Park before the fashionable crowds descended in the afternoon. Sometimes she didn't encounter another soul as she strolled along the pathways in the dappled morning light.

As she was turning for home, a familiar figure called her name, and she paused to see Inspector Ross striding toward her.

"Good morning, Lady Caroline." He swept off his hat and bowed to her. "I was just coming to see the Scuttons."

"Then we can walk back together once I have found all the dogs." Caroline looked around her. "Pippin is refusing to come to me."

"Let me try." Inspector Ross whistled loudly. Pippin appeared in some bushes ahead of them and immediately came loping back to Caroline.

"I wish it wasn't considered unladylike to whistle," Caroline said as she attached the dog's lead to his collar. "It would save me a great deal of time."

"At this time in the morning, I suspect you could whistle away, my lady, and no one would care."

"And to be fair, no one would care anyway, as I am no longer accountable to polite society." Caroline set her hand on the arm he offered her, and they headed to the park gates. "I'll have to practice." She glanced up at him as they passed through the wrought-iron gates. "Have you found the other Mr. Brigham?"

"Not yet, but we have contacted the authorities in Ireland. They've promised to relay our concerns to Mr. Brigham and to warn him not to attempt to leave the country until he has spoken to us."

"Do you think he will pay heed to such instructions?"

"I can only hope he will. If the information you passed on about Miss Smith seeing him only three days ago is correct, then he doesn't appear to be in any hurry to leave."

"I hadn't thought of that," Caroline said. "And Miss Smith told us yesterday that he was in fine form when she saw him."

"If he thinks he's got away with murder, that might account for his high spirits." Inspector Ross paused. "Do I understand you've had more contact with Miss Smith?"

"Mrs. Frogerton was visiting Theydon Bois and offered to deliver Mary's belongings to the Scutton residence in Epping where Miss Smith also lives," Caroline explained.

"Did she now?" Inspector Ross didn't look at all surprised. "And did you learn anything else that might aid my investigation?"

"Nothing in particular, sir, but Miss Smith believed Mary became alienated from her family on the occasion of her marriage."

"Anything else?"

Caroline hesitated. "Miss Smith believed Mary had told Jude her concerns about her brother's quest for the earldom."

"And now both of them are dead and the Brighams were seen at both locations," Inspector Ross said. "And George Brigham claims he has no idea how either of those things happened."

"How bizarre."

They waited until a hackney cab went past before crossing the road and turning into the relative quietness of Half Moon Street. It was a bright morning, and the sun was reflected off the many windows and filtered through the greenness of the trees.

Mr. Jenkins opened the front door for them and greeted them. Inspector Ross began to converse with the butler as he escorted him into the dining room. Caroline took the dogs down to the kitchen, and by the time she returned, Inspector Ross was being rigorously questioned by the Scuttons.

"How can George claim that he has no knowledge of what happened?" Mrs. Scutton's tone was irate. "I saw him in Mary's bedchamber. Has he run mad?"

"He maintains that he did see Mrs. Brigham that evening, but that when he left, she was perfectly fine and still happily conversing with his brother."

"That's ridiculous," Mr. Scutton added his voice to the discussion. "How can he expect to be believed when we all know he's lying?"

"Is it possible, Mrs. Scutton, that George Brigham might have left before his brother murdered Mrs. Brigham?" Inspector Ross asked.

The color rose alarmingly on Mrs. Scutton's face. "I told you not to bother me until you had a full confession from both of the Brighams. Yet you turn up and ask me *this*?"

"I ask because sometimes in a moment of tragedy, our memories can be unreliable. You told me yourself that you had no recollection of George having any part in the murder, and I wondered whether he was, in fact, present during the incident itself."

Mrs. Scutton ignored the question and looked at her son. "You must go at once to this man's superiors and *demand* that someone competent is put in his place!"

"I'll do better than that, Mother. I'll accompany him back to his place of work and denounce him in front of everyone."

Inspector Ross inclined his head an icy inch. "If you wish to accompany me, Mr. Scutton, I cannot stop you. But I can assure you that I am doing all that is necessary to bring the Brighams to justice."

"Balderdash," Mrs. Scutton snapped. "You're allowing George to get away with spinning fairy tales while his brother leaves the country!"

Inspector Ross looked at Mr. Scutton. "Do you believe Mr. Brigham took his wife's jewelry and possessions, sir? They were not in her bedroom."

"Of course he did." Mr. Scutton looked equally displeased. "Now, have you finished asking your useless questions? I'll walk back to Scotland Yard with you and seek out your superiors."

"As you wish, sir." Inspector Ross bowed to Mrs. Frogerton. "Good morning, ma'am. And thank you for seeing me."

He turned and left with Mr. Scutton on his heels.

Mrs. Frogerton raised her eyebrows and looked at Caroline. "Such excitement so early in the morning. It's quite put me off my breakfast."

"Poor Inspector Ross." Caroline helped herself to some toast and marmalade.

"Inspector Ross is incompetent." Mrs. Scutton was still angry. "But of course you would choose to sympathize with him, Caroline, being of the same class."

"A class your son aspires to join, ma'am," Caroline said.

"That is a different matter entirely," Mrs. Scutton said. "When Thomas assumes the title, he will outrank your inspector and will have nothing to do with him."

Mrs. Frogerton set down her cup and regarded her guest. "I've learned a lot about society while watching my

Dotty find a husband, ma'am. All these families are connected in some way. If your son is seen to be condescending toward a member of a highly respected aristocratic family, it won't reflect well on *him*."

"With all due respect, Mrs. Frogerton, your opinion on this matter is hardly relevant," Mrs. Scutton said. "Your . . . origins are rather lowly."

"And I'm proud of that, but it doesn't make any difference as to what my own two eyes tell me. You'd do better not to offend Inspector Ross. If his brother dies, he'll be the next marquess, and then where will you be?"

Mrs. Scutton took a steadying breath. "Perhaps we should agree to disagree and change the subject, Mrs. Frogerton. I hate to argue when you have been so kind to us."

Mrs. Frogerton wasn't smiling, but she inclined her head in acquiescence.

After a moment, Mrs. Scutton spoke again. "Do you have any further news about the improvements to Morton House?"

"I haven't heard that anything has gone wrong since I last spoke to Mr. Murphy, but I will contact him today and ask him when he intends to be done."

"That is most obliging of you," Mrs. Scutton said and went as if to rise from the table.

"Oh!" Mrs. Frogerton exclaimed. "I forgot! Miss Smith gave me a letter for you. I still have it in my pocket."

Mrs. Scutton took the letter, and her face went pale. "Good Lord. This is Mary's handwriting, not Miss Smith's."

"Is it?" Mrs. Frogerton asked. "I would not know the difference. It was in Miss Smith's possession. She said Jude had it in his trunk from Mary when he was in London."

Mrs. Scutton turned the envelope over in her hands, which were trembling slightly. "I never expected to see her handwriting again."

"It must be quite a shock, ma'am. Perhaps you should stay in your seat while you read it in case you are quite understandably overcome," Mrs. Frogerton suggested.

"No, I think I will retire and read this in my room." Mrs. Scutton shot to her feet. "Pray excuse me."

Mrs. Frogerton grimaced after Mrs. Scutton disappeared through the door. "I handled that badly. She wasn't in the best of moods with me after our previous discussion and not prepared to be consoled."

"There's always the chance she might share the letter with us after she's read it," Caroline said.

"Or leave it open on her dressing table." Mrs. Frogerton looked hopeful. "I wouldn't be above reading it if she did." She paused. "There's something not right about all this, Caroline. Inspector Ross asked the correct questions even if Mrs. Scutton took offense at them."

"Which particular questions?"

"Whether George Brigham was still with his brother when the fatal blows were struck. I cannot imagine why he would claim otherwise unless he truly was not there."

"Perhaps he's lying?" Caroline countered. "And stalling to give his brother time to escape the authorities."

"But that's another odd thing, Caroline. Why didn't Albert depart immediately for Ireland after he'd stabbed his wife? Why did he take the time to visit the house in Epping?"

"I assume there were things he wanted from Epping that he hadn't been able to get from Mary in London."

Mrs. Frogerton considered her. "Things Mary had given Jude to take to Epping *for* him, or things to hide from him?"

"That's the real question, ma'am. We should have asked Miss Smith whether Albert took anything from Jude's trunk when he visited."

"Perhaps you might write her a note and ask? I can have it delivered tonight. The messenger can wait for her reply and bring it straight back to us," Mrs. Frogerton suggested. "Is there anything else we should ask her?"

"I can't think of anything, ma'am. Although I can't help wondering why Mary found it necessary to give some of her possessions to Jude in the first place."

"Presumably because she was scared of something—or someone," Mrs. Frogerton said. "But who was it, her family or her husband?"

Mr. Scutton arrived back with a face as sour as a gooseberry and reported that all his efforts to remove Inspector Ross from the case had been ignored.

"And what is worse," he said, "I was told to stop interfering!"

Mrs. Frogerton tried to look sympathetic but couldn't quite manage it. Caroline didn't even make the attempt. In her opinion, the sooner the Scuttons were gone from Half Moon Street, the better.

"Perhaps it is wise to leave these things to the professionals, Mr. Scutton," Mrs. Frogerton said. "I'm sure your mother will be most understanding when you explain it to her."

"I won't say anything to her at all unless she asks me directly, ma'am," Mr. Scutton said. "I prefer not to worry her."

"How very wise of you, sir," Mrs. Frogerton murmured. "I suppose that's why you didn't mention those empty jewelry boxes to her earlier."

The glance Mr. Scutton threw her was sharp. "Exactly."

"Did you ever find out what happened to the contents?" Mrs. Frogerton asked.

"I assume Albert took the jewelry back at some point and then sold or pawned it." He paused. "It would be just like my sister to believe him if he said he'd get the jewelry back for her. That's probably why she kept the boxes."

"The poor child," Mrs. Frogerton said softly. "To be so cruelly deceived."

Mr. Scutton swallowed hard and looked anywhere but at Mrs. Frogerton. "By the way, where is my mother?"

"She retired to her room earlier." Mrs. Frogerton paused. "Yesterday, when we delivered Mary's belongings to Epping, Miss Smith entrusted a letter to us that Mary had written to her mother."

Mr. Scutton raised his eyebrows. "A *letter*?"

"Apparently, Mary gave it to Jude to take back to Epping with him, and it arrived safely in his trunk, even though he did not," Mrs. Frogerton explained. "As you might imagine, Mrs. Scutton was quite overset by this."

"I must go to her." Mr. Scutton turned on his heel and left the room at some speed.

Mrs. Frogerton raised her eyebrows and gestured to the door. "Hurry along, lass. If you go into the spare bedchamber next to Mrs. Scutton's, you might overhear what is being said."

Caroline did as she was asked, but not without an element of doubt. Being caught eavesdropping by the Scuttons wouldn't endear her to either of them. She tried to walk nonchalantly along the corridor as if she had a legitimate purpose and only diverted into the spare room at the last second. It took her a moment to slow her breathing and to consider how best she might hear what was going on next door.

The fireplace adjoined the one in Mrs. Scutton's room and was separated only by only a thin brick wall. Feeling slightly ridiculous, Caroline knelt on the hearthrug and leaned in toward the chimney. Unfortunately, she could barely distinguish between the two voices, let alone hear what they might be saying to each other. She let out a frustrated breath, stirring the soot. She devoutly hoped she wasn't now coated with it.

As she gazed down at her gown, she caught sight of something stuck in the grate, and she bent to examine it. A piece of slightly singed metallic cord was tangled between the grate's bars. She tried to ease it out, but it was attached at both ends. She followed the line of the cord and discovered it was knotted around what appeared to be the back of an earring. At the other end there was the scrap of a label or note of some kind.

Caroline slowly untangled the cord and wrapped her find within the folds of her handkerchief. She stood up just in time to hear someone leave Mrs. Scutton's room. She prayed she would remain undiscovered as footsteps went past her and another door opened farther along the corridor. After a few moments, when all had gone quiet, she left the room, tiptoed past Mrs. Scutton's door, and went down to the drawing room, where Mrs. Frogerton awaited her.

"Well? Did you hear anything interesting?" Mrs. Frogerton asked. She was sitting at her writing desk, her pen poised over the paper.

"No, they were speaking too quietly, but I did recover something odd from the fireplace." Caroline went to sit beside Mrs. Frogerton and took out her handkerchief. "How it didn't get completely burned, I'll never know."

"What is it?" Mrs. Frogerton put on her spectacles and poked the chain. "Is that part of an earring?"

"I believe so, and there's a remnant of a tag on the other end." Caroline attempted to remove some of the soot from the item. "I can't tell if it's a maker's label or some kind of note."

"It is difficult to tell," Mrs. Frogerton peered closely at the earring. "There's a hallmark on there. That might help."

"If it's from one of the emptied jewelry boxes, I could take it to Rundell's and see if they recognize it," Caroline suggested.

"What a good idea," Mrs. Frogerton said. "Although why Mary would be throwing perfectly good jewelry into the fire is beyond me."

"I doubt she was the person throwing it, ma'am. It's more likely that whoever took the jewelry from the boxes discarded anything they didn't think was valuable."

"Then it must have been a man, because any woman would know to take the earring back part to the jewelers and ask them to fix it." Mrs. Frogerton said. "One earring is far less valuable than a pair. Once you've had your lunch, you can take the carriage and make a call on Rundell's in Ludgate Hill."

"Yes, ma'am."

"And, by the way. Mr. Lewis is coming to eat with us and wishes to speak to you."

Caroline concealed a sigh and offered her employer a bright smile. "How very pleasant. I'll just arrange for a messenger to take your note to Miss Smith, and I'll be back to greet Mr. Lewis when he arrives."

Mr. Lewis was in a jovial mood and more inclined to chat over lunch than bother Caroline with business. As Mr. Scutton had joined them, Caroline was relieved Mr. Lewis kept his counsel.

After his second slice of lemon soufflé, he patted his stomach and looked over at Caroline. "Can you spare me a few moments, my lady? I have news from South Africa."

"Of course, Mr. Lewis." Caroline rose to her feet. "We can speak in Mrs. Frogerton's study."

Mr. Scutton cleared his throat. "Would you like me to accompany Lady Caroline, Mr. Lewis? I am the head of the Morton family."

"That won't be necessary, sir," Caroline spoke for herself. "I will deal with this matter."

She left the dining room and opened the door into Mrs. Frogerton's study to allow Mr. Lewis to follow her in.

"Scutton seems a decent enough chap," Mr. Lewis commented after they entered the study. "Very respectful and quite rightly concerned about your prospects."

"My prospects have nothing to do with the Morton estate," Caroline said.

"I'm quite aware of that, my lady. I can assure you he'll get no information out of me without your agreement." Mr. Lewis smiled. "Mr. Scutton has already tried to assert his right to know your business, and I very politely put him off."

"Thank you." Caroline smiled. "Now, what is it you wish to speak to me about?"

He indicated the two chairs in front of the fire, waited until she sat down, and then took the other seat.

"I've had more information from the potential buyer of the mines and the adjoining land." He took out a packet of letters from his pocket and handed them over to Caroline. "Here is all the correspondence between my office and the buyers for you to read at your leisure. My clerk has already made me copies."

"Do you think they are serious buyers?" Caroline asked.

"Yes, indeed. They are a young company, but they have big ambitions to succeed and appear to be fulfilling them. Miss DeBloom's lawyers gave me an excellent report on their financial status and prospects."

"But Miss DeBloom simply wants to get rid of her share of the business," Caroline pointed out. "She'd probably be willing to believe anyone."

"Which is why I consulted other mining experts both in England and Africa to verify their claims." He smiled at her. "I'm not going to allow anyone to beggar you a second time, my lady, I can promise you that." He rose to his feet. "Please read the letters and my notes and let me know if you have any questions. I believe this is an excellent opportunity that will offer you a substantial financial reward."

"Thank you." Caroline stood, too. "I'll let you know my thoughts when I've thoroughly reviewed this information."

"I'd expect no less of you." He headed for the entrance hall. "I won't bother Mrs. Frogerton again, so I'll see myself out." He collected his hat and gloves from the table beside the front door. "Good afternoon, Lady Caroline."

"Good afternoon, sir."

Caroline went back up to the drawing room, the packet of letters in her hand.

"Was Mr. Lewis helpful?" Mrs. Frogerton asked.

"He believes there is a serious buyer for the DeBloom land and mines and wishes me to consider their offer."

"How exciting! Did he mention the name of this company?"

Caroline extracted the first letter from the pile and spread it out to read it. "They are called DeBeers."

"DeBeers?" Mr. Scutton, whom Caroline hadn't realized was standing by the far window overlooking the street, turned to stare at her. "I believe I've read about them in *The Times*."

"Then they must be legitimate if *The Times* mentioned them," Mrs. Frogerton said as Caroline wished she hadn't opened her mouth before assuring herself that they were alone. "I'll have to look out for that name when I read the business news."

Mr. Scutton came over to Mrs. Frogerton's chair. "I wish you would use your influence, ma'am, to impress on my cousin that I am more than willing to be her advisor in these complicated matters."

Mrs. Frogerton chuckled. "I am the last person you should ask to intercede for you, Mr. Scutton. I am firmly of the opinion that women are perfectly capable of managing their own affairs."

"With respect, ma'am, Lady Caroline is not like you. She's been gently brought up and—"

Caroline stood up. "Mr. Scutton, I was managing my father's household from the age of fourteen when my mother died. I paid the wages, did the accounts, tried to stop my father from stealing the very food from our mouths, *and* dealt with the staff. I am perfectly capable of understanding the ramifications of a financial deal."

"That is all very commendable, but—"

"I do not need your advice, sir, and I am becoming tired of repeating myself."

Mr. Scutton drew himself up. "You are insulting me."

"No, I am asking you to let me manage my own affairs without your interference." Caroline kept her voice calm. She didn't want Mr. Scutton accusing her of behaving like a hysterical female who didn't know her own silly mind.

"I fear you will regret turning my offer of help away, my lady." Mr. Scutton glared at her. "Your lack of femininity appalls me."

"That's quite enough, Mr. Scutton," Mrs. Frogerton snapped. "May I remind you that you are a guest in my house and that insulting a member of my household is not acceptable."

Mr. Scutton bowed. "I apologize to you, ma'am, but not to my cousin. My mother said she was willful. I made excuses for her, but not anymore."

"If you truly feel like that, sir, I suggest you speak to your mother forthwith and find alternate accommodation." Mrs. Frogerton wasn't finished. "I am tired of your attempts to assert your rights in my house when all I have done is try to help you."

Mr. Scutton stormed out, glaring at Caroline as he went past, as if it was all her fault.

"I'm sorry, lass, but he deserved that," Mrs. Frogerton said.

"I'm glad you spoke up, ma'am. He deserved every word. Perhaps we should both go to the jewelers while Mr. Scutton speaks to his mother?"

Mrs. Frogerton looked up. "Oh, no, lass. If they're leaving, I want to be here to witness it myself."

"Then perhaps I should stay?" Caroline suggested.

"It's not me they dislike, dear. You're better off out of it." Mrs. Frogerton folded her hands in her lap and sat up straight. "They'll not be besting me, lass. Don't you worry about that."

Chapter 13

When Caroline entered the jewelers' premises, there was no one to greet her, so she rang the bell on the counter. The shop was almost entirely empty of merchandise, and Caroline wondered what had happened to the once preeminent jewelers in London. While she waited, she looked out of the window at the heavy traffic trundling constantly up the hill.

There was a gentle cough behind her. "May I help you . . . miss?"

Caroline turned to find a young man looking down his nose at her. "Good afternoon, I was hoping you might help me with a damaged earring."

He raised an eyebrow. "Repairs can be managed for most trinkets at any shop, miss."

"I believe this item might have been purchased here."

"Are you here on behalf of your employer?" His skeptical expression made her feel angry all over again.

Caroline raised her chin. "I am here because I mistakenly assumed you might assist me with a query about a piece of jewelry that came from your workshop. But if it is too much trouble—"

"Might I intrude, Mr. Brown?" An older gentleman came

up alongside the first man and bowed to Caroline. "Am I correct that I am addressing Lady Caroline Morton?"

"Yes, sir."

He smiled. "I thought I recognized you. I'm Mr. Spindler. I had the pleasure of meeting you and your mother at Morton House, my lady. I believe your father commissioned a special necklace for you on the occasion of your coming out in society."

"That's correct, sir," Caroline said. "I do hope my father paid for it."

Mr. Spindler winced. "I suspect he did not," He waved his hand at the barren shelves. "Hence our current predicament. No one of worth comes to us anymore. They all go to Garrard, but we still offer repair services."

"Then you might be able to help me." Caroline took out her handkerchief and unwrapped the damaged earring. "There is a hallmark visible on the back. I was hoping you could identify the piece and whether it came from your workshop."

Mr. Spindler raised the loupe he wore around his neck and examined the mangled earring. "I can see our unique maker's mark stamped clearly in the gold, so it did come from us. The rest is harder to read, but if I give the piece a good clean, I might be able to decipher more."

"That would be most helpful, sir," Caroline said. "And, unlike my father, I will pay you for your time."

After leaving her address with him, she exited the shop and returned to Half Moon Street in the carriage. Mrs. Frogerton would be very interested to hear that the earring was from the Rundell workshop. Mr. Spindler had detached the note from the metal parts and given it back into her care. Curious now to see if she could decipher anything further, Caroline peered at the cardboard, using her gloved finger to brush away the soot.

"*To my darl*..." she read out loud. "To my darling who?"

She turned the card over and noticed part of what appeared to be a heavily embellished letter *M*.

"M for Mary?" Caroline wondered.

It seemed likely that at some point Mr. Brigham had given his wife some rather expensive jewelry and had probably reclaimed it in his hour of need. Caroline's father had freely plundered his wife's jewelry box when in need of funds and had never replaced any of the valuable family heirlooms he'd stolen without thought. Caroline had taken to hiding the very few pieces she had left in the nursery because she knew her father would never look there.

Despite her care, when her father died, everything had been taken to pay his debts anyway. She'd saved her mother's pearl necklace and a silver bracelet only by sewing them into the hem of her gown before the bailiffs arrived. Theoretically, those pieces might belong to the Morton estate, but she had no intention of giving them back. In truth, she'd given Susan the bracelet to take to America as a memento of their mother.

Caroline reflected on how much she had changed since her father's death. She'd once believed losing her fiancé and her social status was the worst thing that could happen to her. Accepting a job as a paid companion rather than living on her aunt's charity had been her first act of rebellion, and she didn't regret it. She'd learned to stand up for herself and not allow others to dictate how her life would progress.

Of course, being employed by Mrs. Frogerton was a blessing—one she'd appreciated from the start and had come to value greatly as time passed. Mrs. Frogerton had encouraged her to step outside the narrow confines of being the sheltered daughter of a peer and embrace her independence. Standing up to men like Thomas Scutton and Mr. Potkins would never have occurred to her before her change in circumstances, but now she almost relished the opportunity to set them straight.

Her mother would've been horrified to see her oldest daughter behave so boldly. . . .

The carriage drew up in front of the familiar facade of the Half Moon Street house, and Caroline stepped down from the carriage. The front door opened as she approached, and Mr. Jenkins bowed to her. "Welcome back, miss."

To Caroline's disappointment, there was no sign of any luggage piled in the hall indicating that the Scuttons might be moving out. As Mrs. Scutton was prone to take offense, Caroline could only wonder what was stopping her from leaving. She untied the ribbons of her bonnet and took it off as she walked up the stairs. Perhaps the Scuttons were still packing. She'd been away barely an hour.

She decided to go into the drawing room to assure Mrs. Frogerton that she had successfully accomplished her mission.

"Good afternoon, ma'am, I—" She stopped speaking, as she noted the Scuttons were flanking Mrs. Frogerton's chair.

Mrs. Scutton came forward. "Caroline? Thomas has something to say to you."

"I wish to apologize unreservedly for my behavior earlier." He swallowed hard. "My mother informs me that I was ill-mannered and ungrateful to both you and our hostess."

Caroline's gaze flicked to Mrs. Frogerton, but for once she could gain no insight from her employer's usually expressive face.

Mr. Scutton took her silence as a reason to keep talking. "I am a man of deep passions, my lady, and when I come to . . . care about someone, those emotions sometimes get the better of me. I have already apologized profusely to Mrs. Frogerton, who has been gracious enough to accept my request for forgiveness. I pray that you will do the same."

"My needs are secondary to those of Mrs. Frogerton,

sir," Caroline replied. "If she has forgiven you, I can only do the same."

"I will ensure that Thomas minds his manners until we move into Morton House, my dear," Mrs. Scutton said. "And if he offends you again, please do come and tell me."

Mrs. Frogerton nodded. "Then that's all settled. Caroline, would you order some tea?"

"Yes, ma'am."

To Caroline's relief, both the Scuttons left the room, and she didn't have to converse with them further. She sat opposite her employer, who was looking rather thoughtful.

"I wonder why dear Mr. Scutton felt the need to apologize?" Mrs. Frogerton asked. "Earlier, he seemed quite willing to be cast out onto the street rather than moderate his views."

"Perhaps he has the good sense to listen to his mother," Caroline suggested. "Morton House is in no fit state to receive them yet, and I doubt Mrs. Scutton would care to move into a hotel."

"I suppose that makes sense." Mrs. Frogerton sighed. "Now, how did it go with the jewelers? Did they recognize the piece?"

"Yes, they recognized their unique maker's mark on the gold," Caroline said. "Mr. Spindler said he would contact me when he'd cleaned the earring and assessed the value of the repair."

"That at least is good news." Mrs. Frogerton said as the tea tray was brought in. "I still can't imagine why anyone would be so careless with a piece of jewelry as to throw it on the fire."

"Perhaps that person was in a hurry, ma'am," Caroline said. She took out the piece of card that had been attached to the earring back. "I managed to decipher a small part of this message." She handed it over to Mrs. Frogerton. "I assume the item was a gift from someone."

"It looks like an 'M'." Mrs. Frogerton confirmed Caroline's observation. "Perhaps for Mary?" She sighed. "I doubt it's worth mentioning to Inspector Ross at this point. We'd better wait until your Mr. Spindler gives us more information about the earring."

"Yes, I don't think Inspector Ross would consider this relevant to his investigation," Caroline agreed. "Have you heard from him at all?"

Mrs. Frogerton chuckled. "You know the best way to summon Inspector Ross, lass. Just ask him. He'll come here for you."

Dinner was a subdued affair with both the Scuttons on their best behavior. None of the topics Mrs. Frogerton introduced seemed to interest them, and eventually even she gave up and talked to Caroline about Dorothy's latest letter.

"She seems to be enjoying the west country, although she complains about all the visits to the Lingards' extended family they have to make."

"Society honeymoons can last for months, if not years, if they go abroad," Caroline said. "I've known couples to return home with their first child on the way."

Mrs. Frogerton chuckled. "I can't imagine Dotty's face if that happened to her. I suspect she means to return to London and become known as a great society hostess before she settles down and has her children."

"That would seem quite in character," Caroline agreed.

The butler came in and bowed. "Inspector Ross is asking if you'd see him, ma'am."

"Then send him in." Mrs. Frogerton gestured with her fork.

Caroline set down her wineglass and turned to the door as Inspector Ross came in.

He bowed briefly and turned his attention to the Scuttons. "I'm pleased to inform you that we have Albert Brigham in our custody."

"About time, too," Mrs. Scutton said. "And has he confessed to murdering my daughter?"

"Not yet, ma'am."

Mr. Scutton frowned. "I assume you have at least charged him with the murder?"

"Yes, sir," Inspector Ross said.

"Did you have to go all the way to Ireland to force him to face his crimes?" Mrs. Scutton asked.

"No, he came back voluntarily."

"Isn't that an odd thing to do?" Mrs. Frogerton wondered. "He must have known he'd be held on the charge of murder."

"Mr. Brigham insists he has no knowledge of the crime."

"Another lie." Mrs. Scutton shook her head. "I hope you'll be more successful at getting him to confess than you were with his brother."

"I'm sure Inspector Ross will do his best," Mrs. Frogerton said.

"But how can Albert even claim such a thing?" Mrs. Scutton wasn't finished. "Does he think we are all stupid? That we have collectively forgotten how he deceived us, stole from us, and ultimately murdered my daughter?"

"Mama . . ." Mr. Scutton murmured. "Please don't upset yourself."

"I am merely trying to understand how that . . . *man* can deny murdering Mary." Mrs. Scutton dabbed at her eyes with her handkerchief. "Is he aware that I am still alive, or did he assume his brother finished me off, too?"

"I will certainly find that out, ma'am," Inspector Ross said. "At some point, Mr. Brigham will begin to understand that we have all the evidence we need to convict him and will confess his crimes."

"I'll testify against him in court, Inspector, don't you worry about that," Mrs. Scutton said. "It would give me immense pleasure to watch him hang!"

For a brief moment, Inspector Ross's gaze met Caroline's, and she noted his distaste for Mrs. Scutton's declarations.

He quickly assumed a more neutral expression. "Your testimony would be most valuable, Mrs. Scutton."

"I expect you to keep us informed as to exactly what Albert is saying, Inspector," Mr. Scutton said.

"I will do what I can, sir." Inspector Ross inclined his head. "You must understand that I can't give away information that should first be heard in a court of law."

"Surely you can tell us?" Mr. Scutton countered. "We're hardly going to broadcast it on the street."

"As I said, I'll do my best to keep you informed." He turned to Mrs. Frogerton. "I apologize for interrupting your dinner, but I thought it important to inform your guests as soon as possible."

"That was very thoughtful of you, Inspector." Mrs. Frogerton smiled at him. "It will be interesting to see how Mr. Brigham thinks to wiggle out of this."

"Indeed, ma'am." Inspector Ross turned to the door. "I'll wish you all a good evening."

After a nod from Mrs. Frogerton, Caroline followed him out of the room and into the entrance hall. He was reclaiming his hat and gloves and didn't see her immediately. She was struck by the lines of strain on his face.

She moved instinctively toward him. "Is everything all right, Inspector?"

He almost startled as she reached out to him. "Lady Caroline."

"You seem rather tired."

He half-smiled. "My brother is dying in agony. I'm spending all my free time with him while attempting to keep my job and secure a conviction against Albert Brigham."

"I'm so sorry." She met his gaze. "Is there anything I can do to help?"

"If there was anything, you'd be the first person I'd ask," he said softly. "You have a great deal of kindness inside you, my lady."

"Hardly that," Caroline demurred. "I'm simply . . . worried about *you*."

He bent his head and brushed a kiss over her forehead. "I cannot tell you how much I appreciate your concern at this moment. It is one of the few things keeping me going."

"If you wish me to sit with your brother—"

His faint smile disappeared. "I wouldn't expose you to his vitriol as he rages against the death he's been seeking for years."

"Ah, but it wouldn't affect me as profoundly as it does you because he means nothing to me. If you or your family need help, please don't hesitate to ask. I have some slight acquaintance with your mother, the marchioness, and I'm certain Mrs. Frogerton wouldn't object."

He took her hand and kissed her knuckles. "You are a strong and resilient woman, Lady Caroline." He reluctantly released her. "And there is much more I would like to say on this subject, but this is hardly the right time or place."

He picked up his hat. "Tell Mrs. Frogerton that I'll keep you informed about the investigation. If I can't come myself, I'll send Sergeant Dawson in my stead."

"Is there any hope that your brother will rally?" Caroline asked.

"No. This is the end for him." He grimaced. "He has hours, maybe days? All I know is that I am expected to be there when the worst happens, and it's the last place I'd ever wanted to be in my life." He turned to the door. "I must go, or I'll be sobbing on your shoulder like a little boy."

"I wouldn't mind if you did," Caroline said. "You have much to bear."

His expression softened. "You really are a jewel, my dear."

He left, and Caroline stayed where she was, shocked at her temerity. She'd asked Inspector Ross about intimate matters, and he'd willingly answered her. He'd kissed her on the forehead, and she'd offered to comfort him.

After a few moments to compose herself, she went into the dining room and sat back down.

"You took your time," Mrs. Scutton said.

Caroline looked at her. "I beg your pardon?"

"You should watch your reputation, my dear," Mrs. Scutton said. "Allowing yourself to be alone with men will do nothing for your future prospects."

"Inspector Ross is from one of the finest families in the land, ma'am." Caroline refused to back down. "And if Mrs. Frogerton sees no harm in the connection, then I am happy to continue it."

"I see no harm in it," Mrs. Frogerton agreed.

Mrs. Scutton leaned forward. "With respect, ma'am, Lady Caroline belongs to a world that you are perhaps unfamiliar with—"

"Unfamiliar with?" Mrs. Frogerton raised her eyebrows. "My daughter is a viscountess. She has been presented at court. All the best families came to her wedding, didn't they, Caroline?"

"Indeed, they did, ma'am. Including two of the royal dukes." Caroline smiled at her. "And both of them made a point of seeking you out and congratulating you on your daughter's marriage."

"Well, there you are, then." Mrs. Frogerton picked up her wineglass. "Caroline is in excellent company and should continue to behave as she thinks fit."

Mrs. Scutton opened her mouth to speak but, after a glance at her son, closed it again and returned her attention to her dinner.

Mr. Scutton cleared his throat. "At least Albert's been apprehended. That is good news."

"As he turned himself in, the police can hardly claim any credit," Mrs. Scutton couldn't resist adding.

"One assumes he turned himself in because he realized he was unable to leave the country due to police presence at the ports," Mrs. Frogerton said.

"Perhaps he came back because of his brother," Caroline suggested. "I understand they were close."

"Where did you get that idea from?" Mrs. Scutton asked.

"Mary mentioned that her husband came from a large and loving family, ma'am," Caroline explained.

"Loving enough to stick together and murder my only daughter," Mrs. Scutton said. "I warned her that they were no good, but would she listen to me?"

It was a familiar refrain and one that neither Caroline nor Mrs. Frogerton had an answer for. Mrs. Scutton sighed into the awkward silence.

"I think I'll retire."

Mr. Scutton rose to his feet. "I'll accompany you upstairs, Mama."

Caroline barely waited until they'd left before she turned to Mrs. Frogerton. "Inspector Ross's brother is dying."

"Oh, dear. I did wonder if something else was amiss," Mrs. Frogerton said. "The poor man."

"As the potential heir, he is required to be at Richard's bedside and is finding it quite difficult."

"I'm not surprised, lass. He never sought a title." Mrs. Frogerton shook her head.

"I offered to sit with Richard if it helped," Caroline said.

"That was good of you. I doubt he'll take you up on it, but I'm glad you thought to ask."

"I have some acquaintance with his family from the old days," Caroline said. "And I must admit that I hoped releasing him from his brother's sickbed might make it easier for him to conclude his investigation into Mary's murder."

"I don't think it will be long before Mr. Brigham realizes he has nowhere to run, my dear. He cannot continue to lie when all the evidence points in his direction."

"Then why is he bothering to do so?" Caroline asked the obvious question. "What does he gain from refusing to admit the truth?"

"Perhaps he expects to be saved?" Mrs. Frogerton asked. "He does seem to be something of a gambler."

"He can hardly expect the Scuttons to save him this time," Caroline said. "Mr. Scutton already paid off his debts, and look what happened then."

"That's an interesting point, lass." Mrs. Frogerton frowned. "Why *did* Mr. Scutton choose to involve himself in this matter in the first place?"

"He said it was because he wanted Mary to be happy,"

"He didn't tell his mother what he was doing because he must have known she would strenuously object." Mrs. Frogerton fidgeted with the silk fringe of her shawl. "Something about his behavior doesn't sit right with me."

"Are you suggesting Albert Brigham might be telling the truth and had nothing to do with Mary's murder?" Caroline asked.

"Not quite, lass. I'm just wondering whether Mr. Scutton had anything to do with it."

"You think Mr. Scutton was complicit in the murder of his own sister?" Caroline raised her eyebrows. "You've mentioned this before, ma'am, and I thought we came to the conclusion that he wouldn't hurt his sister like that."

"We did." Mrs. Frogerton sighed. "I suppose it's because I can't get around the thought that Mr. Scutton was the person who set this tragedy in motion by releasing Mr. Brigham from the debtors' prison."

Caroline stared at her employer.

"He's always on the periphery, isn't he?" Mrs. Frogerton said and then smiled. "I know what your next question will be. Why would Mr. Scutton conspire with the Brighams to murder Jude and his own sister?"

"To secure the earldom?" Caroline looked at her employer. "We've already discussed that, but I'm still not convinced."

"Neither am I," Mrs. Frogerton conceded. "I think it far more likely that Albert Brigham is living in a dreamland where he believes he'll never pay for his crimes."

"Or he is waiting for Mr. Scutton to save him again," Caroline said slowly.

"Which would indicate Mr. Brigham has information Mr. Scutton would prefer not to be heard."

For a moment, they stared at each other, and then Caroline stood up.

"Perhaps we should focus our attention on preparing Morton House for the Scuttons and let Inspector Ross worry about the Brighams."

Mrs. Frogerton nodded. "I think you're right, lass. All this speculation is giving me a headache."

Chapter 14

At breakfast the next morning, Caroline received a note from the jewelers, and after consulting with Mrs. Frogerton, she arranged for Mr. Spindler to call on them at eleven. She spent the intervening hours walking Mrs. Frogerton's dogs to the receiving office and posting her employer's letters. There was no sign of Dr. Harris in the park, and Caroline wondered, not for the first time, when he would deign to visit them again.

It wasn't unusual for him to disappear when his workload overwhelmed him, but he usually sent a note to reassure Mrs. Frogerton as to his health and whereabouts. He hadn't even told them if he'd been offered the new position at the Royal Free Hospital. Caroline was fairly certain that his absence was directly related to their last meeting when he'd asked for reassurances Caroline was unable to give to him.

Should she write him a note herself? The thought was appealing, but what could she say? It wasn't as if she'd turned down his proposal of marriage or said anything to make him think she expected one. There were well-honed responses for such scenarios that Caroline had learned at her mother's knee. And she wasn't sure what she should be apologizing for when he'd been the one to take offense.

Perhaps a simple note telling him that she'd heard from Susan might suffice. She spent the remainder of her journey mentally composing such a letter in her head and still couldn't quite get the tone right.

Clouds were gathering as Caroline turned into Half Moon Street. She hurried the dogs straight down to the basement as the first few raindrops fell. She walked through into the kitchen, left her muddy boots, gave the dogs to one of the housemaids, and went upstairs to the drawing room.

Mrs. Scutton was sitting with Mrs. Frogerton, which was something of a surprise, and Caroline wished them both a good morning.

"Were the dogs well behaved?" Mrs. Frogerton asked.

"They were very good. I only had to carry Pug from the park exit to the house."

"He is rather precious," Mrs. Frogerton said fondly. "And not as sprightly as he used to be. I think all these stairs in this town house have worn him out."

Caroline glanced at the clock. "Shall I order tea, ma'am, or shall we wait until our visitor arrives?"

"Let's wait," Mrs. Frogerton said. "I don't think this business will take very long." She turned to Mrs. Scutton. "I have just been reassuring our guest that George Brigham will not be allowed in this house and that when she goes out, someone will accompany her at all times."

"I'm sure that is very heartening," Caroline said.

Mrs. Scutton made a face. "I don't understand why Inspector Ross might allow George to leave without being charged with anything."

"Perhaps the inspector feels he has a strong case against Mr. Albert Brigham and doesn't need the brother," Mrs. Frogerton suggested. "In fact, it might be seen as a positive."

Mrs. Scutton didn't look convinced, and the conversation came to an end.

Just as the mantelpiece clock struck eleven times, Mr.

Spindler came in behind the parlor maid and bowed deeply. From the dampness of his clothes and the mud on his boots, it appeared that he had walked all the way from Ludgate Hill.

"Good morning, Lady Caroline, ladies. I am delighted to tell you that I have your jewelry all restored."

"That is excellent news, Mr. Spindler," Caroline said as she gestured him to a seat.

He patted his pockets, took out a small jewelry box, and handed it to Caroline. "Voilà! I took the liberty of reshaping the catch and adding just enough new gold to strengthen the whole piece." He beamed at Caroline. "I do hope you have the rest of the earring. I believe it was one of your mother's favorites."

Caroline didn't dare look at either Mrs. Frogerton or Mrs. Scutton. "To be honest, sir, I wasn't sure what it was. I found it entangled in an old shawl."

"Then it is a pleasure to restore it to its rightful state, and I hope it will soon be reunited with the emerald and diamond drops it belongs with."

Mrs. Frogerton cleared her throat. "I'm impressed that you knew exactly which piece of jewelry that mangled heap of metal came from."

"It all comes down to experience, ma'am," Mr. Spindler said. "And the very specific marks we use for our favored clients, which make it remarkably easy to identify every piece."

"How clever," Mrs. Frogerton said. "Please send us your bill, Mr. Spindler, and we will pay it directly."

"Thank you, ma'am." He rose to his feet. "And now I must be off. We have to vacate our premises by the end of the week."

"That is most unfortunate, sir," Mrs. Frogerton said.

"*That* is due to gross mismanagement by my predecessors, ma'am, and those who should know better not paying their bills." Mr. Spindler bowed. "A pleasure to serve you again, Lady Caroline."

"Thank you, Mr. Spindler." Caroline stood as well, but he waved her back to her seat.

"No need to accompany me, my lady. I'll see myself out."

Caroline took the opportunity to ring the bell for tea and then resumed her seat.

"Well," said Mrs. Scutton. "What was all that about?"

Mrs. Frogerton opened her mouth, but for once, Caroline got in first. "As I mentioned to Mr. Spindler, ma'am, I found the back of an earring entangled in one of my mother's old shawls and took it to Rundell's to see if they could identify it for me."

"Why would you bother about something so small?"

"I suppose it's because the item belonged to my mother, and I have very little left of her," Caroline said. She opened the box and passed it over to Mrs. Scutton.

"If it is a Morton piece of jewelry, surely it belongs to the estate and not you?" Mrs. Scutton asked after viewing the small gold trinket with some disfavor.

"That's a very good question." Caroline smiled at her. "And a complicated one. Some of my mother's jewelry came with her from her own family and was meant for her daughters. Other pieces were Morton heirlooms, and some were bought for her by my father."

Caroline turned to Mrs. Frogerton. "I wonder if Coutts kept any of the Morton jewelry when they purchased the estate? It might be worth asking them."

"Mrs. Scutton?" Mrs. Frogerton looked at her guest. "Are you aware of any jewelry being held in trust for the Morton estate?"

"You'd have to ask Mr. Castle," Mrs. Scutton said. "But if this earring back does belong to something in their possession, then it should be restored to its rightful place."

"I quite agree," Caroline said. "There's no point in me keeping it purely for sentimental reasons."

"That's very sensible of you, my dear." Mrs. Scutton smiled approvingly at her. "I'll write to Coutts and find out what they have in the vault." She left the room intent on her task.

Mrs. Frogerton looked at Caroline. "That was very quick thinking on your part, lass."

"I prefer not to tell falsehoods, but I had to think of something, and Mr. Spindler's assumptions gave me an obvious avenue to explore." Caroline frowned. "How on earth did a piece of jewelry once owned by my mother end up in the fireplace in Mary Brigham's bedchamber?"

"It is quite extraordinary," Mrs. Frogerton acknowledged. "Even if Albert did buy the jewelry secondhand, the chances of him purchasing pieces from the Morton estate are extremely unlikely."

"Extremely," Caroline agreed.

"Which brings us back to Mr. Scutton." Mrs. Frogerton looked at Caroline expectantly. "What if Mr. Castle from Coutts gave Mr. Scutton access to the Morton assets, and he used them to help Albert?"

"But Mr. Scutton didn't know Mr. Castle when Albert was first imprisoned for his debts," Caroline objected.

"Yes, but Mr. Scutton *did* say that he suddenly had enough spare capital to help his brother-in-law. Perhaps he used all his savings to assist Albert and borrowed against his expectations of becoming an earl on the assumption that Mr. Castle would give him access to the Morton money?"

"That's . . ." Reluctant to jump ahead to Mrs. Frogerton's somewhat fanciful conclusions, Caroline considered what they knew. "The Scutton family are connected to the Mortons. Perhaps the jewelry was already in their family, and Mary brought it with her to London."

Mrs. Frogerton raised her eyebrows. "Your mother's jewelry?"

"Mr. Spindler might have mistaken the mark."

"But even if the jewelry did come with Mary, how is it that her own mother and brother didn't recognize it?"

"Perhaps they pretended not to?"

"For what purpose?"

Caroline sat down. "Now you sound like me, ma'am."

"I just don't understand how this has happened," Mrs. Frogerton said. "But my instincts are telling me that Mr. Scutton is involved somehow. Do you remember how the jewelry cases disappeared when they were left in his bedchamber with Mary's other belongings?"

"Perhaps we should simply ask Mr. Scutton what happened to them," Caroline said. "He is already out of charity with me, so nothing I could say would make anything worse."

"Are you quite sure about that, lass? The man has a temper on him."

"I doubt he'll attempt to murder me right in front of you," Caroline said.

"Of course he won't, but he'll find a way to dispose of you regardless." Mrs. Frogerton looked worried. "Perhaps we should just let the matter drop."

"Now you are alarming me, ma'am. You are normally the person forging ahead intent on discovering everything," Caroline said. "And I'm still not convinced Mr. Scutton is involved in any of this."

Mrs. Frogerton pressed her hand to her bosom. "I can't tell you why I believe that he is, Caroline, but I feel it in my bones. Madam Lavinia did say I was a very spiritual person."

The butler came in with a note that he handed to Mrs. Frogerton. "From Inspector Ross, ma'am."

"Thank you." Mrs. Frogerton opened the note and read it through before passing it to Caroline. "It seems Mrs. Scutton was correct. Mr. George Brigham has been released on bail. I wonder who stood surety for that?"

"I wish we could speak to him," Caroline said.

"He stood by while his brother murdered Mary. I hardly think he is worthy of our attention, Caroline."

"I doubt he'd be willing to come within a mile of this house, ma'am. In fact, his appearance here might mean his bail would be revoked for violating the terms of the agreement."

"Did Inspector Ross tell you that?" Mrs. Frogerton asked.

"He did mention such a scenario when I was concerned about Mr. Albert Brigham turning up here and threatening us again."

"No news on Inspector Ross's brother, I assume?"

"There was nothing in the newspapers this morning. I assume Richard is still living."

The door opened, and Mrs. Scutton came back in, looking very pleased with herself.

"I've written to Coutts and sent the kitchen boy off with the letter. I told him to wait for a reply."

It was on the tip of Caroline's tongue to mention to Mrs. Scutton that it wasn't her house and that she should have consulted with Mrs. Frogerton before she ordered her staff around. In the interests of harmony and her desire to know whether Mr. Castle did have answers for them, she let the moment go.

"I wonder if Mr. Scutton has a list of all the items Coutts holds for the earldom?" Mrs. Frogerton asked. "It would be very useful."

"I believe Mr. Potkins has that information on hand." Mrs. Scutton paused. "I wonder if I should write to him as well?"

"Could you not just ask your son?" Mrs. Frogerton asked.

"I'd rather not worry him about such a small matter," Mrs. Scutton said.

"Then would you care to use my desk to compose your letter, ma'am?" Mrs. Frogerton offered. "Or Caroline could go up to your room and bring down your writing desk?"

"I'd be happy to do that, Mrs. Scutton. You mustn't endanger your health." Caroline rose to her feet and was out of the door before Mrs. Scutton could object.

She picked up her skirts and ran up the two flights of

stairs to Mrs. Scutton's bedroom. The door was unlocked, and Caroline went in. Mrs. Scutton's portable writing case stood open on the table, her pen and ink still uncapped, and a fresh sheet of paper secured into the frame.

Aware that she couldn't take too long, Caroline did a quick search through the drawers for the letter from Mary that Jude had taken home with him. There was no sign of it. Caroline was surprised by the volume of correspondence Mrs. Scutton had received about the state of the earldom and its finances from both Mr. Potkins and Coutts Bank. For a woman who often claimed ignorance about the Morton estate, she was remarkably well informed.

Caroline set the inkpot back in its spot, corked the bottle, and set the pen on the blotting paper before closing the lid. A handwritten label on the inner side caught her attention. It read *Henrietta Bryson, her box, Whitechapel, London.*

Was Bryson Mrs. Scutton's maiden name? Miss Smith had mentioned that her first name was Hetty, which seemed to fit. Caroline carefully closed the lid and brought the box down to the drawing room.

"Thank you," Mrs. Scutton took the box and walked over to the window to get the best of the light. "It is always comfortable to have one's own things to use."

"It is a very useful writing case," Caroline observed. "Have you owned it for a long time?"

"It was a birthday present." Mrs. Scutton paused. "From a good friend of the family."

"Your employer?" Mrs. Frogerton asked. "Miss Smith said that you were employed by an aristocratic family in London."

"Miss Smith has no business gossiping about me and mine." Mrs. Scutton sat down and opened the writing case. "And I shall tell her so next time we meet."

"Is it not true?" Mrs. Frogerton persisted. "As you know, I come from humble origins myself, and I see nothing to be ashamed of in owning them."

"I was in service. I met Mr. Scutton when the family moved to their country seat in the summer months." Mrs. Scutton set out her inkpot and pen.

"And you married him before you had to go back to London?" Mrs. Frogerton nodded. "A wise decision."

"Indeed." Mrs. Scutton bent her head to her writing.

"When we passed through Epping, I noticed a fine church at the end of the high street. Was that where you were married?"

"Yes, at St. John the Baptist. Mary was married there, too, God save her soul." Mrs. Scutton wrote slowly and paused to read before scrawling her signature. "There, that's done."

"It is very good of you to go to so much trouble on my behalf, ma'am," Caroline said.

Mrs. Scutton used her sand shaker over the surface of the letter to make sure the ink was dry before she folded it and wrote the address on the back.

"There is so little left of the Morton estate that every little piece might make a difference, Caroline. A whole earring set is worth more than an incomplete one."

"Quite," Mrs. Frogerton agreed. "Did the Scutton family inherit anything directly from their Morton connections? I understand that in aristocratic families, items that are not entailed can be diverted to other members of the family."

"That's correct, ma'am," Caroline said. "My mother's jewelry was supposed to come directly down the female line. Unfortunately, my father ignored that rule and got rid of it anyway."

Mrs. Scutton looked up. "Perhaps your mother was willing to do anything for her husband, including giving him her jewelry."

"When they were first married, I believe she would've done, but years of watching him gamble, drink, and whore his way through his fortune and hers stretched her tolerance beyond bearing."

Mrs. Scutton sniffed. "I would've done anything for Mr. Scutton." She stood up, the letter in her hand. "If you'll excuse me, I'll make sure this gets delivered to Mr. Potkins today."

When the door closed behind her, Mrs. Frogerton said to Caroline, "You notice she didn't answer my question about the inherited jewelry."

"She always picks and chooses which questions to answer, ma'am. I didn't appreciate her attempt to make my mother seem weaker than her. Mrs. Scutton has no idea how difficult my mother's life became because of my father."

"She isn't the kind of woman who can put herself in someone else's shoes. Her views are very settled, and she delights in finding the negative in everything," Mrs. Frogerton agreed. "Which aristocratic families have summer estates around Epping, lass?"

Caroline considered the question. "There used to be a very large estate in Wanstead owned by the Tylney-Long family."

"I read about that." Mrs. Frogerton leaned forward. "The whole place was sold off to pay her awful husband's debts. Who else had a home there?"

"The Marlborough family. The Earl of Essex, obviously. The Duke of Westminster. The DuBois family . . ." Caroline paused to think. "The Mortons owned several farms in the area, but from what Mr. Potkins told me, they were overseen by the land steward who lived in the Scuttons' house. They had no formal residence nearby."

"I wonder whether Mrs. Scutton worked for one of those families?" Mrs. Scutton asked. "I don't suppose there is a way to find out if she did."

"I assume the houses would keep records of their staff, but we don't have access to such things, or the authority to gain access." Caroline frowned.

"Inspector Ross might be able to do so," Mrs. Frogerton said. "And simply sending letters addressed to the housekeepers of those estates might provide some answers, if I suggest I am writing on behalf of a solicitor looking to share good news of a bequest."

"Why do you think it matters where Mrs. Scutton was employed?" Caroline asked.

"Because there is a mystery there, and Mrs. Scutton's avoidance in answering questions makes me wonder what she is trying to conceal."

Caroline nodded, her thoughts far away. "That label."

"Yes, my dear?"

"The one attached to the earring back. The 'M' might have been my father's signature."

"I suspect you might be right." Mrs. Frogerton paused. "Does that upset you, lass?"

"Yes," Caroline said. "For my mother and all her shattered dreams. She gave up in the end, ma'am, and allowed herself to die rather than fight her illness and deal with my father any longer."

"I'm sure she didn't want to leave you and Susan, Caroline."

"Her last words to me were, 'Thank God you're old enough to take care of your sister.'" Caroline drew in a difficult breath. "She placed all the burden of responsibility on a fourteen-year-old."

"That must have been very difficult to deal with, lass," Mrs. Frogerton said softly. "People always say that the good Lord never gives us more than we can bear, but I don't tend to agree with that."

"Neither do I." Caroline summoned a smile. "Sometimes I'm not even sure I believe in a higher power because good rarely seems to win against evil."

She waited for Mrs. Frogerton, who read her bible every day, to condemn her scandalous comment and was surprised when she simply nodded. "Shall we go down and see what Cook's prepared for lunch? I don't know about you, but I'm rather peckish."

They had barely settled in their seats when Mrs. Scutton

came into the dining room carrying a letter. "I've received a reply from Mr. Castle at Coutts."

"And what does Mr. Castle have to say for himself?" Mrs. Frogerton inquired as Mrs. Scutton sat down at the table.

"That the bank does hold some of the Morton jewelry." She looked rather pleased with herself. "And that if we care to call this afternoon, he will ensure that the items are taken from the vault and displayed for our attention."

"That is good news," Mrs. Frogerton said. "At what time would you like me to order the carriage?"

"For three o'clock?" Mrs. Scutton asked. "That should give them time to retrieve the items we wish to see. In truth, I am quite excited to see what the bank has held on to. I remember reading that the Morton jewels were once considered exceptional."

"I wonder if Mr. Castle has the inventory that was taken a year before my father died," Caroline mused. "It was a comprehensive list of all that had been sold, lost, and what still remained."

"That would be most helpful," Mrs. Frogerton said. "Perhaps Mrs. Scutton could ask him."

"I certainly will."

For the first time in quite a while, Mrs. Scutton was in an agreeable mood with her hosts, and Caroline intended to take advantage of it.

The carriage journey to the Strand proved uneventful, and they arrived in good time. Mrs. Frogerton hadn't visited the bank before and seemed duly impressed by both its grandeur and the haughty looks the staff gave her as she ascended the steps.

Mrs. Scutton addressed the clerk at the reception desk with all the assurance of a duchess. "We have an appointment with Mr. Andrew Castle at three. Please let him know that we are here."

"And who might you be, ma'am?" the clerk inquired as Mrs. Frogerton tried not to smile.

"I am Mrs. Scutton, mother of the new Earl of Morton."

"And these ladies?"

"Lady Caroline Morton and Mrs. Frogerton." Caroline spoke up just in case Mrs. Scutton pretended not to know them.

"Lady Caroline." The clerk bowed to her. "Perhaps you would care to wait in the morning room while I fetch Mr. Castle."

"Thank you." Caroline smiled and sailed past Mrs. Scutton into the morning room.

"Well, you think the man might have remembered me after my visits with Thomas." Mrs. Scutton was not pleased.

"At least he recognized Caroline," Mrs. Frogerton said.

Mrs. Scutton walked over to the window to look at the view and ignored them until Mr. Castle entered the room.

He was his usual, affable, smiling self. "Lady Caroline." He came straight over and took her hand. "Always a pleasure."

"Good afternoon, sir. May I remember you to Mrs. Frogerton? I know you are already well acquainted with Mrs. Scutton."

"Yes, indeed." He bowed to the other ladies. "I have the items you wish to see ready in one of our more secure rooms, if you care to follow me?"

He took them down into the basement and along a narrow corridor lined with numbered doors. Outside number six, he produced a key from his pocket and unlocked the door.

They entered the room, and to Caroline's surprise, there were quite a few of the family jewels laid out on the table.

She turned to Mr. Castle. "I thought my father sold most of these."

Mr. Castle cleared his throat. "From what I understand from my predecessor, when the earl was unable to sell an item due to the entail, he sometimes borrowed money against it and left the item in our possession as security for the debt."

"Like a pawnbroker," Mrs. Frogerton commented.

"In a manner of speaking, yes." Mr. Castle looked horrified at the comparison. "I was not aware of this arrangement until I took complete control of the estate after your father's death."

"Do you have an inventory of which pieces belong to which family?" Caroline asked. "My father sometimes forgot that some of the jewelry was not his to pawn."

"That's hardly relevant, Caroline," Mrs. Scutton said. "We are here for a different purpose."

"I am aware of that, ma'am. I just wish to make sure that Mr. Castle knows that some of these pieces might not belong to the Morton estate."

"I'll look for that inventory for you." Mr. Castle bowed and left the room.

Mrs. Scutton looked at Caroline. "I do hope you aren't going to be difficult, dear. There is a time and a place for your concerns, but the needs of the earldom are far more important."

"Yes, of course, ma'am," Caroline said meekly.

Mrs. Frogerton was leaning over the table examining the jewelry. "This is far nicer than Dotty's wedding tiara." As Mrs. Frogerton picked up the delicate diamond tiara, the light caught the facets, and bounced off the walls.

"I believe it was made for my great-grandmother," Caroline said. "That is definitely a Morton piece. Mr. Scutton can offer it to his bride to wear on ceremonial occasions."

"Would you have worn it on your wedding day?" Mrs. Frogerton asked.

"That would depend on whether my fiancé's family had a better one." Caroline smiled at her employer. "Sometimes the politics get quite heated. I do know of one bride who ended up wearing two tiaras to appease both sides of the family."

"Well, thank goodness the Lingards only had the one," Mrs. Frogerton said. "Or Dotty would've worn them all."

Mrs. Scutton was opening jewelry boxes and checking the contents. "Did Mr. Spindler say the earrings in question were emerald?" she asked.

"I believe he did." Caroline studied a cameo brooch her mother had often worn on her collar. She was fairly certain that it had come down the maternal line of the family and belonged to her. She resisted the temptation to slip it in her pocket.

Mrs. Scutton held up an earring made with a swathe of small emeralds and a dangling diamond. "I wonder if it's this one?"

"Check the back," Mrs. Frogerton suggested.

Mrs. Scutton removed the front of the velvet box and looked behind it. "The backs are both here."

"I wonder whether your mother had a replacement made?" Mrs. Frogerton suggested.

"It's possible, ma'am," Caroline said.

Privately, Caroline wasn't surprised that they hadn't found the right piece of jewelry because she suspected Mr. Brigham had already disposed of it. She was far more interested in seeing the extent of the collection and working out how to determine whether any of it should have come to her or Susan.

They checked every box and did not find a single earring without its back.

Mrs. Scutton sighed. "I suppose it was unlikely that we would succeed."

"At least we tried, ma'am," Caroline said.

"And it was nice to see that not all the Morton treasures have been lost," Mrs. Frogerton said. "I wonder how the bank will handle the transfer back to the earl?"

"I'm sure they'll accept a substantial repayment," Caroline said. "Or the estate could take them to court for engaging in such covert activities in the first place."

"I'll make sure to mention that to Thomas," Mrs. Scutton said before heading for the door. "Shall we depart?"

The door locked behind Caroline as she closed it. She followed the other ladies along the quiet corridor and up the stairs to the entrance hall.

Mr. Castle met them at the front desk. "Did you find what you were looking for, ladies?"

"No," Mrs. Scutton said. "But it was pleasant to see the family jewels."

"Indeed." Mr. Castle bowed and handed Caroline a large leather-bound book. "The records you requested, my lady. You can take them with you, if you wish."

"Thank you, sir." Caroline smiled at him.

She had high hopes that the records would prove that she owned some of the jewelry. And once she had that information, she would set Mr. Lewis to securing her claims.

Chapter 15

The next morning, Caroline was just coming down the stairs from her bedroom when she spied one of the maids standing by the open door of what had been Mary's room. The girl looked up as Caroline approached her and bobbed a curtsy. She had red hair and freckles, a wide, generous mouth, and a shy smile.

"Good morning, Ellie," Caroline said.

"Is it true, miss?"

"Is what true?"

"That Mrs. Brigham was murdered right here?" Ellie pointed at the bed.

"Yes, unfortunately that is true," Caroline said gently. "You were away visiting your family, I believe."

"Yes, miss. My mother was due to deliver her baby, so I went to help out."

"Did everything go well?"

"Yes, miss." Ellie smiled. "A lovely baby girl."

"I'm glad to hear it," Caroline said. "What with the sad events happening here."

"But *when* did it happen?" Ellie asked. "I brought Mrs. Brigham her dinner up on my last night before I got the mail coach to Dorset. She was happy as a lark because her husband was coming to see her." Ellie paused. "She told me not to tell anyone about that, but it hardly matters now."

"Mrs. Brigham told you her husband was planning on visiting her?"

"Yes, miss. She was very excited about it and made me lace her into her best dress so that she could welcome him properly."

"Did she ask you to let Mr. Brigham in the house?"

Ellie bit her lip. "Not exactly, miss. She asked me to make sure the back door was open—which it usually was when Cook was preparing a dinner party, because it gets so hot in the kitchen."

"What about the gate at the bottom of the garden into the mews?" Caroline asked. "Did you open that?"

"No, miss."

"Did it occur to you that Mrs. Frogerton should've been told Mr. Brigham was in her house?"

Ellie's cheek went a dull red. "I . . . thought it was romantic, miss. Mrs. Brigham wanted it to be secret, so I promised I wouldn't say anything to anyone."

Caroline tried to gather her thoughts. "So, you brought up Mrs. Brigham's dinner, made sure the Brighams could gain access to the house, and left for your trip before all the screaming started?"

"I never heard any screaming." For the first time, Ellie sounded defensive. "I waited until I saw Mr. Brigham and his brother come down the back stairs, I locked the door behind them, and then left myself."

"You saw Mr. Brigham and his brother *leave*?"

"Yes, miss." Ellie's confusion was plain on her face. "Mr. Brigham winked and tossed me a shilling for my trouble."

"They did not appear to be hurrying or seem agitated in any way?" Caroline asked.

"No, miss."

"Come with me." Caroline took Ellie by the elbow and started for the stairs. "Mrs. Frogerton needs to hear this."

Mrs. Frogerton and both the Scuttons were seated at the breakfast table when Caroline came in with an increasingly reluctant Ellie in tow.

Mrs. Frogerton smiled at the maid. "I'm glad to see you have returned safely, Ellie. Is your mother doing better now?"

Ellie bobbed a curtsy. "Yes, ma'am. She and the baby are thriving, and she has my sister Agnes to help her."

"That is excellent news." Mrs. Frogerton smiled and glanced at Caroline inquiringly. "Is there something amiss?"

Caroline took a slow breath. "Ellie was here on the evening Mary was murdered."

"And?" Mrs. Scutton asked. "What about it?"

"Perhaps Ellie wishes to offer you her condolences in person, ma'am," Mrs. Frogerton said. "Seeing as she was away when the tragedy happened."

"I hardly think—"

Caroline spoke over Mrs. Scutton. "Ellie saw the Brigham brothers."

A peculiar silence settled over the table.

Mrs. Frogerton was the first to break it. She addressed her question directly to Ellie, her voice gentle. "Is that true, lass?"

"Yes, ma'am." Ellie looked distinctly uncomfortable, her gaze moving between Mrs. Scutton and her employer. "I didn't mean any harm...."

"No one is accusing you of anything, Ellie," Mrs. Frogerton reassured her. "It's just that when Inspector Ross interviewed the rest of the staff, no one saw them leave the house."

"I'm more than happy to tell the Inspector what I saw, ma'am," Ellie said in a rush. "They didn't do nothing untoward."

"Nothing untoward?" Mrs. Scutton said. "Except murder my daughter."

Ellie's mouth opened. "What?"

"Mr. Brigham is accused of murdering his wife, Ellie," Caroline said. "I assumed you knew that."

"No, miss. I've hardly had a moment to myself since I got back. Lizzie just told me not to bother cleaning Mrs. Brigham's room because she had been murdered, and that was that." Ellie started sobbing. "I didn't know. I'm so sorry if I've caused offense, ma'am, but—"

"It's quite understandable, Ellie." Mrs. Frogerton came over and patted her on the shoulder. "Now, after you and Lizzie finish your work, ask Cook if she needs you for anything further. If she says no, you are to put on your bonnet and cloak and come find me. I'll take you to see Inspector Ross, and you can tell him exactly what you saw."

"Yes, ma'am. Thank you, ma'am." Ellie curtsied and almost ran out of the room.

Caroline waited until Ellie closed the door behind her before addressing Mrs. Frogerton. "Ellie said Mrs. Brigham swore her to secrecy about Albert coming to visit her. She was asked to make sure that the kitchen door remained open when Mr. Brigham required entry. She insists that she had nothing to do with the door to the mews being unlocked."

"She deliberately let him in," Mrs. Scutton said. "She is almost as guilty as my son-in-law."

"Hardly, Mama," Mr. Scutton said. "She's just a simple serving girl who tried to do what she was asked by a superior who could've had her fired if she didn't. The only person responsible for Mary's death is Mr. Brigham."

"And those who aided him." Mrs. Scutton glared at her son. "Those who willingly paid off debts and released a monster back into the world."

"I have explained my reasons for doing that on numerous occasions, Mama. I refuse to repeat them again." Mr. Scutton glared back at her. "I also refuse to allow you to use me as a scapegoat."

"Then perhaps you prefer the term collaborator?" Mrs. Scutton said.

"Now what?" Mr. Scutton flung up his hands. "What ridiculous new accusation will you lay against me?"

"Perhaps your relationship with Albert went deeper than I thought." Mrs. Scutton rose to her feet. "Think on that, Thomas."

Mr. Scutton shot to his feet, but his mother had already left, slamming the door behind her.

He sat down and looked at Mrs. Frogerton. "Yet again, I must apologize for my mother's behavior at your table, ma'am. As you can tell, she is still struggling with her grief over Mary's death."

"That's quite all right, Mr. Scutton," Mrs. Frogerton said. "When someone dies so tragically, I fear it is inevitable that people look to blame others. You were correct to remind her that the only person responsible for Mrs. Brigham's death was Mary's husband."

"Thank you for your understanding, ma'am." Mr. Scutton inclined his head. "I believe my mother feels guilty that she couldn't save Mary."

"I'm quite sure she does," Mrs. Frogerton agreed. "I would feel the same if anything happened to my daughter."

Mr. Scutton returned to his breakfast and Caroline helped herself to some tea and buttered toast. She wasn't really hungry, as the events of the morning had robbed her of her appetite, but she needed to keep up appearances. She couldn't stop wondering what else Ellie might have to say when faced with Inspector Ross's official questions. Would she admit to unlocking the rear gate or to passing messages to Mr. Brigham from his wife?

Eventually, Mr. Scutton folded up his newspaper, tucked it under his arm, and stood up. "I will go speak to my mother." He sighed. "I doubt it will do much good, but I can't have her telling everyone I colluded in the murder of my own sister."

"I'm sure she doesn't really think that, Mr. Scutton," Mrs. Frogerton said.

"I admire your optimism, ma'am." He bowed and left the room.

Caroline looked at Mrs. Frogerton. "I can't believe Mrs. Scutton voiced out loud the same suspicions we have of Mr. Scutton."

"It was rather a surprise," Mrs. Frogerton agreed. "But grief can do peculiar things to people. Mrs. Scutton is obviously suffering far more than we realized if she feels the need to accuse her son of being an accomplice to murder."

"Perhaps she thinks that when he becomes a peer, he will be immune to prosecution," Caroline said. "And that it doesn't matter what he's done."

"Is that true?" Mrs. Frogerton asked.

"Not quite. He can stand trial in front of a jury of his peers, which in his case would be the House of Lords."

"No lord is going to convict another lord." Mrs. Frogerton made a face. "It's just not done."

"I fear you are correct, ma'am." Caroline hesitated. "Ellie told me that when the Brighams were leaving, they were in high spirits, and that Mr. Brigham gave her a shilling for her help."

"That seems remarkably macabre, does it not?" Mrs. Frogerton asked with a shudder. "Did they enjoy murdering an innocent?"

"It does make them appear heartless, ma'am. Perhaps this isn't the first time they've killed." Caroline sighed. "The sooner we can get Ellie to speak to Inspector Ross, the better."

"I quite agree." Mrs. Frogerton glanced at the clock. "Perhaps I'll ask Cook if she'll let Ellie come with us right now."

Caroline stood up. "Then I'll order the carriage, ma'am, and wait for Ellie in the hall."

She was almost at the door when Mrs. Frogerton made an exasperated sound. "Oh, dear."

"What is it, ma'am?" Caroline turned back.

"I've just remembered I can't come with you," Mrs. Frogerton said. "The manager of my woolen mill is in London today, and he's coming to see me this morning."

"I'm happy to act as your deputy, ma'am," Caroline said.

"I have complete confidence in you, dear." Mrs. Frogerton also rose to her feet. "I'd better go consult my ledgers so I'm prepared to deal with Mr. Ings. He has a very high opinion of himself that I'm not sure is warranted."

Fifteen minutes later, Caroline had settled Ellie in the carriage and was just about to tell the coachman to go, when Mr. Scutton got in.

He nodded at them both. "Mrs. Frogerton asked me to accompany you."

Caroline couldn't think why, but there was little point in arguing about something so trivial. She spent the short journey talking soothingly to Ellie, who had her hands clasped together on her lap and her gaze fixed firmly on her well-patched boots.

"There is no need to be afraid, Ellie," Caroline said. "Just tell Inspector Ross what you saw, and all will be well."

"Yes, miss." Ellie's gaze flicked to Mr. Scutton. "I'm sorry for your loss, sir."

"Thank you. Mr. Scutton didn't even look at her, and she returned her attention to her boots.

Great Scotland Yard was rarely quiet, and today was no exception. There were police constables constantly coming in and out of the entrance, sometimes with reluctant criminals in tow yelling their innocence or defiance. During her various visits to Inspector Ross, Caroline had seen more than one scuffle break out and a few escapees, so she kept a tight hold of Ellie's elbow.

Mr. Scutton forged a path for them to the front desk, where Caroline recognized a familiar face. "Good morning, Sergeant Dawson. Is Inspector Ross available?"

"Morning, your ladyship." Sergeant Dawson winked. "You up to no good again?"

"I'm merely trying to be a good citizen, sergeant." Caroline smiled at him.

"I'll get one of the constables to see if the inspector is in his office." Sergeant Dawson had to raise his voice to be heard above the melee, but it didn't seem to bother him. "If you'd kindly step to one side and watch your belongings, miss, there are a lot of undesirables in here this morning."

His comment was received with predictable jeers, a few minor threats, and a few winks in her direction. Caroline was fairly certain they were insults, but luckily, she couldn't understand them. Mr. Scutton stood in front of her and Ellie, his arms crossed over his chest, his expression threatening enough to ward off any unwelcome advances. For the first time Caroline realized Mrs. Frogerton might have been right to ask Mr. Scutton to accompany them.

To her relief, it didn't take long for Inspector Ross to appear and beckon to them.

Caroline turned to Mr. Scutton. "Thank you for accompanying us. We'll meet you back here as soon as we're finished."

He frowned. "I intend to come in with you—"

"There is no need. I'm sure Ellie will feel more comfortable telling Inspector Ross what happened without your presence."

"But—"

She ignored him and hurried over to Inspector Ross, Ellie at her side.

"Good morning, Inspector."

"Lady Caroline." He bowed with a precision fit for a ballroom.

There were some loud whistles and ribald comments, but neither Caroline nor the Inspector took any notice.

He led them through a locked door into the quieter part

of the building and then into his office. To Caroline it appeared that he had borrowed several items of furniture from his family home, which gave the room an elegance that was absent in the rest of the building.

"Was that Mr. Scutton with you?" Inspector Ross asked.

"Yes." Caroline took a seat next to Ellie in front of the inspector's mahogany desk. "I didn't think his presence would help matters in this interview."

Inspector Ross raised an eyebrow but didn't comment before turning his attention to Ellie.

"I don't believe I've had the pleasure, Miss . . . ?"

"I'm Ellie Noble, sir. I work for Mrs. Frogerton as a housemaid." Ellie glanced at Caroline. "Miss Morton made me come to see you."

"Ellie has just returned from visiting her family in Dorset, Inspector," Caroline explained. "This is why you haven't met her before. She left Half Moon Street on the same evening Mrs. Brigham was killed and had no idea until today that Mr. Brigham had been arrested for the murder of his wife."

"Is that correct, Miss Noble?" Inspector Ross turned to Ellie.

"Yes, sir." She nodded vigorously. "It gave me quite a turn when Miss Morton told me what had happened after I left."

Inspector Ross took out a sheet of paper and his pen and glanced inquiringly at Ellie. "If you don't mind, I'll take notes while you tell me about the last evening you spent at Half Moon Street before your departure for Dorset."

"Yes, sir." Ellie took a deep breath. "I took Mrs. Brigham up her dinner because she didn't want to dine downstairs. I also helped her get dressed in her favorite gown."

"Even though she wasn't planning on going down to dinner?" Inspector Ross asked. "Did that strike you as unusual?"

"Yes, sir, but she told me her husband was coming to visit her and that it was a secret because her mother, Mrs. Scutton, would not approve."

"Ah, so she asked you to keep it a secret, too?"

"Yes." Ellie tried to shrug. "I didn't think there was any harm to it, sir. Mrs. Brigham was in love, and I felt sorry that her mum didn't approve."

"Quite understandable," Inspector Ross agreed. "Did you facilitate Mr. Brigham's entrance to the house?"

"Did I what, sir?" Ellie wrinkled her nose.

"I beg your pardon. Did you help Mr. Brigham gain access to the house for his meeting with his wife?"

"As I told Miss Morton, Cook likes to keep the back door open when she's preparing a big dinner, so I made sure the door was open when Mr. Brigham was expected." Ellie paused. "I also told Mrs. Brigham when the kitchen would be busiest so that her husband could go up the back stairs unobserved."

"Did you pass any messages between Mr. and Mrs. Brigham at any point to arrange this meeting?"

Ellie considered him. "I took one from Mrs. Brigham to the Blue Boar."

"And when was that exactly?"

"The day before I left for Dorset. I think it was to let Mr. Brigham know what time to come," Ellie said. "I didn't read the note. It was sealed."

"I'm sure you didn't." Inspector Ross wrote a few more sentences, and then looked up at Ellie and smiled. "You are being very helpful, Miss Noble. I commend your excellent memory and your attention to detail."

Having been the object of Inspector Ross's charming smile on more than one occasion, Caroline wasn't surprised when Ellie blushed.

"So, on the evening in question, did you see Mr. Brigham arrive?"

"Yes, sir. I was keeping an eye out for him."

"Did you let him in the back gate?"

"No, sir, Mrs. Brigham told me she'd paid one of the stable boys to do that for her."

"Did Mr. Brigham come alone?"

"No, there was another gentleman with him. Mrs. Brigham had mentioned her husband came from a big family, and from his looks, I assumed the other man was his brother."

"You saw them go up the back stairs to Mrs. Brigham's bedroom."

"Well, I didn't follow them up, sir, because I was busy, so I can't say that for certain, but they were heading in the right direction."

"Fair enough." Inspector Ross wrote another few lines. "Did you see them again?"

"Yes, sir, when they were leaving. The kitchen was a lot quieter at that point, and I wanted to make sure they could get out without drawing attention to themselves. I offered to do the washing up in the scullery, which is closest to the back stairs, so that I could hear them coming down and let them out."

"I'll wager everyone was delighted to leave all the washing up to you," Inspector Ross commented with a smile. "How long was it before the Brighams came down again?"

"About an hour, sir?" Ellie paused. "We'd finished serving dinner and everyone was busy clearing up while Cook took a well-earned rest."

"Did Mr. Brigham and his brother appear anxious to leave the house quickly?" Inspector Ross asked.

"Not particularly," Ellie said. "They were whispering to each other as they came down the stairs but in a joking manner."

"Did they see you?"

"Mr. Brigham did. He winked and tossed me a shilling."

"You're referring to Mr. Albert Brigham." Inspector Ross looked up from his writing.

"Yes, sir."

"And just to clarify, the brothers left together?"

"Yes," Ellie said.

Inspector Ross sat back, his expression thoughtful. "This might seem like an odd thing to ask, Miss Noble, but did the Brighams appear worried in any way?"

"Not that I noticed."

"Were they carrying anything you hadn't seen previously?"

"Not that I could see, sir," Ellie said. "I had wondered if they'd come to take some of Mrs. Brigham's belongings, but they didn't have anything that I could see."

"Why would you think that?"

"That they'd take her things? Because Mrs. Brigham told me she planned to run away with her husband, regardless of what her mother thought." Ellie glanced at Caroline. "She asked me if I'd like to come with her as her lady's maid, but I told her I couldn't just up and leave Mrs. Frogerton."

"That was very sensible of you, Miss Noble," Inspector Ross said. "Mrs. Frogerton is an excellent employer."

He took a moment to read through his notes and then looked up again. "There is one more thing, and I apologize in advance for my directness. Were either of the Brighams splattered with blood?"

Ellie shuddered. "No, sir. I would've noticed that right off and screamed the house down myself."

"Thank you." He wrote another line and then turned the page around so that Ellie could see it. "Would you care to read through my notes and tell me if there is anything I've misrepresented or that you wish to amend or elaborate on?"

Ellie took her time reading the notes, one finger under each line so that she could follow along, her mouth shaping the words as she went. "I don't think you missed anything, Inspector."

"Good. Is there anything you'd like to add?"

"I left right after the Brighams to catch the mail coach

to my mother's and didn't know that Mrs. Brigham was dead," Ellie said. "If only I'd gone up there . . ."

"You did nothing wrong, Miss Noble," Inspector Ross reassured her. "No one is accusing you of being remiss in your duties."

"Thank you, because I feel so sorry for the lady. She was so excited to see her husband, and he turned out to be a bad 'un." Ellie sighed. "Now that you've got me thinking about it, who knows what I might remember?"

"If you do think of anything, ask Mrs. Frogerton to send me a note," Inspector Ross said as he handed her the pen. "Would you care to sign your name at the bottom to certify that these are your own words and that you were not coerced into offering this information?"

"Why do I need to do that?" Ellie asked. "You said I wasn't in trouble."

"On the contrary, you have provided valuable evidence that might help convict a murderer. I can only congratulate you for stepping forward."

"All right, then." Ellie took the pen and laboriously signed her name. "Although I only came here because Mrs. Frogerton told me it was important."

"She was correct, and I'm very glad that you came." Inspector Ross glanced over at Caroline. "May I have a word with you outside, Lady Caroline?"

"Yes of course." Caroline smiled at Ellie. "I'll be back in a moment. You did really well, Ellie. I'm proud of you."

Inspector Ross drew her into the empty room next to his office. "Thank you for bringing Ellie here, my lady."

"It seemed like the right thing to do."

"It certainly confirms that the Brighams were on the premises," Inspector Ross said. "But as to the rest of it . . ."

"I suppose it's possible they are so used to killing they thought it amusing and weren't bothered in the slightest."

"I've met murderers like that before," Inspector Ross said. "They are quite terrifying."

"The thing is . . ." Caroline said slowly. "This might

sound indelicate, but why weren't they covered in blood, and what did they do with the knife?"

"Both excellent observations, my lady. We'll make a police constable of you yet. The Brighams were there for a considerable amount of time. I suppose it's possible that after dealing with Mrs. Brigham, they took a moment to wash off the blood, conceal the murder weapon, and stroll downstairs as if nothing had happened."

Caroline shuddered, and Inspector Ross squeezed her shoulder in a reassuring manner. "They might have known Ellie would be looking out for them and decided to show her that nothing untoward had happened upstairs. The last thing they needed was her raising the alarm before they were clear of the premises."

"I suppose that's right," Caroline said reluctantly. "But choosing to make such cold-blooded decisions is somehow worse than murder done in a rage."

"Perhaps that's what Mr. Brigham does—preys on wealthy women, strips them of their assets, and kills them. There are people who can't stop at one." He sighed. "I might send someone to Ireland to ask whether Mr. Brigham's been married before. At least we've got an independent witness to show that both the Brighams were there at the time of the murder. That might wipe the smile off Albert's face and stop him taunting me."

"I'll take Ellie back to Half Moon Street, Inspector, and let you get on," Caroline said. "How is your brother?"

Inspector Ross grimaced. "Defying the odds, as usual, but it can't last much longer. If I was an uncaring brute, I'd beg him to hold on for another week so that I can at least finish building the case against Albert Brigham before I have to attend to family duties."

"You're not uncaring," Caroline said.

"Thank you." He smiled down at her. "Now, I'd better send you back to Mr. Scutton before he convinces Sergeant Dawson I've abducted you."

Caroline collected Ellie and went out into the busy entrance hall. At first, she couldn't see their escort and wondered if he'd gone home in a fit of righteous rage.

"Can you see Mr. Scutton, Ellie?" Caroline asked.

"No, miss."

"Perhaps we should make our way to the exit. He's probably waiting outside."

"Yes, miss." Ellie grabbed Caroline's hand.

Just as they approached the front door, two constables came in dragging a man who was fighting them with all his worth and screaming obscenities at the top of his voice. A loud cheer went up, and several men jostled the officers, causing one of them to lose his grip on the prisoner's arm. Before he could reclaim it, the man punched him in the face, and he went down with a roar and disappeared beneath a sea of bodies.

Caroline dragged Ellie away from the brawling men, shouting to her as they struggled to avoid flailing limbs. "Stay close to the wall and make your way out! I'll find you if we are separated!"

Even as she spoke, someone kicked her ankle and she teetered toward the melee. She was saved only by the helping hand of a bystander.

"Thank you, sir," she gasped as he winked at her and entered the fight, his fist raised.

Holding tightly on to her reticule, Caroline made her way to the front door where blue-coated reinforcements were streaming in, whistles blowing. She almost tripped over the step, and when she straightened, she saw Mr. Scutton standing on the opposite corner of the building, deep in conversation with someone. She immediately looked for Ellie and found her halfway down the steps, breathing hard.

Even though she was fairly certain Mr. Scutton hadn't seen her, Caroline's heart was still pounding when she reached out to Ellie.

"Are you all right?" Caroline asked.

"Yes, miss, although I had to throw a punch or two to get out." Ellie grinned at her. "I have three brothers."

"I'm glad to hear it." Caroline straightened her bonnet and glanced ruefully down at her best blue boots which were now scuffed to the heavens. "Mrs. Frogerton's carriage should be just around the corner. Shall we make our way over there?"

"Yes, miss." Ellie seemed unperturbed by their adventure as she accompanied Caroline around the building.

To Caroline's immense relief, the carriage was still there. She opened the door and was about to climb in when she realized Ellie was staring back at Great Scotland Yard.

"What is it, Ellie?" Caroline asked as the girl came in after her.

"The strangest thing, miss. I was looking to see if Mr. Scutton was still here, and I just saw him across the way." She frowned as she got into the carriage. "I could've sworn he was speaking to Mr. Brigham."

Chapter 16

After their return to Half Moon Street, Caroline sent Ellie back to work and went upstairs to change her boots and redo her hair, which had started to come down after the scuffle. She found Mrs. Frogerton alone in the drawing room and immediately told her about what she and Ellie had seen.

"Mr. Scutton was talking to Albert? Good Lord." Mrs. Frogerton shook her head. "What on earth is going on?"

"I saw them, too," Caroline said. "But I think Ellie was mistaken that it was Albert. I'm fairly certain it was George. They are quite alike. I'm sure Inspector Ross would've mentioned it if Albert had been released."

"More importantly, did Mr. Scutton see you?" Mrs. Frogerton frowned. "I cannot think he would want to be observed speaking to one of the men accused of murdering his sister."

"I'm fairly certain he didn't notice me. He was too intent on his conversation, and his back was turned toward me." Caroline sat down opposite her employer. "Did you ask him to accompany us to the Yard for a particular reason?"

Mrs. Frogerton looked puzzled. "I didn't ask him to do any such thing."

"I'm certain he said you'd sent him to escort us. It does make me wonder whether your suspicions of Mr. Scutton are more on point than I realized."

"Ha!" Mrs. Frogerton clapped her hands. "I am always right in the end, Caroline."

Caroline frowned. "What did Mary know that would force her brother to form an alliance with her husband to murder her?"

Mrs. Frogerton took a while to answer. "It all comes down to the earldom, doesn't it?"

"Which begs the question—what would stop Mr. Scutton from inheriting it?" Caroline asked.

"Roman Catholicism!" Mrs. Frogerton burst out. "Perhaps we've been looking at this from the wrong angle. What if *Mr. Scutton* is the secret Catholic?"

"That wouldn't stop him inheriting the earldom, ma'am. Look at the Duke of Norfolk," Caroline pointed out.

"But what if Mary found out from Albert that her brother was a practicing Catholic? Wouldn't she think the worst of him?"

"As she seemed to be flirting with the idea of converting herself, or had done so in order to marry, I doubt she'd consider it a negative. In truth, I think she'd have been delighted."

Mrs. Frogerton made a face. "Sometimes I wish you weren't so logical, lass. You constantly throw water on all my best ideas."

"I do apologize, ma'am, but we have to make sure we have our facts straight before we jump to conclusions."

"You're right." Mrs. Frogerton sighed. "Which means the whole notion of him being a Catholic might mean nothing at all."

"But there must be something important enough for him to feel he has to conceal it from the College of Arms and everyone else," Caroline conceded.

"Oh!" Mrs. Frogerton sat up straight again. "Perhaps he's illegitimate." She raised her eyebrows when Caroline gaped at her. "From what I understand, if he's not born in wedlock, he can't inherit, correct?"

"Yes, in general terms, you are right."

"How would we find that out?" Mrs. Frogerton asked. "Would they have such records in Epping?"

"I assume the church would have that information, ma'am, but one would hope the College of Arms would check something this important when judging a claim."

"Mr. Scutton might have lied." Mrs. Frogerton held up a finger. "I've just thought of something else. Mrs. Scutton married in some haste."

"We don't know that for certain, ma'am, and we can hardly ask her."

"She met Mr. Scutton when she came down from London with an aristocratic family and married him within weeks."

"But Mrs. Scutton might have met him on previous visits or enjoyed a long-standing correspondence with him, ma'am."

Mrs. Frogerton gave her a severe look. "Caroline, you're doing it again."

"I'm simply trying—"

"We need to go back to Epping immediately." Mrs. Frogerton got up, awakening all the dogs settled around her chair, and rang the bell. "I'll ask Jenkins to tell the coachman to be ready to take us there tomorrow, and not a word to the Scuttons about where we're going."

As lunch commenced, Mr. Scutton came striding into the dining room looking most put out. He stopped beside Caroline. "Did your visit with Inspector Ross go well?"

"Yes, sir. Ellie was able to confirm that the Brighams were present in this house at the time of the murder, which helps Inspector Ross's case immensely."

"Thank goodness for that," Mrs. Scutton commented. "I was beginning to think no one believed me."

"We believed you, Mama," Mr. Scutton said.

"I did wonder where you'd gotten to, Mr. Scutton," Caroline said. "We couldn't find you when we came out, and there was quite a brawl going on."

Mr. Scutton's smile wasn't kind. "I had no desire to hang around Great Scotland Yard waiting to get my pocket picked. And, as you assured me that you didn't require an escort, I decided to walk back."

"Then no harm was done, was it?" Caroline smiled, knowing that he'd stood there, watched the fight in progress, and had made no effort to locate or help them. "Ellie and I managed to escape without injury."

"Thank goodness." Mrs. Frogerton wasn't amused. "I've told you before about wandering around London without an escort, Caroline. That's why I sent Mr. Scutton in the first place."

Caroline waited to see if Mr. Scutton would react to Mrs. Frogerton's comment, but he was already busy helping himself from the serving dishes on the sideboard.

"The hired furniture is arriving tomorrow at Morton House." Mrs. Scutton was the first to break the uncomfortable silence.

"That is good news," Mrs. Frogerton said. "Do you intend to go and supervise its arrival?"

"Thomas and I will both go," Mrs. Scutton said. "Mr. Potkins has also found some staff for me to interview."

"Having once been in service yourself, I'm sure you have strong views as to what makes a good servant, Mrs. Scutton," Mrs. Frogerton said.

"My mother's short experience as a domestic servant is hardly relevant, Mrs. Frogerton," Mr. Scutton said as he sat down with his full plate. "And, in future, when my mother is installed in my house, and I am the earl, I hope you'll respect her privacy and not discuss her affairs with your friends."

"Why would Mrs. Scutton object?" Mrs. Frogerton said. "She has risen very far in life and should be proud of herself."

"I am not ashamed of my past, Thomas," Mrs. Scutton addressed her son. "Everything I have done has led you to this place and the inheritance of a peerage."

"Exactly." Mrs. Frogerton nodded. "Mrs. Scutton is to be commended."

Mr. Scutton's lips thinned, and he applied himself to his food.

"Caroline and I will be out for most of the day tomorrow as well." Mrs. Frogerton said. "Mr. Lewis is taking me to see some property."

"You have decided to buy a house in London?" Mrs. Scutton asked.

"No, I wouldn't waste my money on that," Mrs. Frogerton said. "This is property for business purposes."

Mr. Scutton looked up. "Perhaps Lady Caroline would be better served coming to Morton House and sharing her preferences with us than touring industrial buildings."

"I'm more than happy to go with Mrs. Frogerton, sir," Caroline said. "Morton House is no longer my concern."

He frowned. "Of course it is. You are a Morton."

"I'm a mere female who can inherit nothing and who no longer expects anything from the Morton estate," Caroline said.

"Thomas..." Mrs. Scutton looked at her son. "Perhaps it is time to be more direct."

Mr. Scutton sighed. "Lady Caroline, I have tried to accommodate your desire to appear independent, and, as my mother often reminds me, such confidence is a requirement for a person of rank, but it is past time to stop pretending."

"Pretending what, sir?" Caroline asked.

"That you will not be my wife."

Caroline set her fork down carefully on her plate and tried not to look at Mrs. Frogerton, who had her mouth open.

Mr. Scutton continued. "It is apparently obvious to everyone but you that the best way to safeguard your future reputation and the Morton name is for you to marry me and unite both branches of the family." Mr. Scutton sounded like he had a bad taste in his mouth, and he did not have the look of a man who embraced his future gladly.

"You should be grateful to Thomas for making this offer, Caroline," Mrs. Scutton said. "And your gratitude should continue for the extent of your married life."

"And what if I don't care to be the next countess?" Caroline asked.

"Don't be silly, dear." Mrs. Scutton gave an indulgent laugh. "You're not stupid. You cannot remain as you are."

Caroline stood up, and Mr. Scutton rushed to follow suit. She pushed in her chair and curtsied. "Thank you for your generous offer, Mr. Scutton, but I fear we will not suit."

"You don't mean that," Mr. Scutton said. "This is just hurt pride or some ridiculous sense of false superiority. I am offering you a marriage that will elevate you to the rank you deserve."

"And I believe you should marry someone who deserves *you*, Mr. Scutton, and who will love you in return."

"I am willing to give up love in order to marry," Mr. Scutton said. "Why can't you do the same?"

"Because I wish more than a marriage of convenience for both of us. Thank you again for the offer, but I will not be your wife."

She'd almost reached the door when Mr. Scutton spoke again. "If you think Inspector Ross will marry you when he becomes the heir of a marquess, you'll be disappointed, miss. He's only dallying with you while he pretends to be a common man, but one sniff of that title, and he'll dump you just like your first fiancé did."

"Mr. Scutton!" Mrs. Frogerton said in outraged tones. "How *dare* you?"

"If you refuse me now, Caroline, don't come running back after Inspector Ross destroys your expectations."

Caroline left the room and went upstairs to her bedroom. She made sure to lock the door before she sat down on her bed. She studied her shaking fingers until her breathing calmed down. Mrs. Frogerton had warned her that Mr. Scutton intended to control her, and Caroline hadn't taken her seriously enough.

Of course he wanted to marry her. It was a common practice among aristocratic families for the new heir to select a suitable female relative for a bride. She should have realized Mr. Scutton was no different. At least he hadn't pretended to be pleased about the matter, and her refusal of his proposal had allowed him to insult her with impunity.

Caroline shuddered. He would make a terrible husband. She pitied the poor woman who would end up with him. There was a knock on the door, and she jumped.

"Miss Morton? It's Ellie. Mrs. Frogerton says there is no need to come down this afternoon and that if you wish to have your dinner on a tray, I'm to bring it up for you."

Caroline made herself get up and unlock the door. Ellie looked her up and down, her expression concerned. "Are you all right, miss? There's been a lot of shouting from the dining room. Mrs. Frogerton's in a right temper with the Scuttons."

"I have something of a headache, Ellie. I think I will lie down for a while."

"I'll tell Mrs. Frogerton." Ellie curtsied. "I'll bring your dinner up after your nap, miss."

"Thank you."

Caroline shut the door and locked it again.

She went to lie on her bed but couldn't settle, her mind endlessly replaying the uncomfortable scene with the Scuttons at the dining table. Had she been too rude? Mr. Scutton had certainly thought so, his calm veneer of doing her an immense favor ripped away to show his distaste for her very being. It wasn't pleasant to be seen as a woman chasing a title. She reminded herself that if she truly was materialistic, she could easily accept Mr. Scutton and become a countess like her mother.

Her head throbbed, and she mixed herself a potion of hartshorn and water and swallowed it down. Her gaze fell on the ledger Mr. Castle had lent her from the Morton estate. If she couldn't sleep, she might as well fill her time with something useful. She sat at her writing desk and opened the book.

The earliest writing wasn't familiar, so she assumed it was the housekeeper, the butler, or her grandfather's secretary who had been charged with keeping the books straight. If her father had dealt with such matters in later years, the estate would have been bankrupt far earlier and the accounts not as meticulously maintained.

Forgetting her original purpose of researching the provenance of the current Morton family jewels, Caroline allowed herself to be waylaid into the daily accounts of a leisured life that no longer existed. She smiled as she flipped through the pages, stopping every now and then when she saw her name or Susan's. That life was no longer hers, but it was still precious to remember some of the good times and not just the bad.

But even in the daily accounts, her father's spending loomed large as he borrowed from various funds, leaving the household accounts in disarray and the staff prone to complaining in the margins of the columns.

Had to ask her ladyship for money to pay the butcher. Three months in arrears, one entry read, followed by: *Discuss with his lordship whether to let one of the parlor maids go to save the wages . . .*

As with most aristocratic families, her parents had lived with the previous earl until her father inherited the title. It hadn't always been an easy relationship. Caroline's mother had never raised her voice to her husband, but she had tried to stand up to him, especially when it came to her children's inheritance. Caroline remembered tears and shouting and hiding in her room as her mother tried to pretend nothing was wrong. Caroline turned a few pages, and her gaze fell on another note in the margin.

No need to let a parlor maid go. Hetty Bryson is leaving to get married on Midsummer day.

Caroline read the name twice, her mind in a whirl. Mrs. Scutton had worked for the *Mortons?* Caroline had no recollection of her, as Mrs. Scutton had been there before Caroline was born. She suddenly remembered Mrs. Scutton's familiarity with the house and the secret door into the drawing room that only family members and staff knew about.

How could she have been so stupid? Mrs. Scutton had met and married a man who was also connected to the Morton family, which could hardly have been a coincidence. It made far more sense now, but why hadn't Mrs. Scutton been honest from the start?

Caroline checked the time and realized Mrs. Frogerton would be taking her afternoon nap. Her startling revelation would have to wait until her employer was awake and willing to receive her. Caroline returned her attention to the book. While she waited, she would look Hetty up in the ledger's servants index and, if she had time, she'd research the jewels and make a list of what belonged to her and not the Morton estate.

When Ellie returned later that evening, she told Caroline the Scuttons were dining out with Mr. Potkins, and that if she wished to go downstairs, Mrs. Frogerton would be pleased to see her.

"I'll come down. Thank you, Ellie."

Caroline changed into the plainest of her three evening gowns, picked up the ledger, and brought it with her to the dining room. Mrs. Frogerton sat at the table, looking splendid in her diamonds.

"Glad to see you showing some spirit, lass," Mrs. Frogerton commented as Caroline took her seat. "There's no need to let the Scuttons prevent you from eating in your own home."

"I must confess that I wasn't expecting a proposal over lunch, ma'am."

"It barely even qualified as one." Mrs. Frogerton snorted. "It was a mealymouthed excuse of an offer and not worthy of an answer. I knew Mr. Scutton can be unpleasant, but he really surpassed himself. Even his mother took him to task after you left."

"His mother has far more sense than he does, ma'am."

"She's no better. She's got her eye on those South African mines of yours. She wants you to marry him because she thinks you'll bring in the cash to save her precious son's inheritance."

"I did wonder what made Mr. Scutton propose despite my constantly telling him I wanted nothing to do with him or the earldom," Caroline said. "It seemed as if Mrs. Scutton goaded him into doing it."

"He's a lily-livered fool," Mrs. Frogerton said dismissively, "who got what he deserved. I'm very much hoping they'll move out by the end of the week. Your refusing his proposal might be a blessing in disguise."

"Let's hope so, ma'am." Caroline stopped talking as the footmen set the second course on the table and withdrew. "Although he does have a tendency to follow his bad behavior with an abject apology."

"Would you accept an apology from him, Caroline?" Mrs. Frogerton looked inquiringly at her.

"No, ma'am."

"Would you agree to be his wife?"

"Absolutely not."

"Then you have your answer." Mrs. Frogerton helped herself to creamed spinach and some sliced lamb. "And don't you pay any heed to that nonsense he spouted about Inspector Ross. If that man wants to marry you, he'll do it regardless of a title."

"Thank you, ma'am," Caroline said. "It was rather lowering to hear myself described in such terms."

"I'm surprised Mr. Scutton didn't bring up Dr. Harris as well, seeing as he's appointed himself guardian of your morals."

"Dr. Harris isn't speaking to me," Caroline reminded her.

"He's simply off licking his wounds wondering how to approach you for the next go-around," Mrs. Frogerton said bracingly. "As I keep telling you, if you wish to be married, you just have to snap your fingers."

"That is reassuring, ma'am." Caroline knew it wasn't worth arguing with Mrs. Frogerton's romantic sensibilities. "But I assure you that I am content just as I am."

"I do wish Dr. Harris would come and see us," Mrs. Frogerton said. "I'd love to have his opinion on the likelihood of the Brighams being able to get rid of all traces of blood from their persons before they left the house."

"I did wonder whether Mary had clothes stored for Mr. Brigham somewhere and that they changed completely," Caroline said.

"I suppose that's possible," Mrs. Frogerton said. "Although I'd still like Dr. Harris's thoughts on the matter."

"Perhaps you should write to him?" Caroline suggested. "Or I can do so in your stead."

"Yes, why don't you do that after dinner? It will offer him an opportunity to reconnect with us without losing face. Now, what did you bring the ledger with you for? To ward off the Scuttons?"

"No, ma'am, although the thought of launching it at Mr. Scutton's head is becoming increasingly attractive."

"Let's hope it doesn't come to that." Mrs. Frogerton smiled. "Did you discover anything about the jewelry?"

"Yes, I worked out which pieces belong to me and Susan, and I noted others that might be worth asking Coutts about if Mr. Lewis is willing to act for me."

"He will. He loves a good fight, lass, you know he does."

"There was something else...." Caroline opened the

ledger. "I found several notations about a Hetty Bryson who was employed by my family for two years."

Mrs. Frogerton frowned. "Why does that name sound familiar?"

"It's Mrs. Scutton."

Her employer gasped and dropped her fork to the floor, where it was immediately carried away by one of the dogs. "No! She worked for your family? Why didn't she mention it?"

"That's a very good question, ma'am," Caroline said.

"Perhaps she was too embarrassed to admit she'd been in service to your family."

"That's quite understandable."

"There have been several occasions when she might have mentioned it in passing," Mrs. Frogerton said. "And wouldn't you think it would enhance her claim to be connected to the Mortons? She worked for them, met Mr. Scutton who was also a Morton, and married into the family."

"It does make more sense as to how she became connected to Mr. Scutton, but..." Caroline hesitated. "We had no house in Epping, so the notion that she came down from London with the family and met Mr. Scutton there can't be accurate."

"Maybe she was sent down to help with the harvest at the farm and had to sleep in the barn and hates to be reminded of being required to do manual work," Mrs. Frogerton said. "She is a very proud woman."

"That would certainly be an experience she'd want to hide," Caroline agreed. "Perhaps on our trip to Epping tomorrow we should seek out Miss Smith again and ask her if she remembers exactly how Mr. and Mrs. Scutton met."

"I think that's an excellent idea," Mrs. Frogerton agreed. "I intend to set off quite early tomorrow morning so we'll be spared the sight of the Scuttons at the breakfast table."

"Mr. Scutton does have a tendency to sulk."

"Yes, and it's not attractive in a husband, lass. I'd much rather have someone who stands toe to toe with me and fights it out than a man who sticks out their lip like a three-year-old." She looked up as the butler came into the room. "What is it, Jenkins?"

"A note from Inspector Ross, ma'am." Jenkins gave the letter to Mrs. Frogerton. "The messenger said there is no need for a reply."

Mrs. Frogerton broke the seal, read the short note, and passed it to Caroline, who read it as well. "Richard is dead," Caroline said. "I truly hope he finds the peace in the afterlife that eluded him on earth."

"Amen to that." Mrs. Frogerton sighed. "I suppose this means that the Inspector will have to relinquish his cases to others while he attends to family business."

"It might be even worse than that, ma'am," Caroline said. "If he is proclaimed his father's heir, he might have to resign his position immediately."

Chapter 17

The journey to Epping was accomplished with little trouble, and, after a change of horses in Woodford, where they also took time to eat, they arrived at their destination at midday. The church of St. John the Baptist stood on a corner marking the start of the high street. It looked like a relatively new structure, but the graveyard behind it was far older. After getting down from the carriage, Mrs. Frogerton directed the coachman to the nearest inn and stood back admiring the church.

There was a large door at the front and behind it a central tower with a belfry at the top. The sides of the building appeared to be crenellated like a castle, and the walls were built of stone. It was a fine, if rather stark, building that hadn't quite settled into its environment.

"Shall we try the church or the vicarage first, Caroline?" Mrs. Frogerton asked. "As a non-conformist, I'm unsure of the etiquette in these places."

"Let's try the church," Caroline suggested.

There was a small door on the side that opened with a resounding creak that echoed throughout the church.

A young man dressed in a long black habit and white stock appeared in the side aisle and approached them with a friendly smile. "Good afternoon, ladies, may I be of assistance?"

Mrs. Frogerton had already agreed that Caroline should be the first to speak.

"Good afternoon, sir. Are you the vicar?"

"Yes, I'm Mr. Bowen. How may I be of assistance?"

Caroline gave him her most charming smile. "I'm Lady Caroline Morton, and this is Mrs. Frogerton. A friend of ours in Theydon Bois reminded me that a branch of my family resided in your parish. As I am attempting to compose a detailed family tree, I wondered if I might be allowed to examine your parish records?"

"Yes, of course, my lady." He bowed so low his nose almost hit his knee. "How... delightful! You must come to the vicarage and meet Mrs. Bowen and take some tea while I bring the relevant information to you."

"That would be extremely kind of you, Mr. Bowen," Caroline said. "Have you been in this parish long?"

"Not at all. I only recently took over from Dr. Kendrick, who retired due to ill health." Mr. Bowen held the church door open for them to exit and then hurried ahead of them on a worn path that led to the side of the church. He unlatched a gate and led them through into a small garden. "Here we are. Anna! Come quickly!" He directed them through a set of open French windows and into a charming sitting room. "Please make yourselves comfortable. I'll just find my wife."

"Well done," Mrs. Frogerton whispered to Caroline as he disappeared out of the door. "You charmed him."

"As you always tell me, ma'am, a speck of politeness goes a long way, as does the judicious use of a title." Caroline walked around the room, admiring the paintings on the wall and the beautiful flower arrangement on the mantelpiece. "This is a very pleasant room."

"Indeed," Mrs. Frogerton agreed.

The door opened with something of a bang, and a fair-haired woman rushed in, her cheeks flushed. She wore a dress of crisp blue cotton under an apron that was streaked with soot. She was younger than the vicar and even more flustered.

"I do apologize for not being here when you arrived, my lady." She looked down at herself and gasped as she stripped off the apron. "I was upstairs in the nursery attempting to black the fireplace."

"There's no need to apologize, Mrs. Bowen," Caroline said. "We are remiss for not making an appointment to see you."

Mrs. Bowen bundled the apron up in her hands and then looked as if she didn't know quite what to do with it. "I've ordered some tea, my lady. Dulcie will bring it as soon as it's ready."

"That is very good of you, ma'am." Mrs. Frogerton smiled at her. "We will be glad of some refreshment, having come all the way from London this morning."

"London?" Mrs. Bowen sat down and gestured for them to join her. "That is a long way."

To Caroline's amusement, Mrs. Bowen stuffed the apron behind a cushion as she spoke.

"We are planning on visiting a friend in Theydon Bois," Mrs. Frogerton said. "It was no trouble to come a little farther."

"Theydon Bois?" Mrs. Bowen looked interested. "I have many friends there. Who were you visiting?"

Mrs. Frogerton looked helplessly at Caroline.

Caroline smiled and said, "A relative of the Bois family whom I knew through my parents."

Mrs. Bowen nodded. "That must be Lady Hilda, she is rather frail these days and quite forgetful."

"Yes, indeed, she never even remembers that we visit her," Mrs. Frogerton said with a somewhat high-pitched laugh. "But we persevere."

Before Mrs. Bowen could inquire further, the door opened, and a maid came in with a tray.

"Thank you, Dulcie."

"Yes, ma'am," Dulcie was openly staring at Caroline. "I've never seen a real lady before. I must say I thought she'd look a bit more fancy-like."

"Dulcie," Mrs. Bowen said.

"What?" Dulcie didn't look away from Caroline.

"Would you fetch the cake?"

"Yes, ma'am." Dulcie backed out of the room, her gaze fixed firmly on the guests.

Mrs. Bowen sighed as the door closed. "I can only apologize again for my household. What you must think of me . . ."

"Perhaps you should pour the tea," Mrs. Frogerton suggested. "Before Dulcie comes back and demands to see Caroline's tiara."

Mrs. Bowen started to laugh, and Mrs. Frogerton and Caroline joined her.

"Now," said Mrs. Frogerton. "We can be comfortable with each other. How long have you been married, Mrs. Bowen?"

"Almost two years. Alistair was my father's curate. When he was ordained and offered his own parish, he asked me to marry him."

"How delightful," Mrs. Frogerton said. "And are you happy in Epping?"

"Yes, it is an excellent parish with a godly number of parishioners," Mrs. Bowen said. "My husband also tends to the flock in High Beech."

Dulcie returned with the cake and managed not to linger. The vicar arrived with several leather-bound books under his arm and placed them on the writing desk beneath the window.

"There's no need to hurry yourselves," he said with a fond smile for his wife. "Anna and I are always delighted to welcome new guests to our home."

"Mrs. Bowen entertained us with great kindness," Caroline said. "And is an exemplary hostess."

Caroline hadn't missed the worried glance Mrs. Bowen

had given her husband when he sat down right next to the discarded apron behind the cushion.

"Lady Caroline is acquainted with the Bois family," Mrs. Bowen said in reverential tones.

Mr. Bowen bowed. "How did you find Lady Hilda?"

"Oh, we haven't got to her yet today," Mrs. Frogerton explained in something of a hurry. "We intend to call on her after this."

"Yes, she is in better form in the afternoons," Mr. Bowen agreed as he helped himself to a piece of cake. "This is very good, dearest. Is it my mother's recipe?"

"Indeed, it is." Mrs. Bowen smiled adoringly at him.

Mrs. Frogerton set down her cup and glanced at Caroline. "Perhaps we should peruse the records, my lady."

"Yes, of course." Caroline stood up and went over to the desk. "Thank you for your assistance, Mr. Bowen."

He fussed around as she took her seat.

"There is ink in the well, freshly cut paper in the drawer, and I will cut you a new nib for your pen."

"Thank you, sir." Caroline took the proffered pen and glanced behind her. There was no sign that Mr. and Mrs. Bowen intended to leave her side. "Please do not let me keep you from your work."

"Oh!" Mrs. Bowen jumped. "I should talk to Cook about dinner."

"Perhaps you could show me around your church, Mr. Bowen?" Mrs. Frogerton suggested. "It looks as though it has recently been rebuilt?"

"I'd be delighted to oblige, ma'am." Mr. Bowen offered Mrs. Frogerton his arm. "There has been a chapel on this site since the fourteenth century, and the bell in the belfry was given to the church by William, Lord Grey, in 1650..." His voice trailed away as they exited through the French windows.

Mrs. Bowen retrieved her apron from behind the cushion. "I'd better get on." She smiled at Caroline. "Please don't hesitate to call out if you need anything, my lady."

Caroline opened the parish register and tried to remember roughly how old Mr. Scutton was. She estimated he was in his late thirties, which would make his birth date around 1808. After some searching and backtracking, she found him.

"Baptized on June the sixth, 1811," she murmured and wrote it down on her notes. "I assumed he was far older than thirty."

She turned her attention to the records of marriages. "If Mr. Scutton was born in June of 1811, his parents must have been married by 1810."

She flipped back through the closely written pages that recorded all the joys and sorrows of human life and tried to find the marriage entry. After a few minutes of unsuccessful searching, she sat back. Had the Scuttons married in another church? She was fairly certain she remembered Mrs. Scutton saying she'd been married in the same church as Mary.

Mr. Bowen returned with Mrs. Frogerton, and Caroline drew his attention to the records. "I cannot find a record of a particular marriage, Mr. Bowen. Perhaps you could help me?"

"Of course, my lady." He set a chair next to hers and sat down. "What is the issue at hand?"

"I found a record of a Mr. Thomas Scutton's birth, but no marriage details for his parents," Caroline explained.

"Hmm. . . . that is odd. I know of the Scutton family. They are definitely connected to the Morton line. Let's see if we can trace the father first."

"Mr. William Morton Scutton," Caroline said helpfully as the vicar turned the pages.

"Yes, here he is." Mr. Bowen showed Caroline the baptism record. To her surprise, he was about twenty years older than his wife.

"We also have a record of his death and burial." Mr. Bowen turned to a different page and placed a finger under a line written in cramped script. "Now, as to his marriage..." He looked up after a while. "How odd. I cannot find it either."

Mrs. Frogerton cleared her throat. "Is it possible that Mr. Scutton senior was affiliated with a different faith?"

"Even if he was a Quaker or a Methodist, the law clearly states that the only marriage recognized in England is one performed and recorded by the Church of England." Mr. Bowen paused. "Unless such a marriage is performed in another country where such alliances are legal, and then that marriage is valid here—with the correct paperwork."

"Thank you for explaining," Caroline said. "Do you often have to marry couples who are aligned to a different faith, vicar?"

"It is more common these days, but back then, it could prove very difficult." Mr. Bowen grimaced. "It's possible that even if a couple did wish to formalize their marriage in this church, a vicar might refuse if he believed they were just doing it to comply with the law." He reached for the pile of books. "If you will permit me, all of my predecessors kept daily journals. Someone might have mentioned this matter in their private notes." He studied the spines and picked out the one within the relevant time span. "Mr. Brockle was the incumbent during that time."

"I assume the marriage should've taken place around 1809 or 1810," Caroline said.

"Thank you, that narrows it down a bit." Mr. Bowen said. "Some of these gentlemen were quite prolific writers."

Luckily, Mr. Bowen proved to be a fast reader who could scan the pages quickly.

"Ah, here's something." He started to read out loud. "*Saw William Morton Scutton this morning. He asked about marriage rites. I laughed in his face, and he took umbrage. He said he had the money to pay for a wedding and that I'd be a fool not to do my duty, as the Morton family wouldn't appreciate it. I told him that I answered only to God Almighty and that his sinful and popish ways were known to me.*" He paused and began reading again.

"Visit from the old Earl of Morton himself! Threatened me with dismissal if I didn't perform the marriage. I told him he would burn in hell. He left in a rage, and I prayed for his soul."

Mr. Bowen closed the book. "There doesn't appear to be any more information. One has to wonder if the Earl took a hand in their affairs and helped them marry in London."

"It does seem likely," Caroline said. She wrote a few more notes and turned to Mrs. Frogerton. "I think we should be going, ma'am. We still have several visits to make."

"Indeed, we do."

Caroline rose to her feet and offered Mr. Bowen her hand. "Thank you for all your help. This has been most informative."

"It's been a pleasure, my lady. Let me fetch my wife so that she can say her goodbyes."

Mr. Bowen raced toward the back of the house while Caroline and Mrs. Frogerton awaited him in the hall.

"I suppose we'll have to visit that Bois lady, now," Mrs. Frogerton whispered to Caroline. "Or be thought liars."

"I think we will."

"*Do* you know her?"

"Yes, of course." Caroline raised her eyebrows. "I believe she was one of my father's godparents."

"Naturally." Mrs. Frogerton said. "How silly of me."

Ten minutes later they were sitting in Miss Smith's pleasant kitchen having another cup of tea along with a slab of ham, piccalilli, and a slice of bread.

"What brings you here again?" Miss Smith asked as she joined them at the table. "More letters from Mrs. Scutton?"

"We're visiting Lady Hilda in Theydon Bois and thought we'd pop in," Caroline said. "Lady Hilda isn't well."

"She's as batty as a windmill," Miss Smith said frankly. "But she does no harm to anyone." She sipped her tea. "Any news from London?"

"They've let George Brigham out on bail and charged Albert with murder," Mrs. Frogerton said. "A witness came forward to confirm that the Brighams were at the house on the fateful night."

"What a terrible shame." Miss Smith sighed. "And I thought young Albert was a good 'un."

"Did Mary ever mention if Albert had been married before?" Mrs. Frogerton asked.

"I don't think so." Miss Smith cut into her ham. "Why? Does it matter in some way?"

"Not particularly," Caroline hastened to reassure her.

"One does hear of these papists having wives in Ireland and then coming over here and marrying again with the rites of the Church of England." Mrs. Frogerton was obviously oblivious to offending Miss Smith's feelings.

"In my opinion, people should be allowed to marry in a place of worship of their choosing," Miss Smith declared. "It's ridiculous that they have to pay a fee to be married in a church they don't support simply to avoid having their marriage declared illegal."

"Isn't that what happened when Mr. Scutton tried to marry?" Caroline asked. "I seem to remember some family story about the previous earl having to intervene."

"I wasn't very old when all that was happening, miss, but Jude did tell me there was something of a kerfuffle," Miss Smith said. "Hetty insisted they marry according to the rights of their religion first and then approach the vicar for the service in the church."

Mrs. Frogerton chewed slowly as she nodded. "And did the vicar oblige?"

"No, he didn't. The earl was most displeased."

"So I should imagine," Mrs. Frogerton said. "But with his power and associates, he was probably able to get them married somewhere else."

"I believe that's exactly what he did." Miss Smith poured them all more tea. "Jude did say that William was very anxious to be wed because—" She paused. "Some things just won't wait, will they?"

"Was Hetty expecting?" Mrs. Frogerton asked.

"I won't say that she was, because she'd be furious that I knew, but that's what William told Jude." Miss Smith gave them a sharp look. "Mind that bit of gossip doesn't get back to Hetty, now."

"We will never mention it in her hearing," Mrs. Frogerton promised. "Now, how is everything here? Has Mrs. Scutton decided whether she's selling up or not?"

Several hours later, after a detour to Theydon Bois and a half an hour call on the absolutely eccentric Lady Hilda, Caroline and Mrs. Frogerton were on their way back to London. Caroline hadn't said much, her mind busy untangling what they'd learned, and whether any of it had any implications for Mary's murder.

"Mr. Scutton," Caroline said.

Mrs. Frogerton sat up straight. "Which one?"

"Thomas. He's the one with the most to lose if this matter becomes public."

"Doesn't that depend on the date of his parents' marriage? From what I understand, if he's born after the marriage occurs, he's legitimate, regardless of his religion."

"But we don't know if his parents were properly married in the Church of England," Caroline pointed out. "And if Mrs. Scutton was pregnant, the need for the marriage to take place quickly was paramount."

"That's another thing . . ." Mrs. Frogerton said. "If Hetty only met Mr. Scutton when she came down from London for the summer, how did he get her pregnant in the first place?"

"We don't know how long she was in Epping before he married her," Caroline said. "And we don't know if Mr. Scutton visited her in London. As a connection of the Morton family, he might well have stayed at Morton House when he came up to town."

"It's not uncommon for women to be preyed upon by their betters," Mrs. Frogerton said. "Although from all accounts, it was a happy marriage." She sighed. "How on earth are we supposed to find out whether a church in London married the Scuttons in time for their son to be legitimate? There must be hundreds of them."

"But very few enjoyed the patronage of the Earl of Morton and would be willing to do his bidding, ma'am."

"That's true! Do you think there might be something about it in those family records Mr. Castle lent you, Caroline?" Mrs. Frogerton asked eagerly. "That would be most helpful."

"I'll look when we get back," Caroline assured her employer. "Although what all of this has to do with solving Mary's murder, I don't know."

"Simply put, if Thomas Scutton's parents weren't legally married by the Church of England, Thomas is illegitimate and cannot claim the title."

"Again, surely the College of Arms would have checked all this before proceeding further?" Caroline asked. "They'd need to see a direct line back to the Morton family."

"Perhaps Mr. William Scutton forged a wedding certificate," Mrs. Frogerton suggested.

"Or Thomas did, or we're completely wrong, and there was a legitimate marriage performed in a church before Thomas was born."

"But if that was the case, Caroline, why have Jude and Mary been murdered?" Mrs. Frogerton sat back. "Because they both knew too much, that's why. The way I see it, Mr. Scutton was worried that his lack of legitimacy would prevent him from gaining the earldom, so he decided to ally with the Brighams to make sure Mary and Jude were never given the opportunity to speak out."

"That makes him sound remarkably heartless, ma'am."

"He stands to gain an earldom, lass. That is a powerful position to hold in this country."

"Even an earldom riddled with debt?"

"Yes, even that," Mrs. Frogerton said. "And, if Mr. Scutton succeeds in marrying you and takes control of your South African interests, he could become a very rich man indeed."

"There is no indication that those interests will mature financially," Caroline demurred.

"Mr. Lewis thinks they will, and even if there is nothing in those mines, the DeBeer company is willing to pay you for the land, regardless. I don't think that will be mere pennies."

Caroline sighed. "This is all speculation, ma'am. In truth, we still have nothing but theories."

"Then we'll have to make them into facts," Mrs. Frogerton said. "We can't rely on Inspector Ross to help us at this point, so we'll have to do it ourselves."

Chapter 18

Despite her promise to Mrs. Frogerton, Caroline was too tired to do anything more than fall into bed and sleep when they finally got back to Half Moon Street. She woke earlier than normal and lay in bed listening to the sounds of the household around her. If she'd been employed by a lady other than Mrs. Frogerton, her day would've probably started along with the servants and would have continued long into the night.

Breakfast would be the first time she would see Mr. Scutton since she'd turned down his proposal, and it was bound to be awkward. She resolved to be polite and friendly and pretend nothing untoward had happened. If he truly was cold-blooded enough to arrange the murder of his own sister, then—

Her eyes went wide.

What if Mary wasn't his full sister?

The thought had her sitting up in bed and swinging her legs over the side. The Scutton marriage had been a hasty affair. What if Mrs. Scutton had been pregnant before the marriage, and the baby's father wasn't William? As Mrs. Frogerton had pointed out, it wasn't unusual for a maid to end up pregnant and unmarried in a society that considered female staff fair game. Had Mrs. Scutton met William and persuaded him to marry her during her brief visit to Epping? And how had the Earl of Morton become involved?

Caroline got dressed and hurried down to the hall where the morning post sat on a silver salver beside the door. She took it through to the dining room with her.

"Miss Morton!" Mr. Jenkins said, surprised.

"Good morning, Mr. Jenkins." She glanced at the clock on the mantelpiece. "I didn't realize how early it was. I do apologize."

"There's no need, miss. If you'll kindly take your seat, I'll ask Cook to send up a pot of tea and your usual toast. It won't take but a moment."

"Thank you."

Caroline sat down at the empty table and began to sort out the post. Her attention was caught by a black-edged envelope bearing a coat of arms addressed to her and Mrs. Frogerton. She opened it to discover the formal notification of Lord Richard's death, along with details of his funeral service. She set it to one side for Mrs. Frogerton and picked up another folded note with familiar slapdash handwriting.

Tell Mrs. Frogerton I'll be around to see her tomorrow.
Best, Dr. Harris

Dr. Harris had responded to her equally brief note. Caroline raised an eyebrow. In truth, Mrs. Frogerton wasn't the only one who would be pleased to see Dr. Harris back at Half Moon Street. Caroline had missed him more than she had anticipated.

"Lady Caroline."

She turned in her seat to see Mr. Scutton in the doorway.

"Good morning, sir." She returned her attention to the post.

"I thought if I rose early enough, I would avoid you, but I suppose that was cowardly of me." He came into the room and looked down at her, his expression resolute. "I refuse to apologize for what I said to you."

Caroline didn't reply, but he didn't move away.

"Your behavior is at fault," he said. "Your values are flawed, and your character is . . . apparently irredeemable."

Caroline looked closely at Mr. Scutton and tried to imagine him plotting with the Brighams to murder his sister. In his current state, she could well imagine it.

Instinct told her to tread warily. "I am sorry that I disappoint you, sir, but perhaps it is better that you've seen my character flaws before we married, rather than afterward, when you'd be stuck with me."

"That's the truth." Mr. Scutton finally stepped back. "I'm glad you acknowledge that you are the problem, not me."

"I am my father's daughter, sir."

"Your father was a disgrace to the earldom," Mr. Scutton said.

"On that, at least, we can agree," Caroline said.

Mr. Jenkins came in with a tray. "Here you are, miss." He bowed to Mr. Scutton. "Are you ready for your breakfast, sir? We're just about ready to bring up the serving dishes."

Mr. Scutton ignored Jenkins and took a seat on the opposite side of the table to Caroline. His gaze fell on the black-edged envelope. "Did the marquess's heir die?"

"Yes," Caroline said as she poured the tea. "We've been invited to attend the funeral."

"You should make sure to attend," Mr. Scutton said. "I suspect it will be the last time you'll see Inspector Ross before he forgets all about you."

Caroline returned her attention to the post. There was something unnerving about sitting near Mr. Scutton when he no longer felt it necessary to maintain even the facade of politeness. For the first time ever, she wished Mrs. Scutton was present. She might prevent her son from displaying his hostility so openly.

Mr. Scutton drank the coffee the butler brought him but ignored the morning newspaper to focus his attention on Caroline. If he wished to scare her away, he was doing an excellent job of it. Only sheer stubbornness kept her in her seat.

"Any news of Dr. Harris?" Mr. Scutton asked.

"I believe he's coming to see Mrs. Frogerton tomorrow, sir."

"Perhaps you'll have to settle for him after all." Mr. Scutton got up to fill his plate and then resumed his seat.

"Mr. Scutton . . ."

"What?"

"We have already agreed that we would not suit, so can we move beyond my matrimonial prospects or lack of them?"

"You have to marry someone." Mr. Scutton sipped his coffee.

"I beg to differ."

"At some point, you'll have no choice. You can't keep hanging on Mrs. Frogerton's coattails. She'll move back up north to continue making her fortune, and what will you do then?"

"I'll manage, thank you, sir."

"On your five-hundred-pound inheritance?"

"If I must." Caroline met his gaze. "Mr. Scutton, this is a very personal conversation."

He raised his eyebrows. "We're family, aren't we? Even if you refuse to marry me, you're still part of the Morton family, of which I will be the head." He paused. "And don't think you'll have that DeBeer money to cosset you in your old age, Caroline. I fully intend to take you to court and bring that money right back where it belongs—with the earldom."

"You can certainly try, sir. But Mr. Lewis assures me that I have the right of it." Caroline picked up her own post and left Mrs. Frogerton's pile on the table. "I'll wish you good morning. I have correspondence to attend to."

She was still shaking when she reached her bedroom and again found herself locking the door. The animosity in Mr. Scutton's voice had undermined her confidence and increased her fear that he was exactly what Mrs. Frogerton had always said—a willing accomplice to murder.

When Ellie came up to make her bed, Caroline asked her to let her know when Mrs. Frogerton was established in the drawing room. She'd decided it was wise to steer clear of the breakfast table when the Scuttons were present. To pass the time, she returned her attention to the Morton family records and the observations of her grandfather during Hetty's employment and subsequent marriage to his fourth son.

She also made a note of the three churches her grandfather held an interest in and where he had a say as to who got the position of vicar. Composing a letter to each of the churches asking for the necessary information without revealing her true purpose took a considerable amount of ingenuity, as did the copying out of the letter three times.

When Ellie knocked on her door to let her know Mrs. Frogerton was ensconced in the drawing room, Caroline was able to hand over the letters to be posted. She made her way downstairs and was relieved to see her employer was by herself.

"The Scuttons have gone to Morton House," Mrs. Frogerton informed her. "Mr. Potkins is there to help interview some more staff."

"I'm simply glad they aren't here," Caroline said. "Mr. Scutton was particularly unpleasant to me at the breakfast table."

"That's probably because you turned him down flat, lass," Mrs. Frogerton said.

"It was more than that," Caroline said. "He truly dislikes me."

"Then he is a fool, but considering our suspicions, we should both be wary of him," Mrs. Frogerton said. "Now, come sit down and tell me what you have achieved since we returned from Epping."

Caroline told her about the three parishes and the letters she had written inquiring whether any of the churches had a record of a marriage between Mr. William Scutton and Hetty Bryson.

"I stressed that I was a member of the Morton family who was simply researching my family tree. It seemed to work with Mr. Bowen, who was most obliging."

"I think that was an excellent tactic, lass," Mrs. Frogerton said.

"There was one more thing relating to this matter, ma'am," Caroline said cautiously. "It occurred to me that Mrs. Scutton might have rushed into marriage with a man who wasn't her baby's father."

"The marriage did happen rather fast, didn't it?" Mrs. Frogerton agreed. "It would explain why she originally went to Epping to marry rather than staying in London."

"I wondered if it was possible that she persuaded the first available man she met to marry her."

Mrs. Frogerton looked thoughtful. "I've been thinking about this matter, too, lass, but I reached a different conclusion."

"How so?"

"Hetty married the descendent of the fourth son of an earl."

"An estranged son who gave up his name and was cut out of the family will," Caroline pointed out.

"But as we now know, Hetty worked for the Mortons, and your grandfather was well aware of who she was, whom she was marrying, and gave his permission."

Caroline considered that. "Yes, I suppose he must have known if he took a hand in it."

"Mr. Bowen told us that Mr. Brockle refused to marry Hetty and William even when the earl turned up in person," Caroline said slowly. "A fact that indicates he was very invested in this marriage, indeed."

"That was my conclusion, too." Mrs. Frogerton looked very pleased with herself as she nodded.

"Maybe the earl wished his son to be married and decided Hetty was the perfect candidate," Caroline said. "She was in his employ and was hardly likely to say no."

"Perhaps it was even more personal to him, lass."

Caroline blinked at her. "Are you suggesting the baby might have been the *earl's*?"

"Why not? His involvement would make perfect sense, if so."

"But he was devoted to my grandmother. He chose not to remarry after her death, even though he only had one living son, my father."

"Devoted or not, gentlemen still have needs, and female staff have always been fair game," Mrs. Frogerton said matter-of-factly. "And if he did have only the one son, perhaps planting another heir in the family tree made sense to him at the time. You did say he was a remarkably clever man."

"I..." Caroline shook her head. "I cannot..."

Mrs. Frogerton allowed her to stumble into silence before she continued.

"What if the earl knew that one of the reasons William kept him at arm's length was because of his chosen religion? When the earl discovered Hetty was pregnant and that she, too, was of the popish faith, he might see a match made in heaven, so to speak."

"But why would Hetty and William agree to such a marriage?" Caroline asked.

"Perhaps the old earl offered Hetty a dowry? Remember, she had no hope of the earl marrying her, and she'd be viewed with contempt if she had a child out of wedlock," Mrs. Frogerton speculated. "You might see such a payment in the family books. Didn't Miss Smith mention that William bought the house from the estate on the occasion of his marriage? Maybe the earl gifted it to him as a thank you."

"I hate to say it, ma'am, because I've always had tremendous respect for my grandfather, but I cannot see any other reasons for his behavior other than those you have stated." Caroline sighed. "He *must* have arranged a marriage for them in London, or else all his plans would come to naught."

"If he did, then surely one of the churches you contacted will have the details," Mrs. Frogerton said.

"But if that is the case, and the marriage is totally legal and above board, why on earth would Mr. Scutton be willing to plot to murder his sister because of it?"

"Maybe Mary discovered there was no record of the marriage in Epping and didn't know her parents had been married legally in London. Mr. Scutton might have considered even that knowledge too much of a risk."

Caroline groaned. "I wish Inspector Ross was here to listen to all our theories. He is very good at ascertaining what is pertinent to his investigations and what is not."

"You could always write to him with your observations, Caroline," Mrs. Frogerton suggested.

"I'm not sure if I should intrude on him when his brother has just died," Caroline said. "I'm sure he is dealing with quite a lot."

"We could mention it at the funeral," Mrs. Frogerton said. "Or would that be considered vulgar?"

"If Inspector Ross asked us what was going on, I think it would be perfectly acceptable to answer his question," Caroline said. "As long as we did so discreetly."

"Then perhaps we should wait until we hear back from those churches," Mrs. Frogerton observed.

"I think that is an excellent idea, ma'am," Caroline said. "The Scuttons weren't invited to Lord Richard's funeral, so they will not be able to overhear any of our conversations."

"And they will be leaving permanently for Morton House in the next few days, which means we won't have to encounter them here, either," Mrs. Frogerton reminded her. "I never thought I'd be so pleased to see guests depart."

"They don't deserve your attention, ma'am, and they have abused your hospitality. I wish Mr. Potkins had never introduced them to us in the first place. But now that I have offended them by refusing to marry Thomas, hopefully they will leave me alone."

"They'd certainly leave you alone if we could prove Mr. Scutton should not inherit the earldom," Mrs. Frogerton said.

"That's true, ma'am," Caroline agreed. "I'll write and ask Mr. Castle if Coutts has my grandfather's personal diary. If he did organize the whole affair to suit himself, I should imagine he would have written about it."

"Of course, if the Scuttons were married in the Church of England, it doesn't matter who Thomas's father was," Mrs. Frogerton pointed out. "He is legally a Scutton and the heir to an earldom, and maybe he has nothing to do with the Brighams at all."

"Then why was he meeting George Brigham yesterday?" Caroline asked. "He cannot expect us to believe he was merely passing the time of day with a man who stood by while his sister was being stabbed to death."

"Perhaps he is being blackmailed."

"By the Brighams?" Caroline asked. "For what reason?"

"If I knew that, Caroline, I'd march straight over to Inspector Ross and tell him." Mrs. Frogerton huffed. "It would be so much simpler if we could just *ask* Mr. and Mrs. Scutton what on earth they are playing at."

"I doubt you'd get a convincing answer from either of them, ma'am. They are set on winning the earldom and will allow nothing to get in their way."

Mrs. Frogerton reached down to pat her dogs. "Well, I hope one of those churches provides an answer for us very soon. Otherwise, I might just blurt out a question to Mr. Scutton over breakfast tomorrow."

"I wouldn't recommend it, ma'am." Caroline pictured the scene and shuddered. "We already know that anyone who questions Mr. Scutton's rights meets an untimely end."

"I doubt he'd murder me over the breakfast table, lass." Mrs. Frogerton rose to her feet. "Shall we take the dogs out for a walk? I feel the need to clear my head."

Chapter 19

At four o'clock, Caroline was in the drawing room awaiting Mrs. Frogerton, who had taken a nap after luncheon. Dr. Harris was expected momentarily, and Caroline wondered what had become of her employer. After a few more minutes of indecision, she went back up the stairs and knocked on Mrs. Frogerton's bedroom door. There was no reply. After knocking again, Caroline looked inside.

"Mrs. Frogerton?"

Something about the quality of the silence told her that Mrs. Frogerton was not present. The door into the dressing room was open, and Caroline walked through just to make sure that her employer wasn't simply changing her dress in anticipation of Dr. Harris's visit. The bonnet Mrs. Frogerton had worn earlier was on top of the chest of drawers, red ribbons dangling, along with the matching gloves. A pair of muddy half boots sat beside the door waiting to be cleaned.

Caroline went back into the bedroom, a sense of unease enveloping her. Mrs. Frogerton had looked forward to Dr. Harris's visit, and yet she was nowhere to be found. Had she gone to the kitchen to speak to Cook about the refreshments? Caroline decided to go down the back stairs to the basement and find out.

There was no sign of Mrs. Frogerton in the kitchen, but Ellie jumped up from the table and came toward Caroline. "Mrs. Frogerton gave me a note for you before she went out."

"Thank you." Caroline took the folded piece of paper. "How long ago did she leave?"

"About ten minutes ago I think, miss." Ellie looked over at the clock. "She went in her carriage all proper-like."

"Did she take an escort?"

"No, miss. I did ask if she wanted me to accompany her, but she said she wouldn't be five minutes and to tell you not to worry."

"Is Mr. Scutton here?"

"He went out to see Mr. Castle, miss. He said he might not be back in time for dinner."

"Thank you, Ellie." Caroline managed a smile. "Please ask Mr. Jenkins to bring up the tea tray after he admits Dr. Harris to the house."

"I will, miss." Ellie curtsied.

Caroline went back to the drawing room to await Dr. Harris with the note in her hand. She unfolded it and read Mrs. Frogerton's words.

Dearest Caroline, I have gone to Morton House. It occurred to me that if anyone knows whether the marriage is legal or not, it is Mrs. Scutton. I intend to check for a marriage certificate amongst her belongings. I doubt I'll be long. Please ask Dr. Harris to await my return.

Caroline read the note again. How on earth did Mrs. Frogerton think she would gain access to Mrs. Scutton's personal effects? She already knew her employer was handy with a hairpin, but dealing with Mrs. Scutton was a completely different matter than the friendly and inferior Miss Smith.

Jenkins announced, "Dr. Harris, Miss Morton."

Caroline turned to the door to see Dr. Harris and the butler. "Oh . . . thank you."

Dr. Harris raised his eyebrows. "There's no need to look so pleased to see me, Miss Morton."

"I wasn't thinking of you," Caroline said. "I was worrying about Mrs. Frogerton."

"Is she not at home?" Dr. Harris looked back toward the hall. "I did tell her I'd be here this afternoon. Did she give up and go out, leaving you to deal with my supposed lateness?"

"Oh, for goodness' sake, this isn't about you, sir. Mrs. Frogerton had to go out unexpectedly," Caroline said. "She instructed me to tell you to stay until she returns."

The butler returned with the tea tray and set it on the table in front of the fireplace. Dr. Harris looked inquiringly at Caroline, who had not sat down or invited him to do so.

"Shall I pour? You seem quite distracted."

"I'll do it." She took a seat, poured two cups of tea, and handed one to Dr. Harris, who joined her on the couch.

"What's wrong?" he asked in his usual blunt manner.

"Where would you like me to start?" Caroline asked. "Of course, if you'd bothered to visit more frequently, you'd know how matters currently stand rather than expecting me to tell you everything all at once."

"You're upset." He put his cup down and took her hand, his thumb and forefinger curving around to take her pulse. "How may I help you?"

She pulled her hand free of his. "Mrs. Frogerton has gone to Morton House by herself."

"And?" Dr. Harris looked mystified. "Is she not allowed to make calls without you?"

"She—" Caroline sucked in a breath. "She can sometimes be impulsive, and I am concerned that she might put herself in danger."

"How so?"

"We believe Mr. Scutton might have been involved in the murder of his sister."

Dr. Harris frowned. "I thought they'd charged that Brigham chap."

"They have, but Mrs. Frogerton and I have come to suspect that Mr. Scutton might have wanted his sister murdered to prevent her speaking out about his claims to the earldom."

"Ah, now it makes sense." Dr. Harris nodded. "Is that why Mrs. Frogerton wanted to speak to me?"

"I believe she wished to consult you about the evening when the murder took place."

"What did she want to know?" Dr. Harris asked.

Caroline took a moment to gather her thoughts. "One of the maids observed the Brigham brothers leaving the house. They appeared relaxed, weren't in a hurry to be gone, and, more importantly, there was no sign of blood on their clothing."

Dr. Harris considered this for a moment. "I assume Mrs. Frogerton wanted to know if it was possible to stab someone violently and yet avoid getting that person's blood on you."

"Yes." Caroline nodded.

"From what I observed at the time, the wounds were inflicted by a single blade, which indicates that there was only one person wielding a murder weapon. So it's possible one of the brothers would remain blood free. The other, however . . ." He paused. "The blade struck an artery in the throat, and the blood came out with some force. In my opinion, anyone standing close enough to stab Mrs. Brigham would have been sprayed with blood."

"Which means that Mr. Albert Brigham must have changed his clothes," Caroline said. "I doubt Mr. Scutton would've left a set out for him, so where did he get them?"

"He would've had to strip down to his smalls," Dr. Harris said.

Caroline looked at him. "But how could he have done

that when Mrs. Scutton was right there screaming her head off and raising the alarm?" She paused. "Oh, dear God. The only person covered in blood apart from Mary was Mrs. Scutton."

Dr. Harris stared at her. "Ah . . . there's something I meant to tell you about that."

"What?" Caroline demanded.

"I've dealt with a lot of knife injuries during my time at St. Thomas's, and I've heard many a story from those who insist they were the victim, but the direction of the knife cuts tells a different story."

Caroline shot to her feet and began pacing. "Are you suggesting Mrs. Scutton was lying?"

"Let me put it this way. The amount of blood on her clothing was far worse than the shallow slashes on her arms and hands would have caused. And the angle of those shallow cuts doesn't reflect her story of trying to fight off Mr. Brigham. She was either right by Mr. Brigham's side when he inflicted the final blows, or—"

"She did it herself, and then cut her own arms to make it look like it was the Brighams." Caroline whispered. "Why didn't you mention this earlier?"

"Well—"

"You let your stupid male pride about a conversation with me prevent you from coming forward with information that might prove vital to this murder!"

Dr. Harris stood up and held up his hands in a placatory manner. "Steady on, now. There's no need—"

"There is every need!" Caroline rounded on him. "Do you not understand? Mrs. Frogerton has gone to see Mrs. Scutton. If she is caught meddling with her belongings, God knows what that woman will do to her!" She turned toward the door. "I must go to her."

Dr. Harris came after her. "Then I will accompany you."

Dr. Harris tried to speak to Caroline in the hackney cab, but she was far too worried to take heed of his words.

When they reached Cavendish Square, she left the cab without waiting for his help, and he only caught up with her as she descended the basement steps of Morton House.

"How do you intend to get in?" he asked as she approached the door.

She bent down to move a paving stone and retrieved the key that had been there since she lived in the house.

"Clever," Dr. Harris said approvingly. "What's the plan?"

She finally looked at him. "We'll go in as quietly as we can and use the back stairs to ascend each level until we find them."

"I assume you don't know which bedroom Mrs. Scutton has claimed for her own?" Dr. Harris asked.

"Unfortunately, no. Although, I assume she might use the countess's suite on the third floor until Mr. Scutton takes a bride."

"I thought he intended to marry you."

"I believe he had some notion of doing so. I set him straight about that." They entered the house quietly and came down the dark passageway, past the scullery and washhouse and into the kitchen proper.

"I'll wager Scutton took that well." Dr. Harris kept his voice low as they approached the servants' stairs.

There was no sign of anyone in the basement, although Caroline noticed the new stove had been installed and some rudimentary furniture put in place. The stove had been banked up and sent out warm waves of air into the coldness of the kitchen. A tray with two used cups, a pot of tea, and some sugar sat on the pine table waiting to be cleared away by the nonexistent staff.

"Are there any servants yet?" Dr. Harris asked as if he'd read her mind.

"Not that I know of," Caroline said. "Let's go up to the ground floor."

One of the advantages of the house being so empty was that sound carried well. There were no voices raised or otherwise in the morning room, secretary's office, or other rooms.

Dr. Harris pointed upward, and Caroline nodded. They went up another level via the back stairs and paused again. Caroline cautiously opened the door and stepped out into the corridor. There were two main apartments on this level—the drawing room, which looked over the square and where guests of stature were received, and the countess's suite that occupied the rear of the floor.

Caroline tried to breathe slowly as she strained to hear voices. She was about to move on when Dr. Harris grabbed her hand and squeezed it hard. He gestured toward the countess's apartment and mouthed, "In there?"

There was a faint murmur of sound from behind the closed doors. She considered how they might approach the suite of rooms without being spotted. There were two sets of servants' stairs in the house—one at the front and one at the back. The safest route would be to go back down a level, cross to the other side of the house, and go back up again, which would bring them directly into the countess's dressing room.

But if Mrs. Frogerton had been discovered searching for the marriage certificate, the most obvious place for it to be secured was the dressing room among Mrs. Scutton's personal effects. Caroline didn't wish to walk in on any conversation that was being held there. She headed back to the drawing room, pausing only to make sure Mrs. Scutton wasn't in residence.

Dr. Harris poked her in the arm, and she turned to face him. He raised his eyebrows and pointed back the way they'd come.

Caroline walked to the interior wall, slid her fingers beneath the wainscoting, and released the catch that opened the secret door. Behind her, Dr. Harris muttered an expletive as the door swung open to reveal its secrets.

She stepped into the gloomy interior, placed her hand on the wall, and let her memory guide her along the passageway to the other end, Dr. Harris close behind her. The voices were louder now, and Caroline pressed her finger to her lips to remind Dr. Harris to keep quiet. She could hear Mrs. Frogerton very clearly and guessed she might be standing near the wall where the concealed panel was located.

"I will ask you again, ma'am," Mrs. Scutton said. "What are you doing in my bedchamber? You have wasted quite enough of my time. And please do not repeat your previous excuses, which include having lost your way, to have suddenly felt faint and needed somewhere to lie down, and your latest attempt that you were seeking the necessary."

"Well, in truth, Mrs. Scutton, I was worried about you," Mrs. Frogerton said.

"By what right do you have to be concerned for me at all?" Mrs. Scutton demanded. "We are not related."

"Yet I have cared for you in my own home and thus feel some kind of obligation to you," Mrs. Frogerton continued. "And the actions of your son have caused me to fear for your safety."

"Don't be ridiculous. Thomas is an excellent son. Just because he has taken a dislike to your paid companion doesn't mean you have the right to come to her defense and malign him."

"I'm not worried about that, ma'am," Mrs. Frogerton said. "Caroline is perfectly capable of taking care of herself."

Dr. Harris nudged Caroline in the ribs, but she ignored him.

"Then what is it?" Mrs. Scutton sounded impatient. "Mrs. Frogerton, you pride yourself on speaking plainly, and yet you have still not come up with a single reason why you sneaked into my dressing room while I was taking the tea tray down to the kitchen."

"I saw Mr. Scutton with George Brigham."

There was a sudden silence, and Caroline held her breath.

"*What* did you say?"

"You heard me," Mrs. Frogerton said. "Now, if that doesn't worry you, then I don't know what will. Why would your son be speaking to one of the Brighams?"

"This is yet another lie," Mrs. Scutton snapped.

"Perhaps you should ask him. I would be happy to do it for you, but questioning Mr. Scutton tends to lead to the end of one's life."

"You are being ridiculous."

"Jude died after being seen with your son. Mary died after claiming to know your family secrets. Who will be next? George Brigham? Or once you have served your purpose and made him the earl, will he turn on you?"

"Thomas will be the next Earl of Morton."

There was a note of conviction in Mrs. Scutton's voice that made Caroline tense. Dr. Harris put a hand on her shoulder and leaned close, his breath feathering her ear. "Should I attempt to create a diversion and ring the front doorbell?" he whispered.

Caroline nodded, and he turned and retraced his steps.

"But should he be the next earl?" Mrs. Frogerton asked. "If he has—"

"He has done nothing wrong! It is his birthright."

"Surely not, if he's willing to kill to conceal evidence that he is not the earl."

"What evidence?" Mrs. Scutton laughed. "Is that what you are doing here, Mrs. Frogerton? Looking for clues to use against my son? You'll find nothing here to aid you."

"I would hope that if my son conspired to murder his own sister, someone would try to prevent him from gaining advancement from it," Mrs. Frogerton said in a steady voice. "I can see that I was mistaken. I thought to give you the opportunity to speak to Mr. Scutton and ask him for the truth, but I shouldn't have bothered."

Her voice grew slightly fainter, as if she was moving toward the opposite door. "As you said, this matter has nothing to do with me. I'll leave you to think it over and decide what you wish to do about it."

A door slammed, making Caroline jump.

"You're not going anywhere, Mrs. Frogerton," Mrs. Scutton said. "Do you really think you can traipse in here, hurl a ball of nonsensical suspicions at my son, and simply walk away? I know your sort. You'll be blabbing to Inspector Ross as soon as you leave."

"I have nothing to tell Inspector Ross," Mrs. Frogerton said. "That is for you to do, unless you can forget that your son was a willing co-conspirator in the murder of his sister."

"Half-sister."

"I beg your pardon?" Mrs. Frogerton said.

"Mary is Thomas's half-sister."

"And that makes his crime more acceptable to you?"

"Perhaps. And while I have you trapped, I'd like to know what you were looking for."

Mrs. Frogerton gasped.

Caroline eased the mechanism that operated the panel forward and opened the door a minute fraction so that she could see out. Mrs. Scutton had her back to Caroline, and Mrs. Frogerton was against the door. A glint of light hit the side of the blade Mrs. Scutton had in her raised right hand.

"If you tell me what you were looking for, I might let you live," Mrs. Scutton said in a conversational voice.

"We both know that you will not."

"Then let me guess what you were after." Mrs. Scutton paused. "This weapon, perhaps?"

Mrs. Frogerton slowly shook her head. "I wouldn't have thought you foolish enough to hold on to it. Mary realized the truth when she went to record her marriage at St. John's, didn't she? That there was no record of *your* marriage because the vicar refused to perform the ceremony."

"We were married in the sight of God through our own

rites. That's all I cared about, and William was more than happy to go along with me." Mrs. Scutton sighed. "I do wish you hadn't decided to meddle, Mrs. Frogerton. You were very good to us when we arrived in London."

"I'm glad you appreciate my efforts, but I still don't understand why you are complacent about your son being allied with the Brighams."

"Thomas might be a fool, but he still deserves to be the earl."

Caroline tiptoed out of the concealed door and picked up the first heavy object that came to hand. She briefly met Mrs. Frogerton's gaze.

"No one deserves to succeed if they get there by murder, ma'am," Mrs. Frogerton said. "Now, kindly open this door and let me leave."

"I can't do that." Mrs. Scutton shook her head. "I've come this far. What's another dead body? I've already been forced to do away with two of the people I love most in the world to preserve my son's claim to the earldom."

"The College of Arms won't validate a Roman Catholic marriage," Mrs. Frogerton countered. "All your hopes will be dashed."

"I'm not stupid, Mrs. Frogerton. The late earl arranged a fake marriage certificate through one of his pet vicars."

"One has to wonder why the old earl was so interested in your marriage, ma'am. Was he perhaps the father of your child?"

"Good Lord, Mrs. Frogerton, you have been busy, haven't you?" Mrs. Scutton laughed again. "Once I've disposed of you, I really must pay a visit to Miss Smith. She's obviously been gossiping."

"So, Caroline's grandfather is Thomas's father. Doesn't that make them rather closely related for marriage?" Mrs. Frogerton asked.

Caroline inched closer.

"It's even worse than that, ma'am. Caroline's father is

Thomas's father. The old earl was merely protecting his son from scandal. He arranged everything—the groom, the dowry, and the fake certificate."

"Which the College of Arms have."

"Yes. Thomas will be the next earl. He is the earl's son, after all." Mrs. Scutton raised the blade. "I'll be quick, ma'am. I wouldn't want you to suffer."

The ringing of the doorbell sounded loud in the empty house, but it was enough to make Mrs. Scutton hesitate and misjudge her thrust.

Caroline rushed forward, a heavy book in her hands, and hit Mrs. Scutton hard on the back of the head. Her opponent went down, and Caroline dropped the book and scrambled over to Mrs. Frogerton, who was bleeding.

"Mrs. Frogerton!" Caroline crouched beside her, took out her handkerchief, and pressed it to her employer's shoulder. She placed Mrs. Frogerton's hand over it. "Press down hard on this while I fetch Dr. Harris."

"Yes, lass." Mrs. Frogerton looked as pale as milk, her breathing harried. "I'll be fine."

Caroline checked that Mrs. Scutton was not yet conscious and tied her hands together behind her back with a stocking from the drawer before racing down the stairs to let Dr. Harris in. To her surprise, Mr. Scutton was with him.

"Dr. Harris!" Caroline ignored Mr. Scutton. "Mrs. Frogerton has been stabbed!"

He pushed past her and went up the stairs two at a time.

Mr. Scutton looked down at Caroline, his expression horrified. "It's my mother, isn't it? It was her all the time."

"Yes. Now please go and find a constable with all speed," Caroline said.

Mr. Scutton sped off, his face ashen, and Caroline went back upstairs. She rushed down the corridor and into the dressing room where Dr. Harris was attending to Mrs. Frogerton. He glanced up at her as she came to stand beside him.

"Fetch me a bowl of hot water and some soap and clean linen that I can tear into strips."

Caroline went off to do his bidding. When she returned carrying the items he'd requested, he had Mrs. Frogerton settled into bed in the other room with the top half of her dress unbuttoned to the waist to reveal her shoulder.

"Good girl." He washed and dried his hands with one of the linens and then wet another one to place on Mrs. Frogerton's exposed shoulder. "Don't faint, ma'am."

"I never faint." Mrs. Frogerton's voice was thin as spun thread.

"You'll be pleased to hear it's a clean wound. The blade went straight through the fleshy part of your shoulder and avoided anything life threatening."

"Good." Mrs. Frogerton closed her eyes. "I've never been so frightened in my life. That woman's eyes were as cold as ice when she went to stab me."

Loud voices sounded from the dressing room. Caroline went in to discover Mr. Scutton with Sergeant Dawson and a constable.

"Good afternoon, my lady." Sergeant Dawson touched his hat to her, his gaze on Mrs. Scutton, who was now conscious. "What's been going on 'ere, then?"

"Mrs. Scutton tried to murder Mrs. Frogerton," Caroline said. "I saw the whole thing." She pointed toward the cabinetry. "I kicked the knife away after I hit her with the book. It's probably under the dresser. I believe it's the same weapon used to murder Mrs. Mary Brigham."

"Take a look, please, Constable," Sergeant Dawson said. "Where's Mrs. Frogerton?"

"She's in the next room being attended to by Dr. Harris if you wish to speak to her."

"Dr. Harris? Not 'im as well." Sergeant Dawson sighed and took out his notebook. "Here we go again."

Chapter 20

By eight in the evening, Mrs. Frogerton was comfortably ensconced in her own bed, and Mrs. Scutton was being held at Great Scotland Yard awaiting an interview with Inspector Ross, who had been hurriedly brought back from leave. After Mr. Scutton instructed Mr. Potkins to deal with his mother's affairs, Dr. Harris and Caroline escorted him back to Half Moon Street

Mr. Scutton seemed bewildered and reluctant to settle until Dr. Harris made him eat something and prescribed some medicinal brandy. When they gathered in the drawing room after their hastily prepared meal, Mr. Scutton turned to Caroline.

"I believe you owe me a full explanation of what has gone on."

Dr. Harris scowled. "And I believe you need to moderate your tone when speaking to a lady."

Mr. Scutton sank into a chair and shoved a hand through his hair. "Forgive me," he said with obvious effort. "I am rather overwrought."

"Are you willing to talk to him, Miss Morton?" Dr. Harris asked. "You are under no obligation to oblige this gentleman."

"I am willing to tell him what I know, sir, but only if he

reciprocates in kind," Caroline addressed Dr. Harris, but her words were for Mr. Scutton. "At one point it appeared that Mr. Scutton was in league with the murderers, not his mother."

"*What?*" Mr. Scutton looked up.

"You were observed speaking to Mr. George Brigham after his release from jail, sir." Caroline said. "And you cannot deny that you have done everything in your power to keep the Brighams away from the law."

"I . . . have obligations to the Brighams."

"Obviously," Caroline said.

"I've known Albert for years. I was delighted when he wanted to marry Mary. Things went awry only when Mary insisted on openly embracing his Roman Catholic faith."

"I assume your mother didn't want even a hint of popery attached to you in case someone started questioning the religious beliefs of the entire Scutton family," Caroline said. "Especially the College of Arms. Was your father a Catholic?"

"I think he pretended to embrace his family's popish leanings when he married my mother, who was a practicing Catholic. But he never made us attend any church but St. John's."

"Then your mother must have been horrified when Mary married an Irishman," Dr. Harris said.

"Not at first," Mr. Scutton said. "It was only when she realized the Earl of Morton had no direct heir and that I might be in line for the earldom that she started to worry about the connection. It was why she insisted that Mary pretend to be widowed when we first arrived in London."

"Something Mary didn't agree with and soon denied," Caroline said.

"Yes, Mother was furious with her about that, but Mary hadn't forgiven her for what happened to Albert."

"Mary seemed to believe your mother was instrumental in his incarceration," Caroline said.

"She might have been right." Mr. Scutton sighed. "Mama

deliberately gave Albert bad advice about his investments and then refused to help him when he suffered financial losses. As you might imagine, Mary was furious. She begged me to speak to our mother, but nothing I said made any difference. In truth, Mama told me to keep quiet and focus on gaining the earldom."

"And that didn't raise your suspicions of her at all?" Dr. Harris asked somewhat sarcastically.

"No, I simply thought she was . . ." Mr. Scutton paused. "Trying to do her best for me."

"I suppose she was, in her own way," Dr. Harris said. "Even if it involved murdering her own daughter."

Mr. Scutton winced.

Caroline hastened to intervene. "From what Miss Smith told us, Mary and Jude were very close."

"They were. I suspect Jude confirmed some of Mary's suspicions about our parents' hasty marriage. I assume Mary must have told Albert, who by then had good reason to dislike our mother. Albert did some investigating of his own about the lack of a wedding certificate and threatened to blackmail me if I didn't allow him access to Mary after his release from the debtors' prison."

"Which is why you continued to talk to the Brighams before Mary was murdered. But why did you speak to George so recently?" Caroline asked.

"Despite what you might think, I didn't arrange to meet him at Scotland Yard. He came up to me. I was so shocked that he dared to accost me in public that I gave him the opportunity to start speaking, and once he started, I had to listen. He swore to me that he and his brother had left Mary alive."

"And you believed him?"

"Not at first." Mr. Scutton swallowed hard. "But I did begin to wonder . . ."

"Whether your mother was the murderer," Dr. Harris said. "How astute of you."

Mr. Scutton turned to Caroline. "Why is this man here?

How does he think he has the right to question me about anything?"

"He's here to care for Mrs. Frogerton and because I trust him," Caroline said. "He is also the person who realized your mother's injuries must have been self-inflicted, which is why we immediately came to Morton House and were able to save Mrs. Frogerton before your mother murdered her."

"What will happen to my mother now?" Mr. Scutton asked.

"I assume she'll be tried for murder, sir," Caroline said.

"And will she hang?"

"That's up to the judge," Dr. Harris said far too cheerfully. "I should imagine the Brighams will be witnesses against her, as well as Mrs. Frogerton."

Mr. Scutton grimaced. "I'm glad we didn't sell the house in Epping. At least I have somewhere to hide while this scandal enthralls London."

"I suspect Miss Smith will be very pleased to see you," Caroline said. "She's missed having a family to care for."

"From everything I've heard so far, I'm not even sure if I am a Scutton, which means I have no connection to the earldom at all." Mr. Scutton looked at Caroline. "Did my mother happen to mention whether I was actually her husband's child?"

"She indicated that you were not, sir, and that the marriage was arranged by the old Earl of Morton to avoid ... unpleasantness," Caroline said carefully. "Perhaps you might speak to your mother about this matter."

"Or you could just tell him the truth," Dr. Harris said.

"Which is?" Mr. Scutton looked from Caroline to Dr. Harris. "I'd rather know."

Caroline tried to kick Dr. Harris's ankle, but it made no difference.

"You're Caroline's half-brother," Dr. Harris said. "If you had been legitimate, you'd already be the Earl of Morton."

"Good God!" Mr. Scutton shot to his feet, an expression of revulsion plain on his face. He left the room in some haste.

Dr. Harris turned to Caroline, his eyebrows raised. "I suspect I'd look just like that if my mother was insisting I marry my half-sister."

"You should not have told him," Caroline said. "It was unkind."

"Unkind? He hardly deserves your sympathy. He is a coward who won't even stay in London to support his mother at her trial, and I'm fairly certain it's because he's not entirely innocent in this matter."

"How so?"

"How did Mrs. Scutton murder Jude?" Dr. Harris asked. "Was she seen at the inn?"

"The Brighams frequented the same tavern, and the attacker was masked. It could have been Mrs. Scutton, the Brighams, or a random passerby."

"But Mary liked Jude. Why would her husband murder him?"

"Perhaps because he knew too much?"

"That's a ridiculous idea. Albert must have known that Mary adored Jude. It's far more likely that it was our dear Thomas." Dr. Harris scoffed. "Although I hope your Inspector Ross asks that very question to Mrs. Scutton."

"I'm sure he will. He's very thorough." Caroline rose to her feet. "Do you wish to see Mrs. Frogerton before you leave? I assured her you would want to check on her condition."

"If you wish." Dr. Harris followed her out of the room and up the stairs.

"For a physician, you seem remarkably reluctant to see your patient," Caroline commented.

"In truth, I'm more concerned about you, Miss Morton."

Caroline paused at the top of the stairs and turned to regard him. "Me? I am not the one who was stabbed, sir."

He stopped beside her. "You're trembling like a leaf."

"It's been a difficult day."

He reached out and cupped her chin so she couldn't avoid looking at him. "You don't have to be strong all the time. You've had a terrible shock. It's quite all right to admit that you are upset."

"What would you have me do?" Caroline asked. "Burst into tears and ignore the fact that I am needed to keep this household running to Mrs. Frogerton's standards? What use would I be then?"

"Perhaps you shouldn't value yourself simply for being useful."

"I am paid to ensure that things run smoothly." She swallowed hard. "Now if you will excuse me—"

He slid an arm around her shoulders and drew her close against his chest.

"Caroline . . ."

She inhaled the scent of his cigars and a hint of hospital disinfectants and closed her eyes. The temptation to lean into him and start sobbing was almost overwhelming.

Instead, she drew a shaking breath and eased free of his arms. "Thank you." She managed to smile up at him. "I promise that the moment I get into my bedchamber, I will cry myself to sleep."

He studied her for a long moment and then nodded, his expression unusually serious. "Shall we see how Mrs. Frogerton is doing?" he suggested. "I can't wait to describe Mr. Scutton's expression when he found out he'd proposed marriage to his own half-sister."

He walked along the corridor, knocked on Mrs. Frogerton's door, and went in. After a moment to compose herself, Caroline followed and found her employer sitting up in bed with a shawl around her shoulders concealing the bandages.

Dr. Harris was already sitting beside her taking her pulse. "How is the pain, ma'am?"

"Bearable," Mrs. Frogerton said.

"It will probably feel far worse tomorrow," Dr. Harris said. "I've already consulted with your physician, and he will be paying close attention to the wound to avoid any nasty infections."

Mrs. Frogerton looked over at Caroline. "How are you, lass?"

"I'm fine, ma'am."

"She's not fine, but she won't admit it," Dr. Harris muttered.

"I'm sorry," Mrs. Frogerton said.

"For what, ma'am?" Caroline came over to the bed.

"For rushing in when I should have used my head."

"I'm sure your intentions were good," Dr. Harris said. "You had no way of knowing Mrs. Scutton was capable of murdering her own daughter."

"I should have waited," Mrs. Frogerton repeated. She gestured at some letters on the table beside her bed. "Those churches replied, Caroline, and one of them found something very interesting in their records."

Caroline picked up the letter on the top of the pile and read it before handing it to Dr. Harris.

He summarized it as he read. "This appears to say that the Earl of Morton forced one of his vicars to produce a fake marriage certificate for the Scuttons after the vicar refused to perform the marriage service. Apparently, the vicar confessed on his deathbed and had a note added to the church records to that effect. Which was very good of him. I suppose it was the fake certificate that Mrs. Scutton handed over to the College of Arms."

"We'll have to let Inspector Ross know," Caroline said. "Should I write him a note?"

"You can do that in the morning," Mrs. Frogerton said firmly. "I want to know what Mr. Scutton had to say for himself."

"Well." Dr. Harris settled back in his chair with evident enjoyment. "It was quite a story...."

Chapter 21

Three months later

Mr. Lewis smiled at Mrs. Frogerton. "How are you today, ma'am?'

"I'm perfectly fine." Mrs. Frogerton frowned. "In truth, I'm becoming tired of being treated like an invalid."

They were seated in the drawing room, and Mrs. Frogerton, normally the most amiable of hosts, was in something of a bad mood. "Between Simon and Dotty hovering over me, along with Caroline and Dr. Harris, I'm heartily fed up of being told what I can't do and not what I can."

Mr. Lewis shot Caroline an amused look. "I'm not surprised your employer is a difficult patient, Lady Caroline. She is not used to being constrained."

"So I have gathered," Caroline replied.

Despite receiving the best care available, Mrs. Frogerton had suffered a severe infection and spent several days in a high fever that had worried everyone and obliged Caroline to write to both her children and advise them to come see their mother. Ever since the fever broke, Mrs. Frogerton had been fractious and quite unlike herself. Her mood finally improved when Dr. Harris suggested she be allowed to attend to her accounting books.

Dealing with her businesses and corresponding with her son had enhanced Mrs. Frogerton's mood, but Caroline was still worried that her employer hadn't regained complete use of her left shoulder. Privately, Dr. Harris had warned Caroline that Mrs. Frogerton might never regain full motion in that joint and that only time would tell.

"Inspector Ross, ma'am," Jenkins announced.

The Inspector entered the room, and Mrs. Frogerton extended her hand to him.

He bowed low and kissed it. "Good morning, Mrs. Frogerton. It's good to see you up and about again." He straightened and smiled at Caroline and Mr. Lewis. "My lady. Mr. Lewis."

"Inspector Ross," said Mr. Lewis. "Or should that be Lord Nicholas now? Or the Earl of Craigmore—is that the heir's title?"

"Inspector Ross will do nicely, sir. I must admit I'm still not comfortable with the rest of it."

"Your name is Nicholas?" Mrs. Frogerton asked.

"Yes, ma'am, although those who know me well usually call me Nick." He smiled. "Which some might say is a most appropriate name for an officer of the law."

"I assume you'll have to resign," Mr. Lewis continued. "Which will be a great shame."

"That matter is still being discussed, sir," Inspector Ross said. "Until a decision is reached, I will continue to do my job to the best of my ability."

Mrs. Frogerton waved him to a seat. "Do you have news for us?"

"Yes." His expression sobered. "Mrs. Scutton was found guilty of murdering Mary and was sentenced to death by hanging."

"And may God have mercy on her soul," Mrs. Frogerton murmured. "Although that woman had no mercy for me or her daughter, so I struggle to have any sympathy for her."

"Your evidence helped convict her, as did the Brighams'."

"Was Mr. Scutton in court to hear the verdict?"

"He was, ma'am. I spoke to him briefly, and he said he intends to enter Holy Orders."

"For which denomination?" Mrs. Frogerton asked.

"The Church of England. He has no love for the papists."

"One would assume he does not," Mrs. Frogerton said. "And what of the Brighams?"

"They are returning to Ireland and will remain there," Inspector Ross said.

"I am glad that everything is over," Mrs. Frogerton said. "I feel that it will be easier to move on now." She looked at Caroline. "What is it, lass?"

"There is one thing I was curious about, Inspector," Caroline said. "How did Mary end up with jewelry that belonged to my mother?"

"Ah." Inspector Ross grimaced. "I was hoping you wouldn't ask me that."

"Why?"

His expression softened. "Because you have had enough to bear from the Morton and the Scutton families."

"I'd rather know."

"According to Mrs. Scutton, Mary must have stolen the jewelry from her and given it to Mr. Brigham to pawn or sell to pay for their removal to Ireland."

Caroline nodded. "Which means that Mrs. Scutton probably got them from my father for services rendered."

"Yes. I'm sorry."

"I'm not surprised," Caroline said. "He did far worse things to our family."

Silence fell in the room, which was broken only when Mr. Lewis cleared his throat. "I, too, came with news today, my lady."

Caroline shook off her memories and turned to Mr. Lewis.

"The DeBeers have made an offer for your land and the mines." He smiled at her. "And it is an excellent one. I'll try to negotiate it up a little, but I can tell you now that you and Susan will be financially secure for the rest of your life." He handed Caroline a letter. "The financial details are in here. Please let me know what you think."

"That is excellent news." Mrs. Frogerton's smile held all her old warmth.

Mr. Lewis and Inspector Ross said their goodbyes and exited the drawing room, leaving Caroline and Mrs. Frogerton alone together.

"Well, lass, if Mr. Lewis is right, you won't be needing this job anymore. You'll be an heiress in your own right."

Caroline smiled at Mrs. Frogerton. "I shall echo Inspector Ross's comments and say that until I see money in the bank, I will continue to do my job to the best of my ability."

"That's the spirit, lass." Mrs. Frogerton visibly brightened. "Samuel's been nagging me to go and convalesce away from London. Would you care to accompany me to Brighton or Bath?"

Caroline smiled. "I think I would enjoy that immensely, ma'am."